As Long As You Both Shall Live

A Christian Contemporary Romance with Suspense

Linda K. Rodante

Linda R. Rodante

LONE MESA PUBLISHING

Lone Mesa Publishing
www.lonemesapublishing.com

As Long As You Both Shall Live
ISBN: 978-0692639047

For information, contact the author at linda@lindarodante.com.

Unless otherwise noted, Scripture quotations are taken from the HOLY BIBLE, NEW INTERNATIONAL VERSION, Copyright 1973, 1978, 1984, by International Bible Society. Use by permission of Zondervan. All rights reserved.

Dedication

- This book is dedicated to the **Father** and to **Lord Jesus Christ** without whom there would be no Christmas, no new life, no eternal life. Thank you for forming me, loving me, shaping and guiding me. May the words of my mouth (and computer) and the meditation of my heart be acceptable in your sight, my Lord and my God.

- And to my mother, Elaine Knadle, for her constant love for her children, and her enthusiastic love of Christ, for her courage in following him and being a witness in Jerusalem, in Judea, in Samaria, and to the ends of the earth.

Thank you to so many!

- The Word Weavers critique group of Tampa for all the love, encouragement and critiques through the years!
- The Tarpon Springs Fiction Writers' Group, especially our leader David Edmunds, retired homicide detective Ken Dye, and all the rest of you "go get 'em" critiquers.
- The Christian Indie Author and the Clean Indie Reads Facebook groups.
- Teri Burns, editor at Lone Mesa Publishing, for doing the impossible and bringing all my ideas and the needs of this manuscript together.
- Beta Readers, reviewers, and encouragers—without you, I would have died on the vine. ☺ You know who you are. Thank you!
- ACFW (American Christian Fiction Writers) and the FCWC (Florida Christian Writers Conference) classes on writing, critiquing, and life--and meeting other struggling and not-so-struggling authors, thank you!
- My husband, Frank, my sons, Justin and Matthew, my daughter-in-law, Melissa and extended family. Thank you all

for your love and support and encouragement, and in putting up with me through all the trials!

- Oldsmar Baptist Church leadership and congregation for their love through the years.
- And to the leadership and congregation of Highest Praise Family Church for their constant quest for God and their passion to serve Him.

Prologue

S he was always on time.

He could see the church parking lot from the edge of the woods. Glancing at his watch, he shifted position and made sure the trees concealed him. Cars exited the main road, bumped down the drive, and pulled in for the evening service. A steady stream of people parked and entered the building.

The woman who called earlier had not given her name—only a message. "Sharee's getting engaged. She's going to get married. Just thought you'd want to know." And although he'd fought the urge to come, he had surrendered to the rising anger before the afternoon ended.

His fists clenched. Just like anyone else, he had a right to be here. He could even walk into the church. They couldn't do anything about it. She couldn't. Not like before. He contemplated doing that, going in, finding a seat near her, and listening to the sermon.

No.

He didn't want to play games.

His head rose in time to see her Honda CR-V turn into the long drive. Parking next to the side door, she jumped out and hurried inside. She hadn't changed. Same petite body, same untamed hair and, he was sure, the same puritanical attitudes.

No, he didn't want to play games. What he wanted was not nearly so innocent.

Chapter 1

John Jergenson's head bounced against the window when the airplane's wheels hit the runway in Tampa. He tried stretching his six-foot-two body in the cramped seat as he'd done numerous times over the last twenty-seven hours. The long flight had taken a toll.

As buildings and cement roared past outside, he shoved the tiredness away. For four weeks he'd flown into the jungles of Indonesia and hiked through muddy terrain to reach villages lost to time. Tired and dirty, his group had emerged from the wild to be met as if they were kings or royalty. Being put on such a pedestal had humbled him, and that taste of humility had not left him. He wouldn't ruin it by complaining.

"Home." His eyes focused on familiar objects. "And home safely."

In the seat next to him, Bob Ferguson chuckled. "Did you doubt it?"

John sent him a sardonic smile. "Only a half dozen times."

"One time being that crocodile and another that logging mess we got caught in. Dugout canoes aren't the safest transportation in a river full of logs."

"I wish they'd warned us."

"And taken the chance that we'd back out?"

John's mouth lifted. They'd have made that downriver trip no matter what. The month he'd spent under Bob Ferguson's tutelage had brought appreciation for the man's wit, intelligence, and spirituality. At times, though, he'd questioned his mentor's sanity.

His smile widened. "With you, they had no fear of that."

"God was with us."

"That He was."

John grabbed the backpack from under the seat in front of him. He'd come through situations he'd never faced before, and each one had sent him to his knees in thanksgiving and praise.

He shifted his gaze to the airplane window. Sharee should have been there. At night, after a long day of work and ministry, he'd lie on

the dirt floor in a crowded hut and think about her. He wanted her
beside him. Her love of helping others would fit perfectly with the
work that needed to be done. Next time… Next time, she would be
with him.

Something stilled inside him. Had the ring he bought in Jakarta
arrived? Had Bruce picked it up as he'd asked?

Around him now, people began to stand and edge into the aisles.
The phone conversations swirled and rose and then grew silent as the
passengers dragged baggage from the overhead bins.

Bob rose. "Sharee meeting you?"

"Yes." John met his friend's grin with his own, squeezed into the
aisle and joined the assembly line inching forward.

They passed through the gangway and caught the tram. When the
doors opened again, he stepped out and let his gaze slip from person to
person until he saw the mass of auburn curls. She wore a blue dress of
some shiny material and the gold necklace he'd given her before he
left. Heels lifted her five-foot-two-inch frame to average height. A
frown creased her forehead, but even with the serious expression, she
looked beautiful. His heart kicked up a notch.

As their eyes met, relief flooded her countenance. He side-stepped
Bob's family reunion and continued forward to stop in front of her.
Her head tilted back, eyes looking deep into his. She'd worried about
him. He saw it in the way she searched his face, and he dropped his
bag and pulled her into his arms.

They turned in at Howard Park, drove past the oaks, pines, and palms
that surrounded the picnic shelters, then headed across the causeway to
the small island beach. On either side, sunbathers stretched out on
beach towels, catching the last rays of the sun. In the water,
windsurfers flaunted their aerial stunts and flipped their boards over in
quick, broad arcs. The spray from their acrobatics swept like long fish
tails behind them.

Sharee sighed—content and relaxed as she hadn't been for weeks.
Maybe since he was home, her concern about their relationship would
cease. Her heart stumbled as she thought about Dean. She'd made a
mistake that time. She'd allowed herself to be rushed into an
engagement. She wouldn't do that again.

She studied John's profile. She'd tell him about the phone calls.
He'd know what to do.

John caught her gaze and smiled. He parked the truck facing the

Gulf. The white sand glistened in the late afternoon light, and the roughened waters stretched to the horizon. Light sparkled off the wave tops—a million tiny reflectors, shifting, winking, moving.

They kicked off their shoes, climbed out of the truck and walked along the beach. When they stopped, John drew her around to face him.

The wind caught her hair, twirling it in front of her eyes. She moved it behind her ear and studied his coffee-colored hair, the line of his jaw, and his tall, wiry build. "Four weeks was a long time."

"Was it?" Light appeared in his dark eyes. "For me, too, although it was an amazing trip."

"Tell me about it."

He ran his hands up and down her arms. "I wish you'd been there."

"I think I would have liked that." After the last couple of weeks, she had to agree. Instead of spending time in a jungle of emotions, the idea of spending time in a real jungle sounded intriguing.

He took her hand and turned to walk the beach again, his voice deep but passionate as he talked about traveling into the jungles, staying in the villages and helping with needed building projects. "Each evening, we took turns preaching. We'd begin after dark and only had the lanterns, but when we lifted them high during the meeting, we could see that the entire village had gathered there." He stopped and turned to face her. "Sharee, mission trips change people. We both know that. The anointing, the presence of God, seems so strong. I've felt called to overseas missions. You know that. I believe this trip confirmed it."

"I can hear it in your voice."

"I need more flight training, especially landing on those short airstrips. I'm sure we didn't see the shortest ones." He chuckled. "And it takes an extra dose of faith to fly some of the planes. I studied maintenance and repair before, but I need a refresher."

He stopped. Sharee felt his hesitation. She lifted her head, keeping her hair in place with one hand, and searching his face.

"I'd like to go back in six months."

"What?" Something dropped into her stomach. The smell of the sea spray reached them. "But you just got home."

"I know."

She had wanted him home, wanted his confidence in fighting the sudden uneasiness in her life. Why was he talking about leaving again? "What about the schooling you just mentioned? Won't it take a while?"

"I'll start immediately. I was studying aviation mechanics when the crash happened." He paused a moment. "Doing a refresher won't take long."

"And you don't want it to."

Her voice must have risen because he moved his head to inspect her. "No."

The sun's last cusp slipped beneath the horizon, and the gold lights disappeared. "I don't know how you can do all that in six months. You're being unrealistic."

He pulled her close. "We need to talk about it. I'd planned to tell you all that happened on this trip. About the dangers we could face in the jungles, but God is so real there, so present. Not that He isn't everywhere, but you've been on mission trips. You understand. I want to go back, and I want you to go, too."

She put a hand against his chest. "John, I'm not sure about a mission trip. I just...I..." What? How could she say she wasn't sure about anything right now?

"Not just a mission trip." His voice had deepened. His lopsided grin and his next words made his meaning clear. "Marry me."

"What?"

His arms tightened around her. "I love you. You know that. God is calling us both. Don't you feel it?"

Feel it? She didn't know what she felt these days. She just wanted him home, wanted the anxiety gone, wanted things the way they were before he left.

"Marry me. We'll go back together."

She dropped her head. *I'm not ready for this, Lord. Not now. Please.*

"Sharee?"

His puzzlement was clear, but she couldn't look at him. His question was a formality only. In fact, it wasn't even a question, and he expected her to say "yes" with the same enthusiasm he exhibited.

"John, I can't. I..." How could she explain her recent feelings? The uneasiness about their relationship, how she'd messed up before, and then the phone calls... A sudden wave of emotion swamped her.

He put a finger under her chin, lifted it, and pushed the hair from her eyes. His smile disappeared. He studied her face a moment longer and dropped his hand.

৵

What is wrong, Lord? Why do I feel as if I'm on a tilt-a-whirl?

Sharee blew out a ragged breath. John had returned from a life-changing experience feeling certain she'd say yes to marriage, and yes to serving the Lord with him. And before he left, her heart had said the same. How could she explain the feelings that swirled inside now, that had grown over his month-long absence? She couldn't. Instead, she'd asked him to give her time, a week or two at least, before she gave her answer.

On the ride back, she sensed his pain. She wanted to say something, anything to make it better but couldn't.

Her eyes slid to the clock. Just three hours ago. She grabbed another tissue, swiped at her eyes then blew her nose. Why this indecision? Why?

The phone shrilled, and her muscles tensed across her shoulders. She didn't want to talk to anyone. The music came again, and she leaned forward to check the screen. Pastor Alan. No. No way. He'd know something was wrong immediately. But why was he calling? It shrilled again. Was there a problem? Someone homeless with whom he needed her help?

She snatched the phone from the end table. "Hello?"

"Sharee?"

"Yes."

"It's Pastor Alan. We're at the hospital, but don't worry. They're just doing some tests. I'm sure he'll be all right."

"Who will be all right? What are you talking about?"

"John."

"John?" Her voice rose. "What about him?"

"There's been an accident."

Chapter 2

Every muscle froze. The phone threatened to slip, and her other hand shot up to catch it.

"An accident?"

"An automobile accident. Daneen and I are at the hospital. They're taking X-rays. Do you want to come down?"

"All right." The cold spread from core muscles to the rest of her body. *Her fault.* It was her fault. He'd been distracted, torn by her answer to his proposal.

"Which hospital?" she asked.

"Intercoastal. You know where it is?"

"Yes. Is he…" Fear stopped her. Why did they need X-rays? "I'll be there in a few minutes."

"Sharee, it's not life-threatening."

Not life-threatening. Her heart jerked. She took a deep breath. "All right. Thank you."

"You want Daneen to come get you?"

"No, I'm fine."

Her hands tightened on the wheel, and she made another quick turn. Not as fine as she wanted him to think. The silence of the dark car filled her with self-recrimination. She'd prayed for John's safety while he worked and ministered in Indonesia, and, yet, within hours of returning home, he'd had an accident.

Ten minutes later, the lights of the hospital were in front of her. The hospital sign swept past. She parked and hurried across the parking lot. Between the buildings, the inky blackness of the Intercoastal Waterway caught the streetlights' glow.

Thrusting open the double doors, she hurried inside. Light stabbed her eyes, and she squinted toward the waiting room. Pastor Alan and Daneen rose from their chairs.

The pastor's wife hastened forward to embrace her. The women stood for a moment, their heads together. Sharee drew back to search Daneen's eyes.

The other woman met her look. "He's got some cuts and bruises, maybe a twisted ankle, but Alan thinks he's okay. They're checking him over, doing some X-rays." Daneen's short, blonde hair bobbed as if to emphasize the words she said.

The wash of relief almost buckled Sharee's legs. The dark presence hovering around her on the drive over had spoken of head injuries or back problems or broken bones. But he would be okay. *Thank you, Lord.*

"Come sit down." Pastor Alan waved to the empty chairs near them. They moved over to the seats. "The hospital called about forty minutes ago. John gave them our number. They said he would need a ride home." There was a slight question in his tone, and Sharee noticed his quick scrutiny of her red-rimmed eyes. "He was getting out of his truck at his complex, and someone didn't see him and hit him. But the driver took off. A neighbor came to help and called the ambulance. He was here for a while before he called us."

"What did they say?"

"They're doing tests. I saw him for a moment. He was scraped up but didn't look bad. The car sideswiped him as he was crossing the parking lot."

Sharee bowed her head. "Thank you." She directed the words upward and fought back tears.

"Hey." Pastor Alan touched her shoulder. "He's going to be fine."

She swallowed past the pain in her throat. "I thought it was my fault. That he was distracted." She hesitated. The waiting room was almost deserted, and she was glad of that. She leaned closer. "John asked me to marry him. I didn't know what to say. I wasn't expecting it, and...I'm not sure. Since he left, I began to wonder. What if I've missed God again? Like before? And then the calls began. It's just made things...hard."

"What kind of calls?" Daneen asked.

"The kind where no one says anything."

The pastor's wife's brow puckered. "How long has this been going on?"

"Almost since John left."

"Do you have any idea who it is?"

"No."

"Your work? Any of your clients?"

Sharee frowned. Would the homeless clients she worked with do this? "I don't think so."

"Some have cell phones."

"Yes, but I...I don't think they'd take the time or keep it up this long."

Daneen's arm slipped around her shoulders. "Why didn't you tell us?"

Sharee shrugged. "It was just once or twice at first. But this last week, it got crazy. I…I stopped answering my phone unless I knew who it was."

"Did you write the number down?"

"I did, but it changed. In fact, it changed more than once."

"You don't think it could be one of the youth, do you?"

"No. I haven't taught any of their classes for a while, so I'm off their radar. I think."

Daneen gave her another squeeze. "Well, the accident was not your fault. And marriage is a lifetime commitment or should be. So, there's nothing wrong with wanting to make sure before you say, 'yes.' John should have waited. He might have thought a lot about it while he was gone, but to pop the question the day he gets home…" She shook her head.

Sharee caught movement behind Daneen, and she looked past the woman's shoulder. John stood, on crutches, in the doorway to the back rooms of the emergency area. He leaned forward and said something to a nurse who sat at the desk there. A long bandage covered the lower part of his left arm. His jeans on his right leg were split halfway up his calf, and another bandage covered his foot and ankle.

She jumped to her feet, taking two steps towards him, before halting. His eyes rose, and everything about him stilled as their gazes met. His shoulders straightened, and he turned back to the nurse.

"Come on." Pastor Alan and Daneen were on their feet, too. They crossed the room.

Sharee hung behind and waited until the nurse finished speaking. John signed something, picked up a few papers, and settled the crutches under his arms.

"That was quick," Pastor Alan said. "We didn't expect you this soon. You know how slow emergency rooms are."

John's eyes flicked toward Sharee but came back to the pastor and his wife. "Well, I refused half their tests and told them to bandage what they could see and let me out—against doctor's orders. The foot has a fracture. They want me to stay on the crutches for a few weeks, and they have an air cast they want me to get from an orthopedist in a couple of days. It comes off so I can shower or sleep."

"And they had the crutches for you?"

"Not the usual. Someone left them months ago and never came back to get them, so they gave them to me. They fit well. The nurse was glad to see them go."

"Anything else?"

"Just scrapes and bruises."

"Well, you need a ride home. Daneen and I will be glad to take you or…" The Pastor's voice trailed off as he glanced at Sharee.

"Thanks," John said. "I'll take you up on the ride."

Sharee bit her lip and looked down. He had called them, after all, not her. They started for the door.

"What about your arm?" Daneen asked.

"The wrist and right hand took the brunt of the fall. Torn up from the road, and they're sore, but neither is broken. That's a miracle, although it makes it hard to work the crutches. Also, I have a nice gash on my side. Must be from the car. Somehow. They stitched it up. I'll be fine."

Sharee followed. Her heart's erratic pumping sounded loud in her ears. Pain enveloped her. What did she expect? That he would welcome her with open arms?

The double-doors opened, and Pastor Alan and Daneen went out. John turned to her, leaning on the crutches, holding the door open with his back.

"Thank you for coming."

His voice held a detachment that caused her chest to tighten. She dropped her head. He settled the crutches under his arms and began to move forward.

"Sharee."

"Yes?" She forced the word. He didn't need to see the tears that sprang to her eyes. Light spilled through the hospital's glass doors and hit her face, and the wetness on her lids starred. She blinked it away, and John stopped. Quiet settled between them, wavered, and gripped her heart.

He settled the crutches and leaned forward. "This will sound strange, but I think whoever hit me did it on purpose."

Her head rose to meet his wondering look, and he straightened and hobbled forward again.

Sharee slipped into church fifteen minutes late Sunday morning. She found a seat at the back. From across the aisle, Miss Eleanor's silver head turned her way, and the blue eyes studied her. Since she always arrived on time, if not early, Sharee knew some comments might come her way after the service.

Pastor Alan cut short the praise and worship as he usually did when they had guest speakers. Today Bob Ferguson and John filled the role. She settled back in her seat while he introduced Bob. John sat on the platform, too, not far from the podium.

Bob walked to pulpit, his infectious smile enveloping the whole congregation. Sharee's heart swelled as he began to talk about God's love and how he realized God's call on his life at sixteen. A few minutes later, he shared how their daily routine during the last month consisted of long hikes through the jungles—going from village to village—sleeping on dirt floors, and eating rice, rice, and more rice.

"One village," he said, "killed their only chicken for us and added it to the rice. John knew the honor they were doing us, but he didn't realize he'd find the beak and parts of chopped feet in his bowl."

The congregation laughed.

"Indonesia is often called the land of a thousand islands. In truth, it has over 17,000. We took a boat to the first island. From there, we caught a ministry plane." He glanced John's way. "Of course, John was itching to fly, but I think he spent some time in prayer after we boarded that first plane. Some of the planes over there...well, let's say, it takes faith to fly them."

John cleared his throat. "I seem to remember your head bowed as we took off."

Giggles rolled across the room.

Bob grinned. "But what a lush wilderness we found when we landed. The jungles have hundreds of species of orchids. The wildlife is incredible—the endangered elephants, fruit bats, Komodo dragons, orangutans, iguanas. Some animals are found nowhere else on earth. Of course, volcanoes have formed much of the land. They call the islands the Fire Islands."

He stopped and clicked on a video that showed animals unique to the area. After a few minutes, he clicked it off. "We were able to minister often. Some villages had very seldom seen anyone from the outside and had no Christians. We preached and shared the Gospel. Other groups welcomed us back. I had been to some before." He gave a detailed summary of their ministry.

When he finished, he looked over his shoulder at John, a smile widening across his face. "But let me give you a view into one man's experience."

John lifted a brow and straightened in his chair.

"Mission trips are times of discovery—about ourselves and each other. John, I found out, is a clean freak. Not necessarily a good thing in the midst of the jungle. We arrived late at the first village, so John thought he would get up early and go down to the river to wash. He didn't realize the whole village would follow him and stand on the banks to watch." A ripple of laughter rose from the congregation. "We both got used to soaping up with half our clothes on. Soap is a luxury in the villages, and John lost his the second week we were there. He made a mad dash to shore that day getting away from a bull that wanted his place in the river."

More laughter.

"Of course, we were told not to go into the water except where they showed us. Another morning, John decided he was going to bathe in private. So, he got up very early and slipped down to the river, around the bend, and went away from the village. He was about to step into the water when one of the smaller boys, who had followed him, grabbed his arm, and hauled him back. That particular section of the river belonged to a large crocodile." A ripple of amusement moved over the congregation. "Whatever angel God had watching over John had double duty on this trip."

Sharee's eyes rested on John's face. Bob's stories amused, but her breathing deepened. With a different ending, the stories would be tragedies.

Bob's voice changed, and his next story described the time they received small-arms fire as they flew low over one island.

"The persecution of Christians is well documented in parts of Indonesia. Churches have been burned and people killed because of their faith. It is known that missionaries fly not only supplies but also the Word of God into the villages. I thank God for the skill of our pilot that day, and for God's answer to prayer."

Her heart kicked into overdrive. John hadn't mentioned that or the other problems they'd faced. Of course, they hadn't had time. Not with his proposal. If she'd said yes, would she have faith enough to face whatever came? If God gave his assurance...

After the strain of the last couple of weeks, though, she'd found it hard to concentrate much less hear God's voice. Some people said go with peace, but she didn't have peace either way.

She hadn't told anyone about the calls because she'd waited for John to get home. Without thinking it through, she'd planned to dump the whole thing on him—expecting that he would have a solution. But how could she explain it to him now?

Her heart thudded in her ears. She rose, slipped out the back of the church and headed for the field. The bleachers at its edge beckoned her. She climbed up a few rows and sat, her eyes closed. *Just give me a billboard, Lord. Tell me what to do.*

Close at hand, the bleachers creaked as someone else ascended them.

"Sharee?" Pastor Alan sat down near her. "You bolted out of church. Are you okay?"

Her throat tightened, and her mind jumped from one explanation to another.

"John tells me you two haven't spoken since the night of the accident."

"I...no, we haven't." Her heart hurt. John hadn't called, and she hadn't either. Since Tuesday.

The Pastor's face showed concern. "You want to talk about it?"

"I don't know." She cleared her throat. "I'm embarrassed to say that, but I just don't know. I've prayed. I've asked God to show me, but I haven't heard anything. It's like I'm waiting for something to happen, only I don't know what."

"You're praying about whether to marry John or not?"

"Yes."

"Okay. What about the phone calls? Have they stopped?"

"Yes."

"Good."

"Did John tell you he wants to go back to Indonesia in six months?"

"No." The pastor shifted on the bleachers. "And he wants you to go with him?" She nodded. He let out a long sigh. "So he wants to get married and go back in six months? That sounds like him. He's never liked to wait for things."

"Well, I wish he'd waited this time."

"Sharee, confusion's not from God. Look inside and see what you're afraid of. Get into the Word. God's not given you a spirit of fear. He's given you one of power and love and a sound mind."

"I know."

The side of his mouth lifted, and his smile reminded her of John's. They seemed more like brothers than cousins even though ten years separated them.

He put a hand out and helped her to her feet. "Let's get back in church. Listen to what John has to say, to what God did during his trip. You might hear something you need."

"Okay."

They stepped to the ground. "You know, when John makes up his mind about something, he jumps in—with both feet. He's been like that since he was a kid, and he gets a lot accomplished that way. But it also can cause trouble. He could use a good balance."

They walked to the church. Pastor Alan stopped and let her go in alone. She slipped into the back pew.

John was standing at the podium, his crutches resting against the chair behind him. He stopped talking when he saw her, shoved a hand through his hair and cleared his throat.

"I think I need to balance some scales here." His glance skidded to Bob, and a smile started at the corners of his mouth. "I have some stories of my own."

Bob's protestations added to the group's amusement. Sharee laughed along with the others as John told some anecdotes about Bob. Then John's voice changed, and he began to share how the trip they'd planned to bless others had ended by changing his life's priorities.

"I saw God work in so many situations, in so many people; and He used that to touch me deeply. That kind of power and love humbles you and makes it easy to surrender everything to Him. In Philippians 3:7-8, Paul says 'What things were gain to me, those I counted loss for Christ...and I count all things...loss for the excellency of knowing Christ Jesus my Lord.'"

Someone in the congregation murmured, "Amen."

John turned and limped back to his seat as the congregation broke out in applause. Pastor Alan walked to the podium and began to pray.

Sharee didn't hear what he said. Her mind focused on what John had shared, the awe he'd felt and experienced. It stirred her. Her trips as a teenager had excited her, opened new worlds and shown her real poverty; but she hadn't returned as John had, filled with the wonder of God's presence.

Pastor Alan's prayer ended. People rose and brushed past her. She looked up in time to see John hobble out the side door, crutches under his arms; and she smiled. He'd want his space now, his privacy. Bob had pegged. At times, John needed privacy as much as she did.

Someone stopped beside her. Sharee glanced up and smiled. China Summers gave her a shy smile. The girl had graduated high school last year, started college and now helped with the youth group. She'd changed a lot, her dress and hair reflecting the college scene. She'd dyed her rich brown hair black and her eye make-up gave her eyes a slight slant. A tiny diamond rested in her left nostril.

"John was totally awesome. I mean, he's never spoken at the youth meetings. He helps keep the guys in line, that kind of stuff, but I've never heard him speak. But he was awesome today." China's voice sounded rushed and a little high. "And he looked great." Her gaze bounced from Sharee's seat back to her face. "How come you're sitting back here?"

Sharee stood and lifted her Bible and her purse. "Oh, I came in late."

"Hmm…" China studied her. "Bet you're glad he's back, aren't you?"

"Of course." And why aren't I prepared for this type of comment? I knew people would have questions.

"He has a great tan. He's always been pretty hot, but now… Well, he looks even better." China smiled and turned to go.

Miss Eleanor inched her way through the people to stand next to Sharee. Her blue eyes looked out of a wrinkled face surrounded by white hair. "John did himself proud. I think he's going to make a good missionary." She tilted her head. "You remember what I told you?"

Sharee nodded and tightened her grip on the chair in front of her. "Yes." How could she forget? Miss Eleanor hardly ever made phone calls and when she did, you listened.

Miss Eleanor nodded. "Good."

Sharee ignored the texts and calls the rest of the day. She loved her friends, but they could ask hard questions. She'd worked hard to avoid them this week, but today both Lynn Stapleton and Marci Thornton forced her to hit her phone's ignore button all afternoon. Finally, she sent a text telling them she needed their patience and that when she could talk, she'd get in touch. Not that it would silence them but a day or two. She shook her head.

She walked from her apartment's living area to the kitchen and checked the time. As it was, the evening service would bring questions she'd find hard to avoid. They might both descend on her, along with others.

Her phone rang. Won't they ever give up? She reached to hit the ignore button and saw John's picture. Her heart stopped. It rang again and then a third time, and she stabbed the green button.

"John?" Her voice squeaked.

"Are you going to church?"

"What? Oh, yes. I… Are you?"

"I wasn't."

"Oh."

"But I'm working out here. If we don't want a hundred questions from well-meaning friends, perhaps we should."

"We?"

"If you're going, I'll be there."

"I…I was planning on it."

"All right."

Silence dropped, and a minute later, the phone went dead.

She watched while his face disappeared from the phone, her heart thudding. He would be there tonight. Bringing her hands together in a fist, she pressed them hard against her chest and bowed her head.

John slipped the phone back into the case on his belt and stood for a moment in the cool of the work shed, head down. She hadn't called all week. The knife thrust to his gut was just as sharp as on Tuesday when he'd stood looking at her windswept hair and the uncertainty in her eyes. Nothing had prepared him for that. A month of serving God had ended with his hopes slammed against the rocks of her indecision.

He unhooked the shovel from the wall. When he'd left a month ago, she'd whispered "I love you" at the end of their kiss, and it had not been the first time she'd said it. Was he a fool for believing her?

Over the last few days, anger had replaced the pain, replaced the calm peace that flew back with him all the way from Indonesia. He'd lived with that kind of anger before and knew its dangers. If he'd kept talking to her now, it would have found its way into his voice.

No, she hadn't called since Tuesday, but neither had he. That he hadn't was wisdom on his part. He could hurt her with his words, and right now, he wanted to.

Sharee's phone chimed again as she parked the CR-V in the church parking lot. She pulled the phone from her purse. Glancing at it, her heart jolted. Unknown caller. Whoever it was, was back. She stared as it rang again then jabbed it on.

"Would you quit calling, please?" Her voice sounded guttural even to her own ears. "Whoever you are, just stop it." No sound came from the phone, and she stabbed at the face again, turning it off.

Maybe she would get a chance to tell John. He'd called, broken their stalemate. Perhaps they could talk… She thrust the phone back into her purse, slipped her Bible under her arm and climbed from the car. So many times this week, she'd reached for the phone to call him only to put it down. What would she say?

A girl laughed, and Sharee twisted her head in that direction. John, his crutches propped under his arms, looked down at China Summers. They stood in front of the office, across the patch of grass from where she stood. The girl's black hair caught the fading light, its healthy shine shifting with the evening breeze. Two potted azaleas rested between them, and a shovel leaned against a tree.

Crutches or not, it didn't surprise her that John had jumped back into work again, doing maintenance at the church as before.

He said something she couldn't hear and shoved his hand through his dark hair. China laughed again. Sharee's heart squeezed.

She turned and walked to the fellowship hall. She'd wait inside until the service started. Fishing for answers to personal questions was not her forte. Opening the door, she slid into the darkened room and stood for a moment, letting her eyes adjust to the shadows. She started forward but came to an abrupt halt.

Two figures stood outlined against a window, a man and a woman embracing. No one moved.

"Marci?" Sharee heard the hesitancy in her own voice.

The figures parted. One made its way to her. "Sharee, I…"

"What's going on?" Sharee asked before recognizing the other person. *"Ted?"* Alarm sent needles of shock through her. She started to back toward the door.

"Sharee." Ted Hogan's voice was thick. "Don't go anywhere." She stopped. He turned to the other woman. "Marci, go on. Go to church. Stephen will be here soon."

Marci Thornton slipped out the door, not looking at Sharee. Ted moved over to her. "You didn't see anything here. It's not what you think. It's innocent. It…" He stopped, his voice fading away, then in an abrupt, hard tone, "Don't say anything to anyone."

Sharee's heart raced, but shock gave way to anger. She found her voice. "I thought you were going to stay away from Marci. What's been going on since Christmas?"

"Nothing's going on."

"That's not what it looked like."

"She just wanted to talk. I told you it's not what you think. Stephen doesn't listen to her. He doesn't know how to communicate."

"And you do?"

"Yes, I do. She's in a bad way lately and—"

"She doesn't need your help. She can talk to me or Pastor Alan or someone who wants her marriage to work. Leave her alone. If she and Stephen are having problems, then they need to talk about it together." She looked at him in the gray light. "Ted, if you're talking with her, consoling her or whatever, you're creating a stumbling block for her. You're…you're stealing her affections."

"Stealing?" He stepped toward her. "I'm not stealing anything. We were just talking."

"Oh? Can you do that? You told me about your feelings for Marci, remember?" Sharee kept her voice level. "Think about what you're doing. Think of Marci and Stephen, think of the children and all the hurt you could cause."

"I am thinking of Marci."

"Think of God. What would He have you do?"

"God forgives."

"Listen to yourself! If your motives are so pure, what would He have to forgive? You think you can do whatever you want with no consequences? That's a lie from the pit."

Ted's eyes narrowed. "And you always do it right, don't you, Little Miss Self-Righteous? You don't ever—"

Someone opened the door. They both jumped. Matthew Thornton stepped across the threshold. He stopped when he saw them.

"Oh, uh, hi. I was looking for mom. Dad sent me to find her." He eyed Ted, looking as if he'd just eaten a raw egg.

Sharee fought to keep her voice neutral. Marci's sixteen-year-old son didn't need to know what she'd seen. "Marci's in the sanctuary, I think."

"Naw, we already looked there. Maybe I'll look in the office." The door closed after him.

Sharee rounded on Ted. "What if that boy had walked in on you and Marci instead of me?" She started to move away.

Ted grabbed her arm. "Just don't go telling anyone about this."

She yanked her arm free. "I'm not promising anything. Why don't you take a vacation or something? Think things through." Her voice softened. "You know you don't want this. This isn't right."

"You don't know what I want."

"Hopefully, you want God."

He said something under his breath, and pushed past her, letting the door slam as he exited.

She gave him a minute then followed him out and walked toward the front of the church.

John leaned on the shovel now. He'd propped his crutches against the nearby tree. Dirt mounded next to a hole near his feet. His head came up as she made her way to the sanctuary. Sharee felt his eyes follow her as she ducked inside the church.

Her heart did an erratic tap dance inside her chest. Praying that no one would approach her, she moved down the aisle to their regular place. She folded her hands in her lap and thought of Marci and Ted. What had happened back there? Just innocent, Ted said. So why insist she say nothing?

Sharee lifted her head and looked around. She wanted things like they were before John left. No proposal. No pressure. She tried to push the thoughts of her last engagement out of her mind. John was not Dean. She closed her eyes. Stupid, irrational fear!

A few minutes later, John stopped beside her. He took a moment to set the crutches in a way that kept them out of the aisle. He'd changed his shirt, combed his hair. She tried a smile, but his glance held a hard reserve. The wall she'd erected between them remained.

After a moment, his hand moved, touching hers, the briefest of touches. She wanted to tell him what she'd felt this morning when he shared about his trip, and about Ted and Marci, and the phone calls; but the music began, and they rose to sing.

Sharee swallowed. How can we do this? Stand here and praise God and act like nothing's wrong? She took a deep breath and put her concentration on the words of the song and off the man beside her.

When Pastor Alan rose to share, it was as if he'd heard the cries of her heart. "Moses needed courage to face Pharaoh, to take six million people into the wilderness. When he died, God told Joshua, 'Be strong and very courageous.' David needed courage to face Goliath and later to face Saul, and especially when his own army wanted to kill him after their wives and children were taken hostage. Paul and Silas were beaten and thrown in prison. We've known missionaries today who have been killed or jailed because of their faith. Courage is something we need today, too. Courage to do what is right, and courage to do what God wants. We can't run from situations in our lives. We have to stand and allow God to work."

Sharee bowed her head. *I need this, Lord. I need courage. I can't let my life fall apart because I'm scared of another relationship or scared of some pesky phone calls. Please help me.*

As Pastor Alan ended and the worship began again, she touched John's arm and slipped past him out the doors of the church. She didn't want to put on a front for others after the service, and she needed time alone. Sitting next to him, feeling the barriers between them, had left her stomach knotted and empty.

She walked into the evening light, past a large pine, past the bleachers, to the field and the pond beyond. The fragrance from the cypress trees filled her nostrils. They had begun to fill out with new spring growth, and their black silhouettes rose against the sky.

Lord, what are you saying? Something's wrong. What did Miss Eleanor mean? You have her praying for us—for John and me. Why?

She stared at the half moon, drew in its stillness. The sound of crickets' chirping and the smell of the damp earth pushed their way into her consciousness. Lifting her head, she turned and walked back toward the lights of the church.

John waited near the top of the bleachers. She spotted his dark silhouette as she drew near. How did he get up there and where had he put his crutches? She climbed over five rows of seats to get to him. Lowering herself onto the cool seats, she stared back toward the pond.

The night air vibrated with tension. She had asked him to give her a week or two for an answer. And she had no answer. Yet.

"John." His name caught in her throat. She swallowed. "I'm sorry. I never meant to hurt you."

He said nothing. The quiet stretched.

Her chest tightened. "I want you to understand. After you left, I began to feel anxious. I'm not at peace."

She didn't move; neither did he.

His question, when it came, sounded abrupt and rough. "Is that what you want me to understand? That you don't have peace?"

"No, I mean, yes; but..." Her heart squeezed.

He shifted on the bleachers. "Alan told me I should have waited before I asked you, that I jumped in too quick. But you knew before I went what I felt about you...about us. What happened after I left?"

The pit in her stomach opened, and she reached out only to have him draw away. "I don't know, I..."

"Whatever it is, you need to tell me. Is there someone else?"

"No." She closed her eyes. How could she tell him what she didn't understand herself?

"Okay. If you need more time, you have it. If you don't feel God wants us together..." His voice faltered. When it came again, the anger had disappeared leaving just the raw emotion. "As much as I care, I... Neither of us wants this if it's not right."

His pain hurt her. *Lord, I love him. You know that. I thought you wanted me to marry him. I don't understand the fear, the uncertainty.*

John stood to his feet, but she caught his hand. *Don't go.* But the words didn't leave her mouth. He looked down, his face shadowed in moonlight. She drew a long, shuddering breath, fighting the waves of pain spilling through her. He reached and cupped her cheek in his palm. A light breeze caught her hair stroking it across his fingers, and his mouth twisted. His hand slid over her cheekbone and into her hair. She stood even as he pulled her forward, meeting her need with his. The kiss was hard and long and mutually desperate.

"I love you," she whispered.

"Don't." His voice tensed. "Don't say it if you don't mean it. I don't want that."

The ache in her chest increased. "I wish I could make you understand, but I don't myself. I'm not sure what God wants. I—"

His arms dropped. "That's what I mean." The words cut across hers. "You want a week or two. Fine. But don't say something you don't mean."

"But I …"

He swung away from her and off the edge of the bleachers, landing on his good foot. "Sharee, make sure before you give me your answer. We don't want to go through this again." He leaned down on one foot and picked up his crutches.

Her heart slammed hard into her chest. She loved him. She knew that. And God had brought them together. She'd known that before. Something went strong and deep into her chest. Relief washed over her. She stepped to the edge of the bleachers.

"John…"

He swung away from her. "A week. I'll see you in a week."

Her hand went out, but he didn't see it. He went around the big pine tree and was lost to sight.

"John!"

Her heart pounded in her ears. God had answered her prayer. *She knew.* She started down the bleachers, but slowed, stopped. His last words had held anger again.

Maybe I should wait. Give it time, so he's sure I know what I'm saying. I can wait a week. What could happen in a week?

Chapter 3

Nothing could happen because she wasn't waiting a week. Three days were three days too long. She'd tell him at the Wednesday service.

She arrived fifteen minutes before the evening service, heart thumping in her chest. She'd throw herself into John's arms as soon as she saw him.

He hadn't called the last couple of days, but neither had she. She didn't want to say this over the phone. She wanted to see his face when she told him, wanted his arms around her, wanted his kiss.

As the minutes passed, though, her stomach began to churn. Surely he would come. He always came. *They* always came. Once the service started, her heart stopped its excited pounding and plummeted in her chest. He wasn't coming. He had said a week, and that was what he'd meant.

The first song ended, and she dropped into her seat. Miss Eleanor gave her a speculative look before smiling in welcome. Sharee made herself smile in reply, let her eyes slide past her and caught Lynn's gaze. Her friend lifted an eyebrow, and she quickly shook her head. She didn't need any questions. Pastor Alan had put a hand on her arm earlier and said her name in greeting, but with a question in it before he continued up the aisle and onto the platform. John always sat with her. They all knew that. His absence was noticeable.

Sharee stood to her feet and closed her eyes as the second song began. "Oh, how He loves us," the choir sang. Sharee inhaled the words and music like a fragrance. She lifted her hands and worshiped.

I give it to you, Lord. I give the worry, John, and our situation to you. As she sang, the heaviness lifted. John's pain and anger were understandable. If he had said the same thing to her, she would have been devastated. She needed to call him as soon as possible. Why had she waited?

On the drive home, peace and humming filled her heart. God felt close, His love, His comfort surrounded her. Everything would be okay.

"Thank you, Lord. I trust you."

She picked up her phone, pushed in John's number, but then hit "End." No, she didn't want any distractions. She'd call when she got home.

The parking lot in her apartment complex had only a few open spaces. She parked, climbed from her car, and headed across the dark lot. Her heart sang.

Behind her, over her right shoulder, an engine started. Lights flashed on, shooting across the cars and spotlighting her.

Watch out.

The words whipped across her mind. She glanced around but didn't stop. Instead, she picked up her pace. A shiver went through her. At the car's sudden acceleration, she shot a second look over her shoulder. Tires squealed, and the bright eyes of the car rushed at her.

With sudden comprehension, she whirled, leaping for the sidewalk. The car hit the walk, too, and hurdled forward. Its front edge caught her hip and slung her back against the passenger door. She flew off the back fender, legs twisting under her. Her head slammed the sidewalk, and pain exploded throughout her.

The siren's scream woke her. Lights strobed against her eyes. She winced. It took a minute before she recognized the strange instruments and sterile insides of the ambulance. Pain stabbed her head, and she struggled against the straps that held her. Beneath her, a flat, hard board added to her discomfort.

"You're awake?" Someone asked. A woman's unfamiliar face filled her vision. "Don't try to move. You're secured to a spine board, and we've put a neck collar on. You were in an accident. We don't know all your injuries yet, but your vital signs are okay. Do you know your name?"

"Yes." Sharee struggled for words.

"What is it?"

"Sharee Jones." The siren wailed in her ears.

"Your address?"

Sharee told her.

"Okay, good. We have your purse with us." The EMT's voice was professional and crisp. She held up Sharee's purse. "Your phone's inside. Can I call someone?"

"Yes. Call John." Sharee swallowed and shoved the pain aside. "Tap the face. Then…push the green button…twice."

The EMT made the call. Sharee listened to be sure she had reached him. Just his voice, sounding startled, as Sharee's condition was relayed to him sent a wave of reassurance through her.

The woman slipped the phone back into Sharee's purse. "He's on his way. What hurts?"

"My head. My back. The board."

"Okay. Try not to move. We're coming to the hospital now. They'll take care of you."

Sharee gritted her teeth and issued a plea for help. *Jesus.*

The ambulance doors opened, and Sharee felt the rush of air. Hands pulled the stretcher out, and they wheeled her inside.

"They're full tonight. They'll leave you in the hall until they have a room. I'll give your purse to the nurse here and check you in."

A couple minutes later, a masculine face appeared above hers. "I'm Dr. Lawson. You stepped in front of a car, I hear." He leaned over and checked her eyes with a small flashlight. "Here's the plan. In a minute, we'll unstrap you and do a fast 1-2-3 move to a gurney. I'll examine your back and check your spine before we send you up to X-ray and after that a CAT scan."

"Sharee?" A familiar voice reached her, and Pastor Alan's head appeared next to the doctor's.

Relief swept through her once more. She tried to smile.

"You're family?" the doctor asked.

"I'm her pastor."

"Oh...Okay..." He hesitated a moment. "Well, we're about to take her to X-ray. You'll have to move aside."

"All right." He gave Sharee's hand a squeeze. "John called. I was here already—visiting someone. He's on his way. He wasn't at home so it will take him awhile. Did he say you stepped in front of a car? Like John?" A smile formed. "What am I going to do with you two?"

"Okay, Pastor..." another voice intervened, moving up next to the stretcher.

As he moved back, Sharee twisted her hand and caught his. "Alan, please. Tell John it wasn't an accident."

"What?"

"It wasn't an accident."

⨖

The truck ate up the dark road, the yellow lines in the middle whizzing by, the dashes creating one continuous line, but it wasn't fast enough for him. He glanced at the speedometer and struggled with what he knew was right and what he wanted to do.

A car had hit her. Alan said she was coherent, but they were doing X-rays, and that the accident was no accident. Exactly like what happened to him. What did that mean?

The thought of a future without her drove a swirl of blackness to his gut. He'd fought it all week. *What happened between the time he left for Indonesia and his return?*

And how was he supposed to act now? She'd had the paramedic call him, not her parents, not Alan and Daneen, but *him*. Car lights raced his way, tore past and sailed into oblivion. What did *that* mean?

He should call her parents. He'd met them at Christmas and seen the closeness. They'd want to know. He braked at the light, swerved onto US 19 and began to pray.

The chill in the X-ray room enveloped her more the second time than the first. The doctor had ordered more X-rays. Sharee shivered. The cold room and the gurney's hardness added to the pain in her head. She shut her eyes. The hospital's antiseptic odor filled her nostrils.

"You're going to have to lie still," the technician said. "We don't want to do these a third time."

Sharee froze and heard the woman walk away. A door opened and closed. The first time they'd wheeled her into the room, the woman's abrupt tone had surprised her. Now, a jolt of irritation sent adrenalin rushing through her. *I didn't move the first time. It's not my fault if you have to re-do these.*

She heard the hall door open and then nothing else. Had the tech gone out one way and come in another? When no other noise came, she forced her eyelids apart.

John stood propped against the outer door, resting on his crutches. His gaze met hers, and her heart jolted. Relief swept through her.

"John."

He hobbled into the room, maneuvering around the table and stopped close to her head. His hand moved toward hers then stopped. It dropped to his side, and he straightened. "I'm sorry it took so long. I was at Bruce's. He said he'd be in prayer for you."

"I think I need it."

The brown eyes darkened. "What happened?"

"An accident. Like yours. A car tried to run me down in the parking lot. I jumped back but not far enough. It caught me and sent me flying. They're taking X-rays of my back. They did some already, but they have to redo them."

"Why?"

I don't know. I…" She stopped, swallowed. "I want to tell you something. Something else. Not about this.'

The technician stepped into her line of vision. "You can talk to him in a few minutes."

"But I—"

The woman's gaze settled on John. "Would you wait outside, please?"

"I'll stay."

"It would be better if you waited outside."

John repositioned his crutches and lifted a brow. After a moment's stand-off, the technician shrugged and walked to the other side of the bed.

"Good decision," he muttered.

Sharee bit back a smile. She loved him. Of course, she did. Where had the uncertainty come from?

The technician opened a drawer at the side of the gurney and pulled a weighted jacket from it. She handed it to John. "Put this on if you're going to stay."

John took it and slipped his arms through it. Sharee studied him. Accident or not, she had to tell him how she felt.

The tech slipped a rubber wedge under Sharee's legs, and Sharee sucked in her breath. John caught her hand in his.

"Just a couple more." The woman said. "Remain still until I get back."

John's gaze followed the technician as she left the room. He glanced at Sharee again. "Your back? What about your back?"

"There's pain when I move."

"Why is she moving you then?"

"I'm sure she knows what she's doing. They took X-rays earlier. The doctor ordered some more. I don't know if something was wrong or if he wants different pictures, or what. They did a Cat scan for my head—in between the X-rays."

"Why?"

"I might have a concussion. I blacked out for a while, and I can't move my head without setting off an electric current."

"A current?"

"Of pain." She wanted him closer. His words sounded abrupt, and his stance was stiff. Awkward. "Lean down here, will you?"

He shifted the crutches and bent his head toward her just as the technician swung the door open. "Okay. Relax." She walked to the bedside and spent a few moments removing the plates. "I'll look at these then we'll see."

When the tech left, John leaned forward again. "Alan said it wasn't an accident."

Her heart sank. She didn't want to talk about that. "I'm sure it wasn't, but can we discuss it later? I want to—"

"Someone tried to run us both over."

"Yes, but—"

"Tell me exactly what happened."

She shot a glance at the ceiling, back at him, and then rattled off what she remembered.

"Did you see the make of the car?"

She shook her head, and pain exploded inside her skull. She snapped her eyes shut and clenched her teeth. Tears rose, pooled, and drained down the sides of her face.

His hand tightened around hers. "What can I do?"

She couldn't answer, couldn't open her eyes.

He prayed under his breath, and his voice rolled over her, the words massaging, soothing, penetrating. In a minute, the pain began to subside. *Thank you, Jesus.*

When, at last, she opened her eyes, the concern in his face stroked her.

The tech swept into the room. "We need to re-do one of these."

John's head twisted in her direction, and his jaw clenched. Sharee groaned.

"I'm sorry. We'll do two more. Just in case." She adjusted the equipment again. "Please stay the way you are. Don't move."

Just as the technician disappeared through the side door, someone swung the hall door open. "Sharee Jones?"

"Yes?"

A man in a pair of scrubs stepped into her view. "Your parents are here."

"My parents?" The words squeaked from her throat.

"Yes, in the ER, looking for you. Your mother was quite agitated not to be on the HIPPA forms. She's making rather a scene. Do you want to see her or to have her on the disclosure forms?"

"But how did they know I was here?"

John squeezed her shoulder. "I assumed you'd want them to know, so I called on the way." He turned toward the clock on the other wall. "I spent quite a while trying to find you. They wouldn't give me any information. Your parents must have left Orlando right after I called."

She hadn't thought of them. When they asked about the HIPPA forms, she'd given John's name.

"You didn't put them on the forms?"

"No, I..." She stopped a moment. "I put you."

"Me?" His eyes widened. "I never thought to ask. It would have made things easier."

"I'm sorry, I—" She'd only thought of him.

"Was I out of line calling them?"

"No. No, of course not. I forgot."

"Would you like me to see them?"

She sighed. Would she ever get to talk to him? "Yes. Thank you. They'll worry."

"Good." The other man turned and headed out.

John glanced at the technician who had reappeared. His eyes narrowed.

"I'll be fine, John." She glanced at his crutches. "Is it a long way?"

"Not that far." He removed the X-ray jacket and set it at the foot of the gurney, shooting one more glance at the X-ray technician. "I'll be back soon." Propping the crutches under his arms, he made his way out the door.

Sharee stared at the closed door. His protectiveness wrapped her like a warm blanket.

"Look," the tech said, "we need one more to finish this. Hopefully, before he gets back." She adjusted the wedge under Sharee's leg. "Is that your husband? He doesn't like seeing you in pain, does he?"

Husband. Sharee smiled. Not yet, but if she could talk to him, they'd be a step closer. *If* she could talk to him.

Heading back toward the emergency room entrance, John wrestled with the anger inside him. After the hospital personnel and their continued reference to the HIPPA laws—he'd never thought to ask if he was on the forms—he'd been forced to hobble through the halls to find Sharee, and the X-ray technician had found his last nerve.

He swallowed and forced himself to concentrate on the important issue—someone had run her down. On purpose. His hands squeezed the bars on either side of the crutches, and flames shot bright and hot within him. He'd already lost one person he loved; he wasn't going to lose another.

But who'd want to hurt her? Or both of them? It made no sense. And would they try again? His heart stuttered. How could he to protect her? He'd stay with her tonight, if she'd let him, but after that, what?

He slowed his pace and took a deep breath. His eyes went heavenward. God hadn't left them. They'd both been hurt, but they were alive. Since he'd re-surrendered his life to God six months earlier and gone on the month-long mission trip, he should have expected some kind of attack. He didn't know what was happening, but God was with them. Relief freed the knot in his stomach.

He shifted the crutches and made his way to the emergency room. Sharee's parents rose when he came through the door, and her mother rushed forward spraying questions at him. Her dad glanced at the crutches and raised an eyebrow. John managed a short explanation of his injury and waved them back to their chairs.

Sharee's mom started again with a scatter-shot of questions, but her dad—first name Brian, John remembered—remained quiet. Somewhere within the explanation of Sharee's accident, he decided to withhold the information that the incident was intentional. Sharee had referred to her mother as a teddy bear, but that didn't quite fit. More like an uptight cat. He'd get Brian alone later and explain.

When her mother paused for breath, he leaned back in the chair. "I'll stay with her tonight. The care in the X-ray room was not the best, and I'd rather be with her if she needs anything."

Her mother sat forward. "I intended to do that myself."

His gaze met hers. That made sense, of course, but just wasn't happening. Until they knew what was going on, Sharee needed some protection. "I'm sure Sharee would want you to bunk at her place. I'll do fine here."

"I'd rather be with my daughter than 'bunk' anywhere."

Her tone surprised him. The hospital personnel said she'd caused a commotion. Maybe adrenalin running high.

He sat forward. "I know you're concerned. I am, too, which is why I've decided to stay."

Her mom pushed her shoulders back. The teddy bear morphed into a grizzly. "You've decided, have you? Well, I think she'd rather have her mother."

"When she comes home, Mrs. Jones, she'll need you. You don't want to be worn out from sitting in a chair all night." And he'd make sure Sharee had decent locks and an alarm system in that apartment she called home.

"Oh, I don't? And just when did you start making decisions for her?"

Brian put a hand on her shoulder. "If the man wants to stay—"

"I do." John saw the instant fire in her mother's eyes and determined to end the argument. "In fact, I insist."

"Insist?" Her voice rose. "Insist? I will not have some man spending the night with my daughter. She needs her mother."

Some man? He gritted his teeth. "This is a hospital, not a motel. You—"

"I should hope not!"

A couple sitting close by looked their way. John wanted to roll his eyes like Sharee did with him once in awhile. He leaned closer and lowered his voice. "Look, there's nothing improper about this. She's going to be my wife, and—"

"Your wife? What do you mean she's going to be your wife?"

His gaze ricocheted from her mom to her dad and back. Great. Where had that come from? "I've asked her to marry me." That was the truth, at least.

Her father leaned forward. "You—"

"*You're engaged?*" Mrs. Jones voice overrode her husband's. "But…When did this happen? Why hasn't Sharee told us?"

Other people stopped their conversations and looked their way. Sharee's dad put a hand on his wife's arm. "Marilyn, calm down. Sit back and relax."

John glanced from one to the other. Had he just made a bad situation worse? Should he let them believe that lie? If so, he'd need to tell Sharee soon. If she found out before he could explain, what would she think? Or say?

Sputtering, Mrs. Jones glared at John and clutched her purse in balled fists. "I still think—"

Brian made a movement with his hand. "Marilyn, we are not arguing this anymore. John wants to stay with her. They're engaged, and Sharee called him. I'm sure John can get a nurse if needed just as easily as you can."

His wife glowered at him then her shoulders sagged. "I just want to make sure she's okay."

"As I do," John said. Relief flooded him. A flicker of amusement rose. Sharee had inherited more than just petiteness and good looks from her mother. He nodded a thank-you to her dad. "I will make sure they take good care of her."

He stood and grabbed his crutches. "She was in X-ray when I left. Let me go see if she's still there or if she's in a room. I'll call down here or come get you when I know."

Her mom would have protested again, but her husband's agreement stopped it.

John headed back through the labyrinth of hallways. Her mother couldn't protect her. He could. He needed to be there. His steps slowed, and he stopped in the middle of the corridor.

Don't lie to yourself, too, Jergenson. You want her safe, but it's more than that. You want to be with her. This week had proved long and hard. Had he been crazy to think of their life together?

A moment later, he moved to the other problem. The accidents. They needed to put their heads together and see if they could make sense of what had happened.

Two people went by him, talking and laughing; and he hauled his mind back to real time. He adjusted the crutches and started down the corridor again.

They had moved her to a private room. As he entered, the attendant finished adjusting the bed and left.

John leaned forward to draw a thumb down her cheek and stopped. Staying detached was proving hard. "How are you feeling?"

Her eyes showed the strain of the night. "If I don't move, my head's okay."

"Good. Don't move."

"Oh. Gee. Thanks."

He smiled at her sarcasm. "Just wanted to help. Anything else?"

"My back feels out of place, and I have this strange numbing and tingling sensation crawling down my left leg."

"Sounds like sciatica. Anything else?"

"My hip and leg feel bruised—and my backside, too."

He grinned. "Want me to check?"

Her eyes narrowed. "Is that the kind of help you're going to be?"

"Whatever you need, babe."

Her face relaxed, and her eyes warmed. He shifted the crutches and bent over her. The door swung open, and a man in a white coat crossed the room to her bedside.

"I'm Dr. Fernandez."

John straightened and stepped back. He'd almost kissed her. Are you crazy, Jergenson? She's hurt and in pain. She needs you right now. At the end of this, she could still tell you to find someone else to trek through the jungles with. He swallowed and shook hands with the doctor.

"John Jergenson."

The doctor nodded then turned to Sharee. "I'll be handling your case. It's been a long night, but we have some good news. First, no major injuries. Nothing life-threatening. You have a herniated disc in your lower back, and you have a concussion. I am ordering more tests for that. I think it's mild; but since you lost consciousness, I want to make sure. We'll keep you here for another day or two. You have any questions?"

"Not that I can think of right now."

"Okay. Are you in pain?"

"Yes, some."

"I'll prescribe something. Take it if you need it."

Pale morning light sifted through the curtains as the doctor left. When the door closed behind him, John's shoulders relaxed. He settled his crutches against the wall. Maybe they'd have a few minutes to talk. Before he completed the thought, the door swung wide again. A woman in hospital scrubs entered.

He waited, fingers drumming against the windowsill.

The nurse checked her IV and the monitors. "The doctor prescribed some pain medication. I'll get that and be back in a minute."

Before she left, another woman entered. John clenched his jaw. Would the parade never end? The other woman spent time going over what Sharee could or couldn't do, the procedure for ordering dinner, and how to work her bed. She pulled up the railings. The RN returned with two pills.

John relaxed as she swallowed the pills. He'd noticed the tightness in her face and her continual shifting to get comfortable. She'd feel better soon.

Both women left.

Good.

Sharee's eyes closed, and John hesitated. Her look of exhaustion halted his questions. Across the room, the door eased open again.

A policeman stepped into the room. "Ms. Jones?"

Sharee opened her eyes. "Yes?"

"I need to get some information from you."

"Okay."

The officer took down her statement and then listened to John's description of his own accident and his idea that the incidents might be related.

"Did you report this?"

"No. At the time, I tried to pass it off. But with Sharee's accident…"

"Do you know anyone who would want to run you both down? Do you have any enemies?"

John's head turned toward Sharee, but her eyes had closed again.

"Not that we're aware of."

"Did you notice the type of car or who was driving the car that sideswiped you?"

"No, and for the same reason. The lights were in my eyes."

The officer nodded. "Okay." He closed the small book he'd written in and pocketed it. "We'll check this out. See if any of your neighbors saw anything." He left a minute later.

Sharee moaned. "He didn't act too impressed by what we had to say."

He pushed some stray curls from her face. No, he couldn't keep his hands off her. "He probably has a plate full of serious stuff, and ours looks trivial in comparison."

Her eyes, big with pain, caught his and held. Something stirred inside him. He swallowed, moved back from the bed and crossed his arms over his chest. Don't read too much into it. She's hurt and vulnerable. Everything he wanted to talk about disappeared. They stared at each other for a long time. When she reached out, he took her hand and enfolded it in his.

Tears welled in her eyes. "John..." Her voice caught, and she stopped.

He sat down on the edge of the bed, past the railing, and tightened the rein on his emotions. "Sharee, you're going to be okay. The pain medication will kick in soon. "

"I know. That's not the problem. I need to tell you something." She tried to straighten in the bed and winced.

"Give it a few more minutes."

"Will you come closer?"

He tilted his head at the railing and got up to move it.

"John."

"A minute." He shifted the railing down then sat on the bed next to her. "What?"

"When you asked me—"

A noise came from the doorway. Her parents walked into the room. He tightened his jaw. Well, what did he expect? He stood and started to move away, but Sharee's hand squeezed his. He caught the anxious request in her eyes.

"Oh, Sharee!" Her mother's high voice broke the quiet. She stepped next to the bed with a flourish. "You've finally got your own room. I don't know why it took so long."

"I'm sure they did the best they could, Mom." Sharee's voice rose, too.

"John was supposed to tell us." Her look grazed him. "I guess he forgot."

He started to say something, but her mother continued. "How in the world did you get run over? Weren't you looking?"

"I don't know, Mom. I'm sorry."

John glanced at her. What was she apologizing for? Someone else had caused the accident, and Sharee didn't need a guilt trip. Good thing he'd won the battle on who stayed the night.

"Your father and I prayed all the way here." Her mother's voice rose again. "Tell us what the doctors said, and why they did so many tests."

John's gaze met her father's. Hmm. The man was quiet in the face of his wife's over-concern, but she had given way when he'd intervened downstairs. What had he missed during his short visit at Christmas?

"The doctor said I have a herniated disc and a concussion."

Her mother leaned closer. "Really? Then you'll need good care." Her eyes focused on John, and she pulled herself up to her full height—all five feet, two inches, John guessed. He'd seen Sharee take that same defiant stance, and he fought to contain his amusement.

Mrs. Jones cleared her throat. "Of course, John acts like you need a guard or something."

A guard was exactly what she needed, and what he planned to be. He glanced down in time to catch a smile that Sharee tried to hide. That's better. Don't let her intimidate you.

"I don't think this is funny." Mrs. Jones' voice mounted.

"I know, Mom. It isn't."

"And why didn't you call us? You called John."

"Marilyn," her husband interrupted.

She glanced his way. "Well, I can't believe Sharee would rather have John stay the night than her own mother."

John's gaze went from her mom to her dad. Back to that, are we? He noticed the humor in Brian's eyes. Ah. So that's how he handled it.

"And I can't believe you got engaged without telling us!"

Sharee's eyes widened. "What?"

"Yes, we know all about it. John told us."

Sharee raised hazel eyes to his. "Engaged?"

"Yes." Her mother made the word two syllables. "Don't try to pretend. How long has it been?"

Sharee's stare filled the space between them. He felt embarrassed under her scrutiny, but he shrugged. He'd done what he thought he needed to do, even if…. Well, better finish it.

"I'm sorry, babe. I told them about the engagement because your mother seemed concerned with me staying the night. I thought it would make her feel better."

He'd given her the information she needed, but he understood her look. I'm the one who makes such a thing of the truth. After a moment, she managed a smile and turned back at her mom.

"Well, we haven't announced it yet."

"But we're your parents." Her mother's voice arched. "Why didn't you tell us? I mean...to have John tell us. At the hospital."

"It's not official."

"What do you mean, 'not official'? Has he asked you or not?"

Sharee glanced his way. He raised a brow. Oh, he'd asked her, all right. Something sharp jabbed his chest, and he strove to keep his face blank.

Sharee tightened her fingers on his and turned to her mom. "It's not official." She lifted her left hand. "See. No ring yet."

Her mother's eyes rounded, and her father's mouth lifted. He winked at John.

Now what?

"No...ring...yet." Each word hit in time with a nod. Mrs. Jones' gaze locked onto his. "I guess you are embarrassed to say you're engaged when you haven't given my daughter a ring. In fact, I don't know if there's an engagement without a ring. Do you have any idea when there will be a ring?"

He leaned back on his crutches and, for a minute, had no answer.

Sharee squeezed his hand again, and he glanced down. Her face held a mischievous expression, and she stifled a giggle. With one short sentence, she'd turned her mother's attentions—and guilt—from herself to him. He narrowed his eyes as she bit her lip and tried to stop her grin. His head lifted.

"Actually, I planned..." He stopped. No. If either of them thought he'd take this load of guilt, they needed to do some rethinking. He cleared his throat. "Your daughter will have a ring in plenty of time for the wedding."

"In plenty of time? What does that mean?" Indignation flooded her mother's words.

Brian stepped forward. "I'm sure John's capable of furnishing a ring." His eyes, amused still, focused on John and then on his daughter. "Sharee, did you get some pain medication?"

"Yes."

"Good. You'll be able to sleep then. We'll drive to your place and try to get some sleep, too, but we'll be back this afternoon. Even though John told us what happened, we'd like to hear it from you." He turned to John. "You must be tired. You've been up all night, also."

"I'm fine."

"Okay. Marilyn?" He slipped his hand under her arm. She smiled at him, a warm smile that touched her eyes and changed her face.

John watched, surprised. What a difference.

As they turned to go, Mrs. Jones said, "We'll be back, Sharee. I hope you get some rest. And your...fiancé...too." The word seemed more of an insult than otherwise. She flashed him a sugar-sweet smile and went out the door.

Sharee began to laugh. John raised a brow. Both the women had more ups and downs than a basketball tournament. He dropped her hand, stepped back and crossed his arms.

"Well," she said, "who would have thought you would lie like that? You. Of all people."

"I lied for a good reason." He saw her expression. "All right, that's an excuse, but don't try to play innocent. You threw me to the lions—or lioness, as the case may be."

"That did work well, didn't it? But it wasn't intentional."

"Girl, you knew exactly what you were doing with that 'no ring yet' routine. Your dad knew, too."

"Not really. But she loves things done properly. As soon as the words were out, I knew she'd take offense."

"Exactly."

"Well, what else could I say?" Her brows arched in an imitation of his. "You were no help."

Her tone and her look did something inside his chest. His eyes searched hers. Was the medicine making her high or—

"And you survived," Sharee said. "Besides, she wasn't that bad."

"She wasn't? You mean she's—" He stopped himself. Don't criticize the girl's mother if you want to win her back.

"I backed you up, too. Pretty quick thinking, don't you agree?" Again, the impish look. She reached past the railing for him.

He ignored her hand, turned and grabbed his crutches and settled them back under is arms. What was going on? She'd declined his marriage proposal. Did she expect him to laugh and tease about things as she was doing? When he turned back, her look caught him off guard. He stood still.

"John?"

"Yes?"

"I will take you up on your other offer, though."

"What offer?"

"This room?" A man's voice floated in from the hall.

Sharee's gaze shot past him. Her eyes widened.

The man outside said something else and the next minute halted in the doorway. Silence followed. John glanced from the man back to Sharee. The color had drained from her face.

He stopped beside her bed. "Hello, Sharee."

"Hello, Dean." Sharee kept her voice level, but her heart skittered. He looked the same. Just as handsome. Just as confident. The dark suit, tie, and white shirt suited him. He'd unhooked the shirt's top button and loosened the tie.

The man's head lifted, and he studied John before introducing himself. "Dean Strasburg. I'm a friend of Sharee's." He looked back down at her without waiting for a reply. "I saw your parents pull out of the parking lot and decided you must be here. I'm on business but thought I'd check. Everything okay?"

"Yes. I'm fine."

"Your standard answer. You must be here for a reason."

Why had he come? Over two years had passed. *Lord, help me.* "Someone ran me down."

"Really? That's a surprise." He paused fractionally. "Well, maybe not. You do have a way of ruffling people's feathers."

John stepped closer to the bed, his hand finding hers. A wave of relief slid over her. She didn't have to face Dean alone.

"You're here on business?"

"Yes. The medical supply business is still lucrative." He glanced again at John. "I'm sorry. You're...?"

"John Jergenson. Also, a friend."

Dean's gaze held John's a moment before he gave a brief nod. He dropped his head. "So, are you okay?"

Sharee sat straighter in the bed. "A herniated disc and concussion, but I'll heal."

"You really did get knocked down?"

"Yes."

"No doubt you have him locked away by now." The words carried an edge of sarcasm.

"The police have no idea who did it. If someone tries to kill you, they don't leave a business card."

"Tries to kill you?" Dean's voice resonated disbelief. "Sounds like you're overreacting. Again."

John shifted beside her. "Look, I don't know—"

Sharee moved her hand and touched his arm. He stopped and dropped his focus to her. She shook her head and saw his jaw clench.

She glanced back at the other man. "I only go to the police when needed."

Dean's face darkened. He slipped his hands into his pockets, raised his head and stared at John. When he dropped his gaze again, Sharee's heart jolted. His eyes held the anger she'd seen many times before.

"You seem well-supported here. I'll give you a call in a few days to see how you're doing."

Before she could answer, he whirled and walked from the room.

Tension drained from her like flowing oil. *Lord, how can he still rattle me like that?*

"Are you okay?" John's voice sounded rough.

She dipped her head. "Yes."

"Was he trying to upset you or is annoying just part of his character?"

She gave an awkward smile. "Both. And to think I almost married him." She moved and repositioned herself. Dean had baited her, mocked her, and kept her off-balance with his demands and compliments. It had taken time to understand his need to manipulate and control.

"That was your former fiancé?" John's tone was neutral.

Her gaze rose to meet his, but his look told her nothing. She nodded, and quiet settled between them. What was he thinking? Feeling? She shifted position. The pain in her head had increased instead of dissipating, and the bed's softness wrestled with her back's need for something firm. Tiredness swept over her.

"Sharee, the first time I saw you…" The words trailed off.

"I remember."

She did, indeed. Almost two and a half years ago, she'd come from a final, volatile meeting with Dean, and had needed a place to cry and to pray. She drove to the church, walked across the field, and dropped down at the edge of the pond.

She'd cried and let out the pain and confusion. How had she missed God's leading? Had she wanted a relationship so much that she'd ignored His voice?

John stepped from behind a small stand of trees nearby. In her grief and emotional upheaval, she hadn't seen him. He introduced himself, ignoring her red eyes and obvious discomfort. Then somewhere in the midst of his soft, deep voice explaining how Pastor Alan had hired him to do maintenance around the church, she'd relaxed. The whole congregation knew that the pastor had hired someone to take the work off their shoulders. John's gentleness that day had calmed her.

"I remember, but it took two years for you to talk to me again."

He shifted the crutches. "That went both ways, I think."

It had. They'd both had tragedies in their lives that needed dealing with first.

"We've never discussed why you were crying that day."

Sharee tightened her grip on the sheets. Only her parents and Marci knew the extent of all that happened. "Yes, it was Dean; but I don't want to talk about it."

"All right." The neutral tone again. Distant.

Was she shutting him out? He'd assume that. "I…I had a restraining order against him."

"A restraining order?" The notch in his voice didn't surprise her. "What for?"

She waved her hand, trying to dismiss it; and silence dropped over them. Of course, he had questions. "Can we talk about it later? My head's hurting. I'm beat."

He gave a kind of grunt that told her nothing, but dealing with the situation right now was more than she could do. Her head felt like it had cracked open. She leaned back against the pillow. No help. She turned to the side, away from him. Not because she wanted to, but because her head felt better that way. She closed her eyes. Sounds came that told her he was settling into the chair nearby.

Thank you, Lord.

Memories flooded her. The startling thing was the number of people who disapproved of the restraining order. "He's such a nice guy," one woman said. "How could you do that?" Others said she should give him another chance." But a few women—and some men—had stepped forward to stiffen her resolve. "If he doesn't get counseling, don't go back to him. He'll plead and make promises, but unless he gets help, he'll never change."

When she'd suggested counseling, Dean had refused. She'd obtained the restraining order only after his repeated phone calls and persistent appearances at work and church.

Don't think about it, Sharee. It's over, done with. Go to sleep.

John watched as she scrunched her pillow and tugged the sheet higher. He stood up and closed the blinds. When he eased back into the chair again, his eyes never left her.

A restraining order? Why had she needed a restraining order?

The man's visit had upset her, but she didn't want to talk about it—or share the reason for the restraining order. The cut from that came on top of her other rejection. His hands tightened on the chair's arms.

Maybe she had all she could deal with today. An accident, a herniated disc, a concussion. She didn't need him pushing. He'd backburner his questions—and his feelings—until later.

Chapter 4

"Asleep?" Someone barked.

John jumped. His eyes flew open and confusion swirled around him.

"Is this the way you watch after a patient?"

He jerked his head toward the door. Bruce Tomlin grinned at him from his wheelchair. John darted a glance at Sharee. She hadn't stirred.

Bruce rolled into the room. "Boy, when I was in the hospital, I had better care than this."

John yawned then grinned and stood up. The two men shook hands. Behind Bruce stood China Summers. John made an effort not to show surprise. Were she and Sharee close enough to warrant a visit to the hospital?

"Hi, John." China's soft voice had a musical lilt. She held his eyes for a moment before focusing on Sharee. "Hope we didn't wake her."

"No, I think the medication knocked her out. She's been asleep for a while." He moved his arm to see his watch. "As I have. You came together?"

"No chance." Bruce shook his head. "We met downstairs. I don't know why, but no one wants to ride with me."

"Probably because you drive like the devil and twice as fast, and no one knows how you stop that thing."

Bruce's eyes lit with his smile. "The marvels of a specially rigged van." He moved his wheelchair forward. "How's the patient? And what is it with you two? Two accidents in a week? Are you so in love, hombre, that you can't watch where you're going?"

"Hey, I take credit for only one, and that..." His eyes drifted to China. No, he'd wait to share with Bruce. He respected his friend's advice, but they'd talk about it when they were alone.

China stepped farther into the room. "Is she okay?"

John gave them both a brief rundown of her injuries.

China pulled long straight hair over one shoulder. "Pastor Alan told me you'd be staying here until Sharee gets out. 'Setting up camp' is what he said. So I thought I'd come by and offer my assistance." She glanced toward the bed. "Since you'll be taking care of the patient, I thought maybe I could feed Cooper for you and walk him."

John's eyes opened. An answer to prayer? He'd given some thought to his black Lab earlier. The dog had plenty of water, but his stomach must be keeping him awake about now.

"Thanks. I was wondering about getting over to the condo to feed him."

"When it's possible for you to get away for a short time, I could meet you there. Just show me where his food is, and where you walk him, and I'll do that for you—if you don't mind giving me a key."

"That would be a big help." He sent her an appreciative smile. "Perhaps we can do that when Sharee's parents get back from lunch."

"Yeah, that's real nice of you," Bruce's voice held a flat note.

China shot him a sharp look. "I don't mind helping."

"I'm sure you don't."

Quiet settled over the room for a moment. John focused on Bruce. Odd that he would hassle the girl. He'd acted as youth pastor before his accident, and, by all accounts, was a good one.

Sharee stirred and moaned.

Bruce rolled to the end of her bed. "You waking up, Sleeping Beauty?"

Sharee's eyes opened.

John rose from the chair and took a step to her bedside. "You've got company. Bruce and China are here."

Sharee's focus settled on Bruce. "Hey." Her groggy voice sounded as rumpled as the bed. She twisted her head in China's direction, then squeezed her eyes shut and bit her lip.

John put a hand on her shoulder. She needed to remember about moving her head too quickly.

China stepped up next to him. "Looks like you're still hurting."

Sharee nodded then opened her eyes. She gave a lopsided smile. "Just a tad. Mostly when I move. Thank you for coming."

"I heard you stepped in front of a car."

"Actually, I was tried to get out of its way. Just wasn't fast enough."

"God was watching out for you," Bruce said. "You and John both.

"What's this?" Sharee's mother remarked, walking into the room, and fixing him with a stare. "You got hit, too? Is that why you're on crutches? You said an accident, but you didn't mention what kind."

"Mom," Sharee interrupted. "Don't start."

"I just want to know how John's supposed to take care of you when he can't take care of himself." She gave him a skeptical look.

"Of course, he seems to be *taking control* of things here quite nicely."

John grinned.

"Marilyn." Her husband stepped forward. "Don't scare the man off." He put a foam box on the windowsill next to John. "Food here, if you want it."

"Thank you. I'll hold it until later, if you don't mind. Dinner time has slim pickings around here."

John introduced Bruce and China. He studied Sharee's father a moment and made a quick decision. "I need to run home, feed my dog, take a shower, and do a few other things. I'll leave Sharee in your capable hands for an hour or so." The statement contained a question.

Brian nodded, returning John's scrutiny. "Of course."

Sharee slipped her hand into his, and he dropped his gaze to hers, surprised at the anxious look she gave him. "I'll be back as quickly as I can." He bent over and kissed the top of her head. *Have to keep the façade up. Yeah.*

He slipped his crutches under his arms and met her dad's look. "Please keep a close eye on her."

"I'll go down with you," Bruce said.

"Me, too," China added. She touched Sharee's shoulder. "I'm sure you'll be out of here in no time." She nodded to Sharee's parents, and the three disappeared down the hall.

Giving China instructions about the dog took more time than he'd expected. He went with her for a short walk to see how she handled herself and the dog. She wasn't scared of Cooper's size and that encouraged him.

Bruce hung around until China left. The friction between the two resembled a rough board and 40 grit sandpaper. John wondered what initiated it but decided to find out later. He needed to eat, take a shower and get back, but still wanted some time with Bruce.

After China said goodbye, he cooked strips of beef, onion, and green peppers, and threw some potatoes in the microwave while filling Bruce in on the past week.

"You're telling me," Bruce said as John set the plates of beef and potatoes down on the table, "that someone intentionally tried to run over you? And the same thing happened to Sharee?"

"Yes."

"That's crazy. You're sure?"

John nodded, bowed his head and said a quick prayer. "Doesn't make sense, but yes, we're both sure." He cut into his potato.

Bruce started to eat, also. Swallowing a bite of sautéed beef, he said, "There has to be a reason. Someone's taken the time to plan this—to find out where you both live, to wait for you. The police are no help?"

"Not so much. I got the feeling the deputy thought we were trying to pull something ourselves. The accidents are too much alike."

"Someone with a limited imagination." Bruce forked another piece of beef. "But then that could be good for you. Thanks for the meal, by the way. You're a better cook than I am."

They ate in silence for a few minutes. Bruce took a drink of water, lifted his head, and cleared his throat.

"You know, if you need something from me, all you have to do is ask."

John nodded. He finished his food. "I've got to shower and get back."

"I heard about your need for being clean." Bruce gave him a sardonic look then sobered. "You got the ring? I left it on the table in the mailer."

John felt his face stiffen. "Yes. I saw it as soon as I got home."

Bruce nodded. "Okay then. Take a shower. I'll wash these dishes and wait for you."

John moved his crutches out of the way and shoved the unwelcome thoughts aside.

Bruce rolled his wheelchair back from the table. "Keep your guard up with that girl around."

John lifted an eyebrow and limped down the hall.

Neon lights from outside painted the darkened hospital room with multi-colored stripes. John watched Sharee change position as she had numerous times already. A number of visitors had stopped by earlier, and she'd become more exhausted with each one.

She groaned. With all the new medications, why couldn't they give her something that would allow her to rest? Keeping track of the nurse's schedules and Sharee's pain meds did nothing to help with the discomfort she felt.

He sighed and let his mind drift. Something inside told him he needed to heed Bruce's warning about China, even though he must be twelve or more years older than the girl. He had lumped her with all the youth over the last two years, but she'd graduated high school last year, and changed.

When she sidled over to talk to him the other day, he realized that she'd become an attractive young woman. She'd made sure he noticed.

Sharee's groan, this time, brought him from his chair to her bedside.

"I'm sorry, John." Her words were tight. "I don't mean to keep you awake. Why don't you go home? You can't get any sleep here."

He ignored her question. "I'll call the nurse and see if we can get you stronger medication."

"No. I don't want to be groggy."

"I'm not worried about your being groggy."

"I hate groggy."

He ran his fingers over her brow. "All right. I'll remember. I'd like to see you out of pain, though."

She mumbled a reply.

"So, if you can't sleep, what can we talk about to pass the time?" He knew what he wanted to talk about. He'd like to know more about Dean and that whole scenario.

"I can't talk about anything. My head's pounding." She put hands on both sides of her head and whimpered.

"Okay. Let's get the nurse in here, and see what she suggests." He reached over her for the call button.

"No, I'm okay." Sharee grabbed his arm and tried to take the long cord from his fingers.

"No way you're winning this fight, woman."

"Woman?" Her voice was indignant. She tried to slap him, but he ducked and chuckled. The next moment, she closed her eyes and tears slid down her cheeks.

"Hey." He reached for her hand. "What can I do?"

"N...nothing."

Not what he wanted to hear. She began a whispered prayer that sounded like the Twenty-third Psalm. He pulled the call button once more.

"Well, what is it you need?" A voice from the doorway startled them. "You've got your light on." The nurse came to Sharee's bedside, clicked off the call button and turned on the overhead light. Sharee winced.

The nurse's scrub top swam with rubber duckies, but the stern lines of her face, her steel gray hair and her cool eyes contradicted the image. She put her hands on large hips and stared first at him then at Sharee.

John tilted his head to see her name tag. Cindy.

"I...I didn't call." Sharee defended herself.

The nurse's eyes slid back to John.

"I did." He tried his best smile. "Sharee's in a lot of pain. It seems worse tonight. She can't sleep. The meds don't seem to be helping. Is there anything stronger? I know it's not quite time for them yet, but..."

"Well, you're right there. She has over an hour to go. And she can't have anything stronger unless the doctor orders it."

"Is there anything you can do?"

"I can't do anything without a doctor's orders." Her stern voice left him to wonder if she enjoyed giving a negative response. She turned to go.

"You know when a woman, when your fiancé," John corrected, "doesn't want to talk because she's in pain, it has to be serious."

The nurse turned back, took a moment to look him over, and left.

John growled deep in his throat. Would they ever get a break at this hospital?

"She's had a long night, John. It's okay. And she really can't do anything without a doctor's orders. She'd get fired."

"You've had a long night, too."

"I'll be okay."

"Can I rub your back?" He leaned forward.

"Don't touch me!"

His hands shot into the air. "Not a chance."

Sharee gave a wavering smile. "I'm sorry. Everything hurts. I don't want anyone touching me. Laughter is good, though."

"I would try to keep you in stitches, but I'm not a comedian."

"You're doing well so far."

His mouth hitched. "Unintentionally."

"They said the headaches would go away in a few days."

"How about a cold compress for your head?"

"That might work."

"Okay, I'll go see if I can find the dragon lady and get one for you. I'll be back."

When he came back with cold, wet washcloths, relief flooded her eyes. He set his crutches against the wall, took a washcloth, folded it, and put it across her forehead. She closed her eyes. He turned the light out and went to sit in the chair in the corner, stretching out his legs.

As the quiet settled over them, the ache in his foot made itself known. A cold compress would feel good on the foot, too; but he refused to get up again. Tiredness surpassed the ache. He laid his head back against the chair and closed his eyes.

Light flooded the room. He jerked awake, startled, and

straightened in the chair. Bruce was right. What kind of guard was he? He'd fallen asleep the first restful moment he had. Sharee's eyes were open, too.

"All right," the nurse said, as loud as if she'd been at a football game. "I'm back. I thought you couldn't sleep, dear. Turn over. Yeah, toward Sir Galahad over there. You, sir, look the other way. Out the window. I'm going to give your lady here a shot in the rear."

John turned, staring at the neon lights outside. He heard Sharee's intake of breath.

"That's nothing, honey," the nurse continued. "You're fine. Okay, Sir Galahad, you can turn around now. The doctor said thank you, by the way, for waking him at 3:00 in the morning as he just got in from emergency surgery and had just gone to bed. My job's on the line." She looked him over as if to ask if he was worth it. Her gaze moved to Sharee. "If he still wants to talk, honey, you'll be able to do that in about ten minutes...with ease." She turned to walk out but glanced at John. "Talk, huh? Would have thought you had more on your mind than that."

Sharee turned toward him with raised eyebrows. John coughed and grinned but didn't say a word.

Sharee woke the following morning at the sound of her name and to discomfort in her arm. She groaned and opened her eyes.

"Hold still, please." She felt something tighten around her arm, then a sharp prick. At her muttered protest, the male voice said. "Sorry."

She forced herself to focus. The man in the white uniform held her left arm next to his body.

"Just drawing some blood." He smiled at her. "Looks like you slept through breakfast." He indicated the tray on the night table. "If you want them to bring you a fresh one, they will." His fingers unsnapped the white elastic and slid the needle from her arm. "Okay, there you go."

A vial with blood went into a box on his cart. He put a bandage over the pierced site on her arm and raised her hand so that it touched her shoulder. "Hold it like that for a few minutes." He gathered all his stuff together and rolled his cart out the door. "Have a good day."

"Yeah." She inched her head around expecting to see John by the window.

Her father leaned forward. His face creased into a smile, and his blue eyes lit. "How are you this morning?" The tenderness and concern in his eyes touched her heart.

"Better, I think. My head's clear. Where's John?"

"He went home when I came in. He made me promise to stay and keep an eye on you. He said you both had a long night."

Sharee giggled. "I think he did."

Her father cocked his head at her. "That man is very concerned about you."

"I know. Dad, I…" She stopped, wondering if she should tell him the truth about her accident. John had not told them the whole story yet, but she didn't like keeping things from him.

"Yes?'

"Nothing." Better wait. Her dad had been her protector, her teacher for so many years; and she still depended on him in certain areas, but what could he do? "Where's Mom?"

"Getting some breakfast."

"She does like John, doesn't she? Everything was fine when he visited at Christmas."

"Of course, she does. He's just in her way now. Plus, she doesn't like the idea of you leaving the country. And from what he said at Christmas, he's thinking of doing that. So, if you're married, I'm sure you'll go with him." He took a breath. "Neither of us wants to think about that. But it's what God wants that matters."

Sharee nodded.

"You're our only child. It will be hard having you so far away."

"But she can't blame John. I've been out of the house for ten years. College and working and living down here."

"I know, sweetheart, but you've still called us to share what was going on in your life and to tell us if you had any needs. Most of that has ended over the last few months. Or didn't you notice?" She hadn't. He looked at her. "It's how it should be. Doesn't necessarily make it any easier on your mother. When John flew over to Indonesia, she spent hours on the internet, reading about the country; and as much as she loves the Lord, she really questioned Him about whether you should be going or not. God sometimes has a lot of explaining to do to mothers." He studied her. "And fathers."

"But John hadn't asked me to marry him then." And I haven't told him I accept yet.

"Your mother's pretty smart. She knew how things were going."

She reached out to touch his hand. "You know I love you and mom."

He took her smaller one in his big one. "We know, sweetheart.

We want you to be happy."

"John makes me happy."

"I can see that."

Her phone rang, and she pulled it off the bedside table, frowned and hit the ignore button.

"Someone you don't want to talk to?"

"Yeah." Whoever was making the anonymous calls hadn't stopped as she'd hoped. She caught her dad's inquisitive stare and knew she needed to change the subject. "Will you help me up so I can shower before John gets back? He's seeing me at my worst. When China was here yesterday, I felt pretty homely."

"You don't have to worry, sweetheart. You always look good."

"Says the father to the daughter."

"Truth is truth. But you might as well clean up. John said that the dragon lady," he gave her a questioning look and Sharee giggled, "told him before she left that the doctor wanted you to get up and walk today."

She inched her legs to the side of the bed, and with his hand under her arm, tested her back with a step. "Well, I'm not walking anywhere with this gown open in the back. Can you see if they have two cleans ones? I saw someone yesterday with one worn over the other—the second one used like a robe."

"You'll be okay?"

"I'll be fine, Dad."

He was back in a few minutes and handed them to her, along with a bag of soft peppermints.

"Peppermints?" Sharee smiled and took them, giving her dad a careful hug.

"Still your favorites?"

"Of course, and I can use them here, too." She unwrapped one and popped it into her mouth on the way to the shower.

When she stepped into the room again, her mother had returned. Bruce, Pastor Jim, and Miss Eleanor added to her visitors and sat in chairs someone had pilfered from other rooms.

Surprise caused her to pause, eyeing them, before she proceeded to the bed. She lowered herself onto its edge, glad for the extra robe and thankful she'd done her hair and make-up.

"Look who I found in the hall." Her mother indicated Miss Eleanor and Pastor Alan.

"Pastor Alan had pity on me," Miss Eleanor said, "since I don't drive anymore. He took me to breakfast and brought me to see you." Her eyes clouded for just a moment. "I see I need to pray harder."

"Miss Eleanor," Sharee lowered her voice, "if you weren't praying, I might not be here right now."

Miss Eleanor's eyes narrowed. "Well, first John and now you. I guess the battle is on."

Sharee smiled. What had Miss Eleanor said before John came home? "I feel God prompting me to pray for you and John. You need to pray, too, Sharee. Make sure you pray." And she had.

Thank you, Lord, that I have such a warrior on my side. Eighty-five years old and still waging war with the enemy of our souls!

"Actually," Pastor Alan put in, "I don't think I could have kept her at home much longer. She might have taken a bus to come see for herself that you were okay or caught a ride with Bruce."

"And she would have loved it," Bruce put in. "I need someone with me once in awhile who still has some fight in them."

"I'm sure I would have enjoyed it," Miss Eleanor said. "Now, Sharee, tell me what the doctors say about your injuries."

Sharee explained the doctor's prognosis, skirting around their questions about the accident.

Bruce rolled closer. She glanced toward him, noting the Nike t-shirt he wore. His muscled chest and arms were noticeable under it. She recalled how his smile had reappeared right after the Christmas program four months ago—almost two years to the date of the accident.

Now, his blue eyes twinkled at her. "How about you and I going for a walk?"

"Are you up to that?" Her mom asked in alarm.

"Doctor's orders, Marilyn." Brian put a hand on his wife's shoulder.

Bruce nodded. "Walking will help. We won't go far."

"I'd love to." She glanced around the room. "I do have visitors, however…"

"You go," Miss Eleanor said. "I just wanted to make sure Pastor Alan was telling me the truth."

The Pastor grinned, as did Bruce and Sharee.

Bruce put out his hand. "Get your IV pole, then. Let's take a spin." And to the others, "We'll be back soon."

Sharee tugged the pole over next to her. "Okay, Sergeant, let's go."

He laughed and rolled forward. Sharee heard Pastor Alan asking about her father's work as they left. Warmth surged through her. Friends, family, God. How blessed could one person be?

As they headed down the hall, Bruce glanced over his shoulder.

"If you feel like you need to sit down or that your back is going out, let me know. We won't go far. Is this your first walk?"

"Yes."

"Tell me again what the doctor said."

"I have a herniated disc in the lower part of my back. I'm supposed to rest it and give it time to heal. But I need to walk, too. It'll take time, but it should be all right." She felt guilty as she said it, thinking how minor her problem was compared to his.

"You need to do everything they say. Resting, walking a little, icing your back. Later heat. All that will help. Don't do any bending. Stay out of cars for a while."

"You're the expert."

"No expert, but I have done lots of research. I would give anything to get out of this chair, but then, I'm also willing to do whatever God wants. It took awhile to get to that point, though."

"I don't wonder." Her hands tightened on the IV pole, and she swallowed the sudden, surprising tears that sprang to her eyes. Bruce had gone through so much.

"You okay?" he asked, as they reached the elevators and turned to head back.

"Yes."

The elevator doors opened, and John swung forward on his crutches. "Where are you going with my girl?"

Bruce grinned. "Well, slipping down the elevator just got foiled. Guess I'll have to think of something later."

"Yeah. We'll talk about that later."

Bruce's grin held. "Actually, she's doing well. Looking good, too."

"You noticed."

"Couldn't help it."

Sharee rolled her eyes. "Okay, guys, quit. I look like a train wreck."

John put a small bag into her hand. "You look wonderful."

She peered inside. "Peppermints?" She bit her lip, holding back the amusement. She had plenty of the soft candies now.

"I thought I'd get them before you asked."

"Thank you."

His look became serious, and he motioned down the hall to the waiting room. "Let's go find some privacy. I'm glad you're here, Bruce. I'd like you to bounce some things off you." He put a hand on her arm. "Can you make it a little farther?

"Of course."

They moved into an empty waiting room and sat down. John's gaze settled on Sharee, and he frowned.

"What?"

"When I went home, my neighbor George came over. He's the person who kept Cooper while I was in Indonesia. I've always called him George, but I know his real name is Mohammed. He's a Muslim from Indonesia. We talked about Indonesia a lot before I left. He came over today to let me know that some of his friends were upset that I went to Indonesia to share the Gospel. They told him he should not be keeping my dog. In fact, they suggested he poison him."

"Poison Cooper? Why would they do that?"

"I think the idea is that anything...or anyone...that I care about is fair game if I'm trying to share the Gospel with other Muslims."

"You're thinking they could be responsible for the accidents?" Bruce questioned.

"It's a good possibility." His eyes went to Sharee. She saw the contemplation in his eyes.

"What are you going to do?" Bruce asked.

Silence filled the room.

John cleared his throat. "I've been thinking about it." The two men exchanged looks.

"Wait a minute." Sharee sat straighter in her seat and ignored the pain that inched up her back. "You better not be thinking...Look, if you're thinking of breaking our engagement because you assume I'll be safer that way, then just forget it."

Bruce glanced at Sharee's hand before shooting a look at John. "An engagement?"

"There isn't an engagement."

Bruce ricocheted a look back and forth between them.

"There is," Sharee said, "but there isn't."

"O...kay."

John made a noise of dismissal. "Sharee, either way, this still makes sense. You're a target because of me. If we stop seeing each other, then the threat to you should go away."

"You don't know that for sure."

"Why else would anyone try to hurt both of us?"

Lord, what is this? I haven't had a chance to tell him I want to be engaged, and he's already trying to break it off.

She crossed her arms. "The answer is no. Don't even go there."

John's jaw tightened. "It doesn't make any difference. You turned me down anyway."

"I did not. I said—"

"You said you needed more time."

"Well, I've had time."

John paused. His face changed, and silence settled around them. "And?"

Bruce cleared his throat, but they ignored him.

"And," Sharee slipped her hand into his. "I love you. Yes, I'll marry you."

"You will?" His voice notched up slightly, and his gaze held hers. "Yes."

"You're positive?"

"Yes."

"Definite?"

"Yes."

"Sure?"

She leaned forward. "John, yes. I love you."

He closed his eyes, and his hand tightened around hers. A moment later, his eyes opened; and he growled deep in his throat. "I can't believe you put me through this."

"Through what?"

"A week of torture."

"But I…" She bit her lip.

"A week. Seven days."

"Uh, guys," Bruce's voice interrupted. "If you let me out, I'll take off here."

"I didn't mean to. I'm sorry."

John glanced at Bruce. "We need to talk." He turned back to Sharee and touched her cheek. "I love you, too." His gaze dropped to her mouth, but he didn't move.

"Kiss me," she mouthed.

He hesitated, his look lingering on her mouth. Finally, his eyes rose to focus on hers. "Later." He mouthed back.

"Later? What?"

He grinned and pulled her close. He turned to Bruce. "Sorry about the sidetracking."

"Sidetracking?" Sharee let her voice jump.

John winked at her and gave her a squeeze. "We need to figure out who's doing this. Safety first."

Sharee let out a frustrated breath. This was not how she'd planned to tell him. Another thought crossed her mind. "I wonder if it has to do with the phone calls I keep getting."

"What calls?" Both men asked at once.

"Someone calls and never says anything. I've called the number back, but no one answered. I even tried doing a reverse white pages on it, but they didn't have it. It's probably one of those untraceable phones you buy at the discount stores."

John tilted his head at her. "How long has this been going on?"

"Since you left."

"Since I left? You've been getting calls for over a month?" His voice roughened. "Did you tell anyone or call the police?"

"No, I...I was waiting for you to get home." She stopped.

"Sharee—"

"When was the last one?" Bruce edged forward in his wheelchair.

"Today."

"Today?" John's startled response caused her to lean back. "When?"

"An hour or so ago."

"They called here?"

"They called my cell phone. They might not know I'm in the hospital."

"If this is the same person who ran you over, they do."

"Maybe it's not."

"Then we have two problems or is that too much coincidence?"

"I'm with you on that," Bruce said. "But your guess about your neighbor doesn't make sense to me. Let me explain why."

A noise from the doorway caused all their heads to swing around. Sharee's father stood there. The easy smile was absent.

He stepped forward into the room. "Does someone want to tell me what's going on here?"

No one moved or spoke. He walked over to where they sat and put a protective hand on Sharee's shoulder. His gaze moved to John, and his look hardened.

"It's obvious from your actions and words that Sharee's safety concerns you. I think it's about time you told me what this is about."

John took a deep breath. "You're right. Please sit down. I meant to tell you yesterday. Would you like Mrs. Jones here?"

"She's looking for Sharee, as I was. Your Pastor went with her. We were all worried when these two didn't come back." He gave Bruce a hard stare before his eyes settled on John. "I'll wait to see what you have to say before we ask Marilyn to join us."

John described his accident, added what they had omitted about Sharee's, explained George's warning and then the phone calls. When he finished, silence settled over the room. A line between her dad's brows appeared.

"And you say the police don't seem to believe you about these accidents? What about this new information?"

John shrugged. "They don't have it yet. The officer yesterday acted like he thought Sharee and I were trying to pull something. And now, well, I don't believe for one minute, as much as George says he's my friend, that he would be willing to share his information with the police. That's a whole different matter."

Brian put a hand on Sharee's knee as she shifted within John's arm. "You okay, honey?"

John's brow creased. "You're hurting again, aren't you? When are you due for your next meds?"

"I'm fine." Sharee cleared her brow, ignoring the ache in her back and the one that had started again in her head. "I want to hear what Bruce has to say about John's neighbor."

Bruce ran his hands along the side of the wheelchair. "Someone was waiting for both of you to get home in the evening. John, you just returned from overseas. Either they were watching for you or knew your itinerary. And they must have an idea of Sharee's routine, have watched her come and go."

John's arm tightened around her again. "I don't like the idea of that."

"Neither do I." Her father's sentiments followed close on John's.

Bruce crossed his arms. "Let's backtrack some on your neighbor. Tell me more about him."

"He's been at the apartments since I moved here. Two and a half years ago. He works at the electric company. I believe we're friends. In fact, he said as much today. He made sure I understood that he did not agree with his friends. We have talked about our different beliefs, and I am hoping God opens his eyes one day."

"And he told you what his friends said about you?"

"Yes."

"So, why would he tell you what the others said if he was guilty?"

"If I'm scared of doing mission work in Indonesia then perhaps it accomplishes what it's supposed to."

Bruce's head went down for a second. "Here's the part that doesn't make sense. The M.O. If these accidents consisted of car bombs or pipe bombs or something like that—well, that's more the style we've come to expect. But car accidents? So poorly done. It just doesn't fit."

John nodded. "All right. Something to think on, but the phone calls worry me."

"What we need to know is if they're related to the accidents. Your neighbor George would know your itinerary and could have revealed it—intentionally or not—to one of his friends, but why would they call Sharee? Just to harass her?"

"It's been done."

He dad shifted. "But I don't think we should stop there. Who else could it be? What do you have in common besides each other?"

"The church, the people there. Our work is separate."

Her father's brow furrowed. "The church? Is that likely? How many people are we talking?"

"We have about three hundred, including the youth and younger children."

"Anybody hate the thought of you two marrying?" He tilted his head. "John, you have an old girlfriend?"

"No. Everyone in the church would love to see us get married." He sobered and looked at Sharee. "Sharee had a visitor yesterday. Dean something or other."

"What?" Her dad's head came her way. "Dean showed up here?"

Sharee's heart dove. She hadn't wanted to tell him. "Yes."

"The man…" Brian stopped. His eyes narrowed.

John glanced from one to the other. "Sharee, I know you didn't want to share earlier, but if this is someone—"

"It's been over two years. Dean would never—"

"Over two years, but when he thinks you're hurt, he comes immediately." John's voice had deepened.

Sharee stared at him.

Bruce cleared his throat. "I think John's right, Sharee. You have to consider everyone."

"All right." She didn't have the strength to fight them all. The pain inside her head had increased.

Her dad leaned forward. "I have a few friends that owe me favors. If you don't mind, John, I could probably get a background check run on your neighbor George."

John inclined his head. "I have no problem with that. Whatever we can find out will be good."

"We'll see what comes up. I know a few Sheriff's deputies, too. I'll talk to them and see if they can give us some advice. They know Sharee. It's out of their jurisdiction, but they will take it seriously."

"That will help."

"I have to leave in the morning. I don't want to, of course, but I have to. Work calls. Marilyn will be here for a day or so longer. I know I can depend on you…" The unexpressed communication was clear.

Sharee wanted to shake her head but didn't dare. They were treating her like a china plate that needed wrapping in cotton batting.

"Look, I don't need babysitting…" Her voice trailed off as she tried to pull free of John's arm. The pain in her back spiked, and she cut off the words.

John stood. "You need to get back."

Her father stood, too. "Yes, let's break this up for a while. I'll go look for your mother. I'm hoping she hasn't put the whole hospital on alert." He smiled, but his eyes stopped on each of them. "We won't tell Marilyn about this. Yet."

"Understood." John helped Sharee to her feet.

Brian picked up the bag with the candy John had given her. He glanced inside, his brows lifted, and he looked at Sharee. "Is this yours?"

"Yes. John brought them." She took the bag from him, feeling awkward. At home, her dad always kept her supplied with peppermints. Sharee's hand moved and touched his arm. "I have two protectors."

He said nothing.

"Actually three," Bruce interjected and shifted his hands to roll forward.

Chapter 5

Sharee lay flat on her back. The late afternoon sun laid ribbons of yellow across her bed. When they returned to the room earlier, she'd taken the pain medicine and drifted off to sleep.

John rose from the chair near her. "Your visitors left right after you fell asleep. And Lynn called a few minutes ago, but I told her not to come by today."

"You told her not to come by? My best friend?"

"She reminded me of that, but I thought we could use a few minutes alone. We have some unfinished business."

"Unfinished business?"

He set his crutches aside and pulled a curl next to her cheek. "You don't remember?" Leaning over, he settled a hand on either side of her head. "You asked for a kiss."

A knock sounded on the door.

John groaned, straightened and turned. The doctor stood just inside the room. "Sorry to interrupt, but I wondered how my patient was today."

"Better." Sharee felt a flush rise, but smiled and reached for the button to lift the head of her bed.

"Good to hear." The doctor moved to stand next to her bed. "You know you have a slight concussion. Your memory, vision, and coordination all show well. That's what we wanted. My guess is that your head will be fine in a few days, a week at the most. But since you lost consciousness after the accident, I'd like to monitor you for one more night. The herniated disc will take longer, and you'll need to limit what you do, especially for awhile. You told the nurse you have pain most of the time, especially moving, and sciatica, which is expected with this. We can give you an injection for your back that will help. It will relieve the pain and take the swelling down. The injection is not painful, just uncomfortable."

Sharee bit her lip. She'd heard that term before. "Won't this get better by itself?"

"It's a process. A lot depends on you. If you don't want the injection now, you can wait and see what happens when you leave here."

"I think I'd like to do that."

"Okay. You can go home tomorrow. In the meantime, try to get a good night's sleep. Let's see if you can sleep without medication. If you need it, though, ask for it."

"All right. Thank you."

After he left, John caught her hand and rubbed the back of it with his thumb. "Afraid of the shot?"

"No. I…I just don't want it if I don't need it."

"Hmmm."

She could read the amusement in his eyes. "Hey. It's not your back they want to put some needle into."

"Another thing to remember. You don't like shots."

Irritated, she pulled the pillow from behind her head. "If you don't stop grinning, I'll hit you with this."

"And if you do, you'll have a pitcher of ice water over your head."

She studied him. Would he do it? When she hesitated, his eyes crinkled at the corners. She narrowed hers and tucked the pillow back under her head. "You know, when I'm feeling better, you're not going to be able to bully me."

"Uh huh. When you're feeling better, I have other things—"

Sharee gave his hand a squeeze, and he glanced up. Marci Thornton stood in the doorway. She held her two-year-old daughter's wrist in one hand and balanced baby Joshua on her hip. Sharee smiled. Even at six months, Joshua looked like a future football player.

"You brought the babies!"

Marci's face lifted. "Yes. Can you believe they actually let them up here now?"

"I'm glad." Sharee reached up. "Can I hold Joshua?"

"No." Marci's and John's voices echoed each other's.

Sharee looked back and forth between them. She opened her mouth to object but that died as she saw their faces. "Okay, but…"

"No buts," Marci stepped closer to the bed. "I heard the doctor say it would take some time for your back to heal."

Sharee wrinkled her nose, but transferred her attention to Joshua and tickled his feet. John waved at his chair and moved behind it.

"Sit in the chair, Lizzie." Marci hefted Joshua to her other hip, and Elizabeth scrambled into the seat. The child stared up at John. He winked.

"I had to bring them both." Marci stepped next to Sharee's bed.

"Stephen is watching the others. The whole family wanted to come, but you didn't need eight children and two adults here all at once."

"I'd love to see them, but we might get a few objections from the nursing staff."

John laughed. "One, in particular."

"Oh?" Marci gave an inquiring look but John just shook his head. Her gaze went to Sharee. "How're you doing?"

"Better, but they're keeping me one more night."

"That's probably the best thing. And you're really doing better? Not just saying that?"

"Yes.

"Good. I wanted to see for myself. I know how you can blow over some of the important stuff."

"Me?"

"That's why I'm here," John said.

"Keeping her in line, huh?"

Sharee waved her hand. "Hey!"

"Don't deny it. You never watch out for yourself." After a moment, Marci's smile faded, and she cleared her throat. "I wanted to ask you something."

"Ask away."

Marci glanced John's way. "I know you've probably told John about Sunday. But I hope you won't tell anyone else—about what you think you saw. And, Sharee, it's what you thought you saw. Nothing was going on. I know how it looked, but I love Stephen, and I wouldn't do anything to hurt him." Her gaze went to Elizabeth, who played with a toy cell phone.

Sharee shifted her position. She hadn't mentioned anything to John. Her gaze slid his way. He raised a brow and turned to Marci.

"Do you want me to leave? I'll take Lizzie."

"No, it's okay. I know you and Sharee care about me. I have nothing to hide. I just don't want this to hurt Stephen or cause gossip. Ted's easy to talk to. I admit that. He listens much better than Stephen." She shifted Joshua to her other hip. "But, there's nothing going on between us."

Sharee reached for Marci's hand. "You're right, we do care about you, but you and Ted weren't just talking. He had his arms around you. Now wait. I understand what you're saying, but what if Stephen or Matthew walked in right then? And Matthew did come looking for you a few moments later."

"Did he?" Marci's voice changed. She spent a minute bouncing the baby. "Matthew and Ted have had words already."

"And if he'd walked in on you two…"

"We were talking. I was upset. That's all."

John shifted. He dropped his keys in Elizabeth's chair. Her little fingers closed around them, and he looked back at Marci. "I won't make excuses for a husband not listening to his wife—even one who probably feels as overwhelmed as you do with the responsibility of a large family—but it's much easier for Ted to give you comfort. His only responsibility is himself. He's looking for someone to care about, someone who will care for him. The only thing is—you're not available for that role in his life. By allowing him to comfort you, to care for you, you're not only giving him false expectations, but you're also not allowing him to find a legitimate relationship either."

"I…I never thought about that."

Silence settled in the room. Tears formed in Marci's eyes, and Sharee squeezed her hand. "Besides, that's Stephen's role—to comfort you—whether or not he's doing it adequately. The only third party you need in your marriage is Jesus. You know that."

Marci's head buried itself near Joshua's. Her arms tightened around him until he struggled to get free. She loosened her hold.

Holding back a grimace, Sharee sat up higher in bed. "Marci, I didn't say anything to anyone, not even to John."

Marci blinked back tears. "Thank you. What did you say to Ted after I left?"

"I told him that he was stealing your affections."

"Oh. Was that all? He was livid."

"Was he? Perhaps it's because he knows it's true, and it's what he wants. He may not be thinking it through yet, but that is what he's doing."

"Stealing my affections? Strange."

"Nevertheless, it's true."

"I love Stephen. He knows that."

"Then stay away from Ted."

Marci glanced at the floor and nodded.

Sharee touched her hand again. "We've been friends too long for me not to tell you the truth."

The baby reached up and pulled on Marci's hair. She caught his hand and began to loosen the fingers that twined around a long strand. "I know."

"When I get out of here, we need to spend some time together. I haven't seen you except at church for months."

"Yes, I can leave these two with Matthew or Mary, and we can have lunch." Marci put her hand out to Elizabeth, and the two-year-old scrambled down from the chair. She focused on John. "Make her do what the doctor says."

"You can trust me on that."

After she left, Sharee let her mind drift over the last couple of months. I should have kept up with her. I worried so much about John and about the phone calls that I let everything else lapse. No wonder she sought out Ted.

Silence filled the room. She became aware of John's scrutiny and turned her head. His look resembled her dad's the time she'd shown up late from her first date.

"What's wrong with you?" Sharee asked.

"You had a run-in with Ted? When was this?"

"The Sunday you and Bob shared about Indonesia. You were talking to China." She tried to keep her voice level. What was it about the girl that made her uneasy? "I slipped into the Fellowship hall, and there they were."

"I thought we agreed that you'd stay away from Ted after that confrontation back around Christmas. The man has problems."

Sharee rolled her eyes. "I know, but I didn't plan to walk in on them."

"But you had to say something?"

"What was I supposed to do? Just walk out and say nothing?"

"That's what most people would do."

"Well, most people can be wrong. Marci is my friend. I'm not going to sit by while she careens off a cliff."

John scowled. "It's dangerous to confront Ted. You know that. He has anger issues."

"And you don't?"

John moved the crutches forward and pointed his finger at her. "If I'm angry it's because I care about you. Because I don't want you hurt again."

Sharee opened her mouth and closed it. She took in his irritated look and pointing finger and giggled. His face changed. She giggled again, and the annoyed expression dissolved.

"Girl, you are one stubborn human being. What am I going to do with you?"

"Love me?"

"What do you think I'm doing?"

"Badgering me?"

"Badgering you? Well, if I can keep you safe some other way— besides locking you up—let me know."

"Marry me."

"What?"

She'd caught him by surprise. "Marry me."

A second later, he leaned over the bed. "If we could do it here, I would."

"You mean we can't?"

"Don't play with me, or you'll find yourself married in a hospital gown instead of a wedding gown."

She laughed, but the look in his eyes kicked her heartbeat into overtime.

He rested his crutches against the bed and sat down next to her. "When you had the ambulance lady call me, and not Alan or your parents, I wondered. And when your parents came, and you were joking around, I wondered, too; but I wasn't sure. Are you positive about this?"

"Yes."

"You're sure?"

"I said yes this morning—a number of times."

His smile returned. "You did, didn't you?"

"Um hum."

He leaned forward, his mouth covering hers. His lips were warm and gentle, and when he drew back, she protested. Catching his shoulder, she tugged him back down. The kiss, this time, roughened her mouth, moved and lingered and sent waves of longing through her.

When he did pull back, he shook his head. "I'm trying to remind myself that you're hurt, you're in the hospital, but you're not helping."

She smiled and ran her fingers along his bottom lip.

He turned his head and kissed her palm. "So, we're engaged? For real."

Sharee hesitated, smiled and held up her hand. "I don't know. Are we?"

Nurse Cindy walked through the doorway that evening carrying a pillow. "You looked uncomfortable last night, Sir Galahad; and you didn't sleep. I don't want you to keep your lady love awake tonight, so try this." She dumped the pillow in John's lap and turned to Sharee. "How's the Princess?"

Sharee ricocheted a look at John and back to Cindy. Earlier, a young man in hospital scrubs had muscled a large easy chair into the room. John lounged in it now. She had no doubt the chair had come per Cindy's instructions.

"Much better. You and all the staff have been really good to John and me."

"Humph." The nurse's scrubs abounded with pinks, greens, and reds on a black background. Betty Boop pranced all over them. "Doctor says you'll be going home tomorrow. He wants you to sleep tonight with as little medication as possible."

"I will. Being unhooked from the IV and the blood pressure cuff almost guarantees it."

Cindy nodded and left.

Sharee shifted in John's direction. "I think she likes you."

"What?" His eyes widened. "Not a chance."

"Oh, yeah. You made an impression last night."

"Not the impression you're thinking. And you'd better get some sleep tonight, or I'll be toast in the morning."

She poked her pillow. "I'll be glad to leave tomorrow."

"Understandable."

"I told Lynn about our engagement, you know."

"I heard."

"Everybody will know tomorrow."

"You knew that when you told her."

Sharee giggled. "I did. Better than the internet."

"It will be on the internet—Facebook, Pinterest, Instagram. And whatever the youth use these days. "

She yawned and snuggled down under the cover. "I wish you'd sleep."

"Sleep is overrated. Except for you." He rose, moved across the room and shut off the light.

✒

Time crawled by before her soft, rhythmic breathing drew his attention. Good. Time to start thinking about tomorrow, about a more secure lock for her apartment door.

Sharee twisted away from him and threw off the covers. He rose and tugged them back over her, letting his fingers linger against the soft, warmth of her neck. He hadn't foreseen the personal problems when he decided to stay at the hospital.

Her sleep deepened over the next hour, but after that, the restlessness returned. She twisted back and forth and threw the covers off again. Her mass of curls circled her head, standing out against the white pillow. The neon light from the window reminded him of moonlight, bathing her in shadowed illumination. Even in the hospital gown, she looked beautiful.

She stretched and moaned. "John?"

"Yeah?" His voice sounded hoarse. He'd been watching her far too long. "Yes?"

"Did I wake you?"

"No."

"Is anything the matter?"

"No." Nothing that a honeymoon wouldn't help. He remembered Cindy's words and felt the twitch of his mouth.

"Oh."

He heard the hesitation. She couldn't see him well. He knew that, but she must be questioning the roughness of his voice.

"Would you close those drapes, please?"

He rose and pulled them together. "Yes, sorry. I should have done it before." He could use a long jog, but that wasn't happening anytime soon. "Look, I'm going to walk the halls, stretch a little. I'll keep the room in sight."

"Okay." She turned over just as her phone rang.

He grabbed it from the nightstand and handed it to her. "Do you want to answer this or wait until morning?"

She yawned, took it from his hand and glanced at the screen. Her head rose. "It's no one I know."

He snatched the phone from her. "Hello? Who is this? Hello?"

A beep sounded, and the line went dead.

Chapter 6

The next morning bright sunlight filled her room. Someone had opened the drapes. She stirred. Her head felt clear. She experimented, inching it sideways to the left, then the right. A twinge, but no stabbing pain.

John sat a few feet away. His Bible lay open in his lap. She could see another Bible, the Gideon Bible she had discovered earlier in the chest of drawers, beside him on the windowsill.

He smiled, but the meditative look in his dark-shadowed eyes reminded her of last night's phone call. He'd gone into protective mode, wanting to buy her a new phone as soon as the stores opened today; but she'd managed to hold him off. After that, with her hand in his, she must have fallen into a deep sleep.

"You slept well the last couple of hours."

"I did. And you?"

"Long night."

"I'm sorry."

"Not your fault." He paused and contemplated her a minute. "Well, actually…" He let it trail off. "I'll go down and get some coffee and let you get dressed."

"I look that bad, huh?"

"You look beautiful."

"Liar."

He winked at her, put the crutches under his arms and headed into the hall.

She rose at a snail's pace from the bed and walked to the window. His NIV Bible lay open on the windowsill to 1st Thessalonians 4. She scanned a few verses. Her eyes stopped halfway down the page.

"It is God's will that you should avoid sexual immorality; that each of you should learn to control his own body in a way that is holy and honorable, not in passionate lust…" She lifted it and glanced at the Gideon Bible. Its KJV was open to the same scripture. He'd been reading…this?

She raised her eyes to look out the window. She had enjoyed their constant togetherness, in spite of the hospital and her pain. But to him?

"Sharee," she whispered to herself, "you have been pretty clueless here." She looked down and reread the scriptures.

When he came back, she was dressed and sitting in his high-backed chair. His brows lifted.

"Well, they said I'd go home today. I'm ready." And, hopefully, not causing any problems you don't need.

He set his crutches against the wall and sat on the edge of the bed, facing her. His eyes fell on the Bible she'd closed and laid back on the windowsill, and his face became serious. He trailed a finger along her jaw and leaned forward to capture her mouth with his.

When he pulled away, he glanced at the Bibles again. "You are beautiful and tempting."

She felt the heat start in her face. "I didn't realize."

His mouth quirked. "Miss Innocent."

Sharee fingered her bottom lip. His kisses lit fires of their own. "Not that innocent, Mr. Jergenson."

John inserted the key into his condo door. Behind it, Cooper barked and yapped. Lynn had stopped by Sharee's room soon after their talk, and he'd decided to take advantage of that, run home, grab what he needed and head back. He settled the crutches under his arms, made sure his good foot supported him then thrust the door open. The dog jumped at him.

"Down, boy, down. I'm glad to see you, too." He chuckled and rubbed the dog's head and moved inside. Cooper danced against his legs, but John stopped at the sight of the girl stretched out on his sofa.

"China."

She sat up, yawning, lifting her hands above her head, stretching her legs in front of her. The shorts she wore left a long stretch of leg exposed.

"Hi." A smile dimpled her cheeks.

He bent and patted the dog again then straightened. "What are you doing here?" He hadn't meant the question to come out as abrupt as it sounded, but every sense he had shouted caution.

"Waiting for my mom. You don't mind, do you?" She lifted her arms again, and the short t-shirt exposed two inches of bare skin near her waist. "I had trouble with my car. Mom dropped me off and is coming back in a while."

He nodded, but the unease didn't disappear. "She dropped you off so you could walk Cooper?"

"Yes." She reached for the dog, but the Lab ignored her, pushing against John's hand. "We had a good walk. I was just napping until mom came back."

"Okay. I appreciate all you've done. You'll be glad to know this is the last day. Sharee's going home today."

"Oh, really? I enjoyed being here—walking Cooper and all."

He kept his face neutral not wanting to interpret what she said the wrong way. "Well, I dropped by to pick up something then I'm running back to take Sharee home."

She slid off the sofa and stood in front of him. "You're leaving right away? But you've spent every day and night there."

"Which is why I'm grateful for your offer to feed and walk Cooper." Her shorts hadn't lengthened any when she stood up. The long black hair hung loose, and she'd shadowed her brown eyes with some smoky color. She stood so close to him, he could feel her warmth. He averted his gaze, stepped back and propped the crutches against the wall. "I'll be right back. I need to get something from the bedroom."

He came to an abrupt stop just inside the doorway. He'd seen her offer to help as a problem-solver, but had it just become a problem-maker? The quick shower and change of clothes he'd planned would wait.

He crossed the room and pulled out the bureau drawer. His hand froze over the box, and his jaw tightened. Someone had moved it. Had she taken the liberty not only to sleep on his couch but also to rifle through his stuff? He opened the box, eyed the contents, and snapped it shut. Closing his fingers around it, he slid the drawer closed and turned.

· She had followed and now watched him from the doorway.

"When's your mom coming?" He asked, slipping the box into his jeans' pocket.

China settled against the door jam. A small smile lifted her mouth. "Not for a while."

He heard the meaning behind her words and grunted. She blocked the doorway. He envisioned what might happen if he tried to get past her. No wonder Bruce had warned him. His height topped hers by six inches at least, and his weight by a good fifty pounds. Yet, here he stood, like a fish in the fisher's net.

Cooper had followed them, too. The dog shoved past China and circled, tail wagging, in front of John.

John patted his head. "Get me the dog's leash, will you?"

"Why?" Her voice wavered, making the word sound like two syllables. "I took him for a walk already." She came away from the door and stepped into the room, her eyes focused on his.

Well, that hadn't worked. The girl's open invitation set him back a moment. The difference in age didn't matter to her, wouldn't matter to a lot of men. But he wasn't interested. He had someone he loved, someone worth more than what she was offering.

Trapped by the Girl from Youth Group. What a joke. He chuckled at himself and saw her eyes widen. He wasn't going to let her try anything else. Grabbing Cooper's collar and keeping him between them, he pulled the dog past her into the living area.

"China, call your mom and have her come get you." He released the dog, settled his crutches under his arms again and turned at the front door. "I appreciate your care of Cooper, but don't think that appreciation is anything more than it is. Lock up when you leave, will you?"

He closed the door behind him, grinned at the muscles relaxing throughout his shoulders and headed for his truck.

John watched Sharee's expression as she climbed from the hospital wheelchair into her older model Honda CR-V. Good thing he had stopped to get her car. Ridiculous to think of her climbing into his truck right now. She could use a step stool at the best of times; but—he smiled to himself—since he valued his life, he had never suggested it to her.

What would she think if he told her about China? Could he have misread the situation? He didn't believe he had, but the possibility existed. Lassoing his mind from where it had wandered, he brought it to the present.

The hospital aide said goodbye and rolled the wheelchair away. Sharee leaned her head against the seat and drew in a deep breath.

"How's the pain?" he asked.

"Not bad." She stared out the car windows. "I'm thankful to be free. It feels like I've been cooped up for weeks instead of days. The weather's beautiful."

"Spring is here."

"I'm glad. Winter this year was long."

He glanced across at her, then back to the road. "Well, the heat and humidity are back. You'll love it."

"I will."

He wheeled out onto the main roadway and slid a look her way. "The doctor gave a long list of do's and don'ts. Are you going to follow them?"

Her smile changed to a frown. "Housebound for ten days? That's ridiculous."

"No housework."

"I heard. No vacuuming, no loading the dishwasher, etcetera, etcetera. Just lie around and ice my back. I'll go crazy."

Just what he thought. Some people would see it as a God-sent time to catch up on their reading or sleeping but not her. "You'll do worse if you don't follow instructions."

"Yeah, well, we'll see."

"Sharee…"

"All right, all right."

He reached out and mussed her hair, and she slapped his hand away. "Hey, don't take those frustrations out on me."

"I'm sorry. It's hard to hit the doctor."

He chuckled. "You said your head was clearer today, your back better and you've been sprung from the hospital. Now you're a crab? What gives?"

"I don't have my life back. Whoever did this to me, to us, is still winning."

"Winning? That's an odd way of putting it."

"Well, if they meant to hurt us, they accomplished that."

"So, you were exaggerating when you told Dean you were fine?"

"That's the other irritation. I can't believe he stopped by."

He checked her face. "You want to talk about it yet?"

"No. It just annoys me." Her hand touched his. "I am being a grouch, and you've missed sleep and meals because of me. I'm sorry."

"Don't worry about it. A home cooked meal will make up for it. I haven't had one since I got back."

"Then I owe you about a dozen."

He reached for her. "Scoot over and sit next to me. What else are these bench seats for?" When she did, he slid his arm around her shoulders. "Are you up to a short walk?"

"A walk?" She sat straighter. "Seriously?"

"A short one. The doctor did say you needed a short walk daily."

"What about your foot?"

"I'm fine. I get the air cast on tomorrow. No more crutches."

"Mother will have our heads if we don't get there soon. She's probably cooked dinner. A home cooked meal just like you want."

He gave her a squeeze, and she snuggled into his shoulder. They rode in silence for a few minutes.

"I'm going to put an extra lock on your door."

"John—"

"Not up for debate. And be careful. Don't open the door to anyone you don't know. Don't allow your mother to either. She won't understand, but just act a little paranoid."

"Here you go again."

He tilted his head. "Sharee, until we find out what's going on, it's better to be safe."

"Okay. Okay."

He shook his head at her tone. In a few minutes, they pulled in at the church. His shoulders tightened. He glanced across at Sharee. She looked tired. Perhaps he'd planned this wrong. Perhaps...

"What are we doing here?"

No backing out now. "Well, unless Alan is here working on his sermon, we should have the place to ourselves. Come on."

They climbed out of the truck and made their way around the bleachers, across the field, to the pond that edged the back acre. An April wind ruffled the cusp of water. Cypress trees cast their long reflections into the shadows at the far end. He propped himself on one crutch and slipped his arm around her. They stood holding each other, not speaking. The mirror image of a red-tailed hawk sailed across the pond's surface.

"Oh, look." Sharee's head rose. The hawk glided just above the tree tops.

John dug into the pocket of his jeans. When she dropped her gaze, he held out the small box. Down on one knee would prove awkward. She'd have to accept it as it came. Her eyes rounded.

"I thought this might be a good time." He opened the box.

A large diamond caught the sun, throwing flashes of light in every direction. A wide gold band made of three smaller, separate bands curved and swirled together in a free-form pattern. The intricate design highlighted the solitary diamond.

"Oh, John." Her voice trailed off in complete surprise.

He watched her, waiting, nerves drawn tight.

"It's beautiful."

Relief loosened the tension. He and the jeweler had worked on the design a long time. He took her hand and slid it on. She turned it back and forth in the sunlight, her smile widening as she studied it.

He took her hand again. "I love you more than I thought possible, and I was devastated when you said you needed time. But now that I've done this right, will you marry me?"

She nodded once and again and a third time. The rest of the tension dropped away. His emotional control over three long days and two nights dropped, and he bent to find her mouth. Her answering hunger stirred him, and he dropped his arm around her waist, holding her close. The small box fell to the ground.

At last, she broke free. "John, I…we…" Her breathing was ragged.

She'd said yes; she liked the ring. He wanted to shout. Instead, he took two long breaths. "I love you."

"I love you, too." The emotion in her voice slammed his heart into overdrive.

"A wedding date would be good."

Her eyes rounded. "You want a date now?"

"You don't want to put this off for a year or something, do you?"

The surprise in her eyes changed to amusement. "A year's too long?"

"Way too long. Six months?" Before she could reply, he said, "But if we go back to Indonesia, that might be too long, too."

"Will you give me a minute? Is everything going to be like this? Make a decision—*now*?"

"I think so. Sorry."

"No wonder Pastor Alan said you needed some balance."

"He said that, did he? Hmm. How about three months?"

"Three months? You're serious?"

"I'm sure you can do it. We can do it. And by the way, the dragon lady said to tell you congratulations, that she'll be watching the papers for the wedding announcement. She appears to agree with your mother. She said even *I* should know no engagement is complete without a ring."

Chapter 7

She rode home staring at the ring. So unique and beautiful. Mrs. Sharee Jergenson. That name would be a change. Although, the youth group could still call her Ms. J. No, Mrs. J. She smiled and caught John's glance.

"I'm glad you like it. It would be hard to send back."

She shook her head. "You were that sure?"

"Not sure at all. Desperate, I think."

She laughed.

Exhaustion hovered near the surface of her laugh. He parked in front of her apartment, and she leaned her head against his shoulder. "I'm worn out. Completely."

"I'm glad you told me. Why don't you get some sleep then? I've got to pick up some things at the store. I'll give you a couple of hours. Think your mother will hold dinner?"

"She'll have to."

He chuckled. "Good. I'm looking forward to the home-cooked meal."

Later, when she woke, the tiredness had disappeared. She changed her clothes and wandered into the living area to talk to her mom.

"Someone called, Sharee," Mrs. Jones said. "They wanted to know if you were home from the hospital yet."

"Who was it?"

"I don't know. They didn't leave a name. They just hung up when I told them you were home and in bed already."

Sharee's brow wrinkled. Not like the other calls, but still strange. "Well…" She lifted the phone from the end table near her and stared at the caller ID. The ID merely showed "RING." She waited a moment longer then punched in John's number.

"Hello?" A girl's voice answered.

Sharee frowned. Wrong number?

"Hello?" The voice said again. "Sharee?"

"China?"

"Yes, hi, it's me. John's out—taking Cooper for a walk. I'm just waiting 'till he gets back. He left his phone."

"Oh." Complete surprise. What to say?

"Do you want me to tell him you called?"

"No…" She glanced down at her hands. The diamond on her left hand winked at her. "I mean, yes. Yes, please tell him I called. It's important. China, what are you doing there?"

China laughed then giggled, making her seem younger than her nineteen years. "You know I've been feeding Cooper for him while you've been in the hospital, right?" Sharee said nothing. "Well, I didn't realize you were coming home today until he told me. My mom dropped me off a while ago, but hasn't been back to get me, so I'm waiting for John to take me home."

"Where's your car?"

"Well," China drew out the word, sounding young again, and embarrassed. "My car is having some work done on it. So, I had my mom drop me off on her way to play Bingo. She was going to pick me up on the way back. But then John showed up again, and he said he would take me home. Mom won't be back for another hour or two."

"You were going to be there for hours just feeding the dog?"

"Yes. Well, I would have to, wouldn't I?"

"Yes, I guess you would. Please make sure you tell John I called. She stopped for a minute. "China, you didn't try to call me before, did you?"

"No. Why would I call? Don't you have Caller ID, anyway?"

"The Caller ID was blocked. My mother answered the phone."

"You live with your mother?" China's voice sounded startled.

Sharee smiled at the tone. "No, she's here because I was in the accident."

"Oh."

"You'll tell John?"

"Yes, yes, goodness."

"Thank you, China," Sharee forced a sweet tone but hated it. "All right. Goodbye."

She looked heavenward. *Lord, I'm sorry; you're going to have to work on me in this area.* She turned around.

Her mother was standing by the sofa. "There's some girl at John's apartment?"

"Don't worry about it." Sharee moved over to her favorite chair and sank down. She looked at the Caller ID again. Ring? She questioned. What's that?

"You know, Sharee...."

"Mom."

"I don't know what to think of that man."

"I love him."

"Yeah, well, in your current condition, you may be excused for that."

"Mom, I want you to be nice to John."

"Oh, I will. After I tell him..."

"You're not going to tell him anything."

"Sharee." Her mother's voice changed, and the bantering stopped. She slid into a chair, also. "I don't want you to get hurt again. You know I liked John when we met him at Christmas. He seemed like...well, like someone with a head on his shoulders. Now, I'd just like to shake him."

Lord, help me. I don't need this. She flung her legs over the side of the chair and squirmed around until she felt some relief for her back. I'm supposed to put ice on it. Then she looked at her hand again and held it up toward her mom.

"What?" her mom started. The next moment, she jumped from the chair. "Sharee! You have a ring! And a nice one, too! Why didn't you tell me? When did he give it to you?"

Sharee giggled. "On the way home."

"Today? Goodness, and I was wondering what was taking you two so long. I thought there was another hold up at the hospital. Why didn't you tell me right away?"

"Well, I wanted to, but you're always picking on him; and I was too tired."

Her mother kneeled down and hugged her. "Sharee, I love you, and I want you to be happy. You know that. If this man does that for you—and for some unknown reason, he seems to—then he's welcome in this family, and you know it."

Sharee giggled again. "I know."

Her mom sat back. "Well, we've got to plan a wedding."

"Yeah, in three months."

"Three months? That's outrageous. You can't plan a wedding in three months."

"Mom, three months."

"Sharee, that's almost embarrassing. Can't you wait a little longer? It takes time to plan a wedding."

"I've waited thirty years. Why would I want to wait any longer?"

"Well...well..." And then to Sharee's surprise, her mom giggled.

Forty-five minutes later, Sharee leaned against the chair cushions once more. The ache in her back had returned. The wedding discussion had replaced needed pain medication for a while. She'd remember that.

A sharp rap on the door interrupted them. When her mother rose, Sharee put her hand out. "Mom, wait. Make sure you know who it is before you open the door."

"I think I know how to answer a door." She looked through the peephole, flipped the lock, and pulled it open.

John gave them both a smile as he entered. He set down a bag on the entry table, along with some tools he carried.

His eyes met Sharee's. "I got your message. You okay?" When she nodded, he went on. "I've got to run China home, but I wanted to come here first. Put another lock on. I'm sorry to hold dinner up. Better yet, you two eat without me. I'll be back after I drop China off." He pulled some articles out of the shopping bag.

"Where is she?" Mrs. Jones asked.

"Mother."

"Well, he's not getting off that easy."

John raised an eyebrow at Sharee then turned back to the door, using a ruler and pencil to mark something off.

"Young man, I see you finally asked my daughter to marry you in an appropriate way."

He turned back to her, the grin in place. "I did. I'm glad to tell you that she accepted…again."

"Yes, so she said. However, a wedding in three months is…very rushed…almost embarrassingly so."

He turned back to the door, lifting some pieces of hardware he had brought with him. "How so?"

"Well...well..." She stumbled over the word. "Well, it is."

"We could live together like a lot of people these days and then get married next year." He glanced over his shoulder.

Her mother's eyes narrowed. "If you were so carefree in your relationships, you wouldn't be rushing into a marriage."

John didn't glance around but continued working. "You've got me there."

"Ha! I knew it. Well, there's one good thing to say for you, anyway."

"Mom!"

"So where's China?"

"In the car, Mrs. Jones. She said she thought it better if she just waited there." He glanced at Sharee, then back at the door, and picked up a screwdriver. "Would you like to go down and talk to her, Mrs.

Jones?"

"I don't think so."

"She's been feeding my dog while I was at the hospital."

"Humph."

"Mother, please." Sharee laid her head back against the chair. Had she filled the prescription for her pain meds? No. She'd forgotten everything after John had given her the ring. She raised her hand and glanced at it again. It would be her pain med for tonight. Her mother sat down on the couch, and they watched John finish with the lock.

"Sharee, walk me out?" John asked.

"No, no," Mrs. Jones said. "I'm going to run my bath. We'll eat when you get back." She got up, came to where John was standing and gave him a kiss on the cheek. "Welcome to the family, John." Then she laughed at his expression and went out.

He shook his head as Sharee came over. "She really does like you, you know. That's why she gives you such a hard time."

"She does that." His eyes focused on hers. "Are you okay? You're awfully quiet."

"It threw me, I guess. The phone call. They asked if I was home from the hospital. The Caller ID didn't show who it was. It just said RING...R...I...N...G."

"I don't like it."

"I don't like you driving around either. It seemed safer, somehow, in the hospital. Be careful driving...China...home."

He took her hand and rubbed his thumb over her ring. "You have nothing to worry about there. Did she say something to upset you?"

"No, it's not what she said, it's..." She grimaced. "It's all right. It doesn't matter."

"All right." He hugged her, collected his tools. "This is a deadbolt, but it only works from the inside, and only if you use it. No one should be able to get in after you're inside. You've got the chain lock and the deadbolt with your key, too. Use all three."

"Okay. Be careful getting into the car."

"Yes, will do."

She set the locks and went to the window as he left. He climbed into his truck, reversed out of the parking space and headed for the highway.

China turned in her seat and waved.

◆

The next day, Sharee set her Bible down on the end table, leaned her head back against the couch, and listened to the silence. John had driven her mom halfway to Ocala to meet her dad. As much as she loved them both, being alone had its advantages. She wondered how she'd do once she and John were married. She'd lived alone over eight years.

Well, Lord, this is what I've prayed for. Help me to be all that John wants and needs, and help us not to drive each other crazy. Amusement rose inside her. *You see how over-protective he is. He bought and installed a new lock.*

She sighed at being housebound for a week or two. Rising, she walked to her front window. The large stand of trees in the center of the parking lot drew her attention. Two squirrels chased each other around the trunk of one pine. Through the years, the squirrels and birds and occasional rabbits had entertained her. But for ten days?

John had installed a motion light above her apartment door after returning from dropping China off yesterday evening. Hmm. Was the girl playing at something or serious? Or was she just jealous? *Lord, don't let me see things that are not there.*

She whirled and headed to the kitchen. Get your mind off it, Sharee. Better clean up before John or Lynn arrive. Lynn's text earlier stated that she had a number of home-cooked meals from the ladies at church to drop off today. And John would be here soon, with her prescription and groceries from the market.

She put glasses and silverware into the dishwasher. This morning's breakfast and lunch had not left much of a mess, and the texts between she and Lynn had flown in-between the meals.

Lynn wanted to discuss details about the wedding. Planning a wedding in this short time would stretch them all—and Lynn had volunteered her services as wedding planner.

Leaning to put a small pan into the washer, she remembered to bend over with one leg lifted straight behind her. Like a golfer, the nurse had said. Sharee tried it and noticed the pull in her back lessened immediately.

She lifted her head as a rap sounded on the door. A key turned the lock, and John entered. She'd given him the key when he left. He had bags in both hands and shoved the door closed with his good foot. She leaned to put another dish in the dishwasher.

"You should use the bolts, babe, even when you expect me back." He hefted the bags and headed her way. "I managed to get you a ripe— What are you doing?"

Sharee straightened. "Just loading a few things. I'm being

careful."

The bags dropped with a "thunk" onto the table, "Go sit down."

"I'm being careful."

"You call it careful when you're doing exactly what the doctor told you not to do?"

She rolled her eyes at him. "The nurse told me how to bend over if I had to pick up anything."

He frowned. "*If* you had to pick up something. Go sit down. And don't roll your eyes at me."

She backed a little at his tone.

He pointed to the couch in the living area. "Sit. I'll do this."

She inched away, toward the couch, and lowered herself in slow motion. He began to load the dirty dishes, moving much faster than she had. As the dishes clunked together, though, she cringed. Would there be any without chips?

"Well, this bodes well for the marriage."

He swung round toward her. "What?"

She couldn't help but laugh. "Getting you to do the dishes."

He was across the room in a half-second. "Girl." The tone was a threat.

She laughed again, and he reached for her.

"Remember my back!" She scooted away.

"You obviously didn't remember it." He straightened but slanted a menacing look at her before returning to the kitchen. In another minute, when he finished with the dishes, he folded his arms across his chest. An arrogant smile spread across his face. "The twenty-first-century male. We do it all."

She rolled her eyes once more, and he narrowed his.

"If I come in here again and find you loading dishes or vacuuming or whatever, I'll revert to caveman mentality. Is that clear?"

"Yes, Mother."

"You've only been home a day. Do you think you could try to do what the doctor ordered?"

"Okay. Okay. I'll be good, but it's going drive me crazy."

"Patience, babe, is a virtue."

She threw a decorative pillow at him. He ducked, and it hit the wall with a thud.

Tap, tap, tap.

Both their heads shot around.

"I'll check it." John went over, glanced through the keyhole, and sent her a sardonic look. When he opened the door, Lynn eased across the threshold, eyes wide, a large shopping bag in her hand. "Did I hear something hit the wall?" she asked.

John waved his hand at Sharee. "Ask your friend."

Lynn glanced her way, but Sharee just shrugged. Lynn inspected the pillow on the floor and gave John an inquiring look.

He raised his hands in a "Don't ask me" gesture. "I've got lots of work to catch up on. Pedro has been pitching in for me while I've been at the hospital, so I'm heading back to church."

"Pedro was helping you?" Sharee asked. "You didn't tell me. How's he doing?"

"He's doing well. Very handy, as you know. As long as..." he glanced at Lynn and stopped.

"I know all about it. As long as he's sober."

John nodded. "I didn't feel it was my place to say anything if you didn't know."

"I knew. Sharee's been picking up homeless people for quite a while, and somehow manages to twist someone's arm to find them food or a job or something."

"Lynn." Sharee interrupted, her voice a warning.

Too late. John was already eyeing her in that half-concerned, half-angry way he had. "I know."

It took all her willpower not to laugh because the struggle he had not to say more was written on his face. He'd expressed his objections to her picking up hitchhikers a number of times. Silence filled the room, and with what appeared extreme effort, he turned to Lynn.

"There are some bags on the table. I would appreciate it if you put away the things that are in them. Sharee is not supposed to do anything besides resting on the couch. Do you think you can handle that?"

"Yes, sir, I can." She gave him a little salute.

"Good." He ignored her mocking tone and moved to the couch to plant a kiss on Sharee's head. The door closed after him, leaving them smirking at each other.

"Tell me what you did." Lynn moved over to the couch.

"I think I hit a male hormone without knowing it. I was putting dishes into the dishwasher."

"And you weren't supposed to? Well, he's all for keeping you safe, that's for sure. And by the look on your face, you don't mind too much."

"I don't—most of the time. It's rather endearing." Sharee held up her hand to Lynn. "What do you think? Better than the picture I sent you?"

Lynn grabbed her hand. "It's gorgeous! Different and sophisticated."

"And you still want to be the wedding planner?"

"You know I do."

"This could challenge an eight-year friendship."

"We'll have a great time. When I called you at the hospital…"

"I think I'd had too much medication when I agreed to this."

"I am the best organizer and decorator you know."

"Best rumor-monger, you mean."

Lynn feigned hurt. "I only deal in truth. Besides, this is the best rumor going. You and John are engaged!"

Sharee laughed and sat back in her chair. "Did you bring a book to write in? John and I have a few ideas of our own. And Mother does, too.

"Your mother, too?"

"Be nice. Mom has a high opinion of you. Although, I'm not sure why…"

"Hey, that week I spent with you last year turned out great. Your parents love me."

"Yea, they do." She hesitated. "I haven't met John's parents yet."

"They'll love you, too."

"Hmm. I hope. He doesn't say much about his parents. But…"

"What?"

"John is still in touch with Janice's parents. His in-laws, ex-in-laws. He calls them almost every week. He said at first, after Janice died, that it just seemed right, and he's kept it up all this time. Only now, of course, he has to do something to sever that tie. I don't think it's going to be easy for any of them."

"Do they know about you?"

"Yeah. When he told them about his trip to Indonesia last January, He told them about me, about us. He even told them he was going to ask me to marry him when he got back." She looked at Lynn.

"You're kidding. Before he actually asked you?"

Sharee made herself smile. "Yeah, but he said he wanted to give them time to get used to the idea while he was gone."

"Wow. How did it go?"

"You know what they said? They want to meet me."

Lynn's eyes widened. "They want to meet you? You're kidding."

"No. Janice was their only daughter, but they have a son. When she died, I think they kind of took John on as another son."

"But still…meeting the woman he's now going to marry." Lynn shook her head. "Does the fact that John was married before bother you?"

"You mean because she was obviously wonderful, and they

seemed to have had a great marriage?" She had tried to make it funny, but her own voice trailed off. Did it bother her? More perhaps than she wanted to admit. "What if I don't measure up?"

Lynn went to her and hugged her. "You don't have to worry about that. John loves you. I'm sorry I brought it up."

"I am having a hard time with the thought of meeting Janice's parents. I think it threw John, too, but what could he say? It will be awkward. I feel so sorry for them, to lose their daughter that way."

"Well, maybe they'll realize how crazy it is and change their minds."

"I hope so. Does that sound terrible? I guess it is, but I don't know how meeting me could cause them anything but pain."

Wednesday evening, Sharee slipped her hand into John's as they mounted the church steps together. She had insisted on coming, countering all his objections.

"I know what the doctor said, but I'm going crazy. I need to get out. I need church. You're working. You have no idea how bored I'm getting. I called work today and told them to send someone over with my laptop and some paperwork. Anything!"

"Your idea of rest and the doctor's are miles apart. You realize that, don't you?"

"And I've been making my own decisions for years now."

"Um huh. That streak of independence could get you in trouble one day, you know."

"John."

"All right. I won't argue anymore. Come to church and suffer through the night, but I'll need to pick you up a half hour early. Don asked me to speak to the youth tonight."

"Don asked you? Really?" Her voice rose. Quiet came from the other end of the line. "John?"

"Don't take this wrong, babe, but I was not planning on you being there tonight. I think it would hamper me if you were there."

"Hamper you?" Her heart stilled. He didn't want her there?

"Yes." He drew the word out. "Look, the talk I'm doing with the teens... It's probably better if I do this without you."

"But I'd like to hear what you're going to say."

"I'm flattered, you know that; but can you do it another time?" When she didn't answer, he said, "Sharee?"

Cold moved from her chest downward. He didn't want her there.

"But I…" She swallowed. Don't act thirteen. Go with it. "I…all right."

"Good. Would it be better for your back to take your car?"

"No, the truck's fine."

When she climbed into his Dodge Ram later, he reached over and drew her to him. "Is this going to cause a problem?"

"No."

"'No,'" he repeated, mocking her voice. "Can I do something to change that tone?" He lifted her chin, brushing her mouth with his.

"But John…" She stopped and swallowed the distress, and reached up to touch his jaw. "If you don't want me…"

"You know I want you." His eyes crinkled at the corners. "But I appreciate your understanding about this."

"All right." Perhaps he'd tell her about it later.

He put the truck in gear and pulled onto the road. "I'm counting the days until we get married."

"Me, too."

"Well, choose a date, my love. Any date is fine with me as long as it's soon."

Once parked at the church, he circled her hand with his and led the way up the church steps. "I've got to go to the youth hall and make sure about the podium and microphone. Also, I need to talk to Don and his wife before the teens get here." He dropped her hand. "See you after church."

The disappointment raced back, but she fought it. "Okay. All right. I'll go for a walk and see how my back feels."

She went back down the steps and headed for the walkway that skirted the premises. Every once in a while, she felt a pull in her back; but she sent a whispered thank you to God for how much better she was. She rounded the far side of the fellowship hall and halted.

Ted Hogan stood in her way, giving the odd impression that he'd waited for her. He crossed his arms and remained in her path. "I heard you were involved in a little run-in, Sharee." His voice mocked her.

"Yes."

"You spent some time in the hospital?"

"Yes." And why did he care? She took another step forward, but he didn't move.

"Well, those things happen to people who don't mind their own business."

"What does that mean?"

"I think it was clear."

"Are you saying you had something to do with it?"

He laughed and stepped forward. "Oh, no, I never *said* that, but you might be safer if you keep your opinions to yourself from now on. Like telling Marci she needed to stay away from me."

Sharee stared at him, shocked that Marci had shared her advice and wondering if what he was implying was true. Was John right about Ted, after all? Was she naïve?

"Makes you think twice, doesn't it?"

"You should be thinking twice, Ted. What are you implying?"

He leaned forward. "I'm not implying anything. I'm telling you to stay away from Marci, and out of our business."

Sharee took a step back and fought to keep her expression under control.

He laughed again. "Do I scare you?"

"You don't scare anybody, Ted." Bruce's voice came from behind her. His wheelchair rolled up and stopped.

Relief flooded like a warm bath over her.

"Coming to the rescue?" Ted's voice held disdain.

"If needed." Bruce wore his usual sleeveless t-shirt and jeans. The scripture tattoos on each arm stood out against his tan, and the penetrating look he gave Ted held confidence.

Ted sneered. He let his eyes rake the wheelchair. "You know, since you've been in that thing, you've gotten way too religious."

Bruce smiled. "So, you're saying this is what you need in your life?"

"No, I didn't say that." The words came like a dog's snarl. "Just tell your friend here to stay out of my business." He whirled and lurched away from them. When he reached the parking lot, he climbed into his truck and screeched down the drive.

"My goodness. What is his problem?"

Bruce touched her hand. "Are you okay?"

"Yeah. He wanted to scare me, though. Did you hear what he said about my accident?"

"No."

"He said something about accidents happen to people who don't mind their own business. Implying he could have caused it."

"He seems to be hitting the repeat button on that theme. Pastor Alan talked with him about Marci, too, and Ted threatened him and the congregation."

"You're serious?"

"Yes. Alan asked him to leave and not come back." They both looked back at the drive where Ted's truck had disappeared. "You need to be careful around him."

Sharee nodded, thinking how much like John he sounded. In the mouths of two or three witnesses... *Okay, Lord, I'm listening.*

"Please don't tell John about this." She saw his look. "At least, not until after he speaks with the youth tonight. I know it would distract him."

"No problem, but only until the service is over. I think he needs to know."

"Yes, but you know John. His tendency to...safeguard me...is already over-the-top."

"He needs to know."

"I agree." She let out a long breath. "Thank you for coming to my rescue."

"I was available."

They made their way to the front of the church. "Do you think that Ted could have caused the accidents?"

"Well, his anger has gotten him into trouble in the past, and he seems to be letting it have its way again. But did he run you down? That's a different question. I can see him trying to scare you. After all, you've confronted him on two or three occasions."

"But..." she started.

"And you reported his relationship with Marci to the pastor. That's why Alan had a talk with him."

"Wait a minute. Why do you think that? I didn't tell Pastor Alan anything."

"You didn't?"

"No. What makes you think I did?"

"I happened to overhear Ted's argument with him. He accused you, but if you didn't say anything, who did?" His brow furrowed. "Do you suppose Marci did herself?"

"She talked with John and me about it when I was in the hospital."

"Hmm. Maybe she felt convicted and went to see Pastor Alan."

"Well, she did tell Ted that I told her to stay away from him. But someone else could have seen them together and mentioned it."

"Could be."

"You and Marci go back a long way, don't you?"

"Actually, the three of us go back a long way. Marci, Ted, and I all went to the same high school. We got saved about the same time." He paused. "Ted and Marci were close for a while, but his temper got him in trouble even then. Marci finally broke it off."

They made their way into the sanctuary. A few people had gathered inside and talked together in quiet voices. Sharee glanced at her watch. It was early yet. Bruce halted beside her as she slipped into a seat.

"Sharee, you need to listen to John about Ted." He glanced at her. "It's just like women. They know other women better than a man does. It works both ways."

"Okay. I hear you."

She studied him for a minute. This side of Bruce was one she hadn't seen before—as protective as John in some ways. His friendship with John had tightened between Christmas and now. It looked like it would hold. The man's accident, the wheelchair, and all the pain he'd been through swept over her. She blinked back sudden tears.

He straightened in his chair; his face hardened. "Don't feel sorry for me. Don't pity me."

She shook her head. "No, I won't. But you said in the hospital that you…" Her words trailed off.

People walked past, down the aisle to other seats.

"That I wished I could walk again?" Bruce finished for her. "Of course. But if the Lord were going to do a miracle, he would have. Although, I'm always open. I refuse, though, to give in to the limitations of this thing. That's why I don't use the electric wheelchair often. I want the physical strength in my arms to do as much as I can for myself. I'm not giving into self-pity. That would get me nowhere. Besides, I've felt the presence of God more during this time than ever before. For instance—and you can do what you want with this—I knew I should be outside just a few minutes ago. I knew it."

"I believe you."

"I feel his presence with me every day. Like a force, a driving but grace-filled force."

Sharee smiled. "Well, Obi-Wan Kenobi, the Force was certainly with you today."

Bruce's face altered. He looked thoughtful for a minute. "This Force is much greater than anything George Lucas ever thought of."

Music startled them. They glanced toward the platform. The worship group had stepped up to the microphones. Bruce rolled backward, winked at her, and moved off.

Sharee sat down, her mind full. The music brought peace, soothing her like a cool, spring rain. When the praise started, she rose and silently thanked God for all the good in her life—for John, for Bruce, for her parents, her friends, her health. The list went on in her mind as the congregation sang.

More people arrived and filled the chairs near her. Their voices rose in adoration. The words and music filled her ears.

"Great is the Lord," the congregation sang, "and greatly to be praised."

When Pastor Alan preached, his message was on forgiveness. *Are you telling me to forgive Ted, Lord? Whether he tried to run me down or not?* Silence surrounded her, but she knew what God would have her do.

She looked up as someone patted her shoulder. Lynn gave her a quick smile, sat down, and turned to listen to the sermon.

When the service ended, Lynn hugged her. "Where's John? And what are you doing back in church already?"

"John's talking with the kids tonight." She slanted a look at Lynn between her lashes. "And I'm in church because it's where I want to be, and I don't need another mother. Got enough of those."

"Ooh! Snippy, aren't we?" Lynn's smile widened. "Okay, girlfriend, I get the message, but just remember that when someone wants to protect you from yourself, it's not always a bad thing. That's my piece. So, do you have a date for the wedding yet?'

"No, but we will soon. We just haven't pulled out a calendar. Oh, here come the youth. I wonder how everything went."

They watched as the teens began to file past the podium. They moved up the aisle, past where Sharee and Lynn sat. Sharee noticed sideways glances, and a couple of the younger teen boys elbowed each other as they strolled by. A few of the girls gave her a thumbs-up.

Lynn put a hand on her arm. "What's going on?"

"I don't know, but here comes Ryann. Maybe I can find out."

Ryann Byrd passed close to her seat, but when Sharee tried to ask a question, Ryann glanced over her shoulder. John had just come through the door. The girl's hand shot out and dropped a note into Sharee's lap. Sharee closed her fingers over it and glanced at John, too. What in the world had he said?

She unfolded the blue note paper as Ryann continued up the aisle to the back doors. Large block letters formed three words: HE'S A KEEPER!

Sharee bit back a laugh and showed the paper to Lynn, who elbowed her. Sharee folded the note and stuck it in her purse.

Lynn gathered her own purse and her Bible. "I'm glad you were here. Thrilled about the upcoming wedding. I'll call you tomorrow, and we'll talk."

Sharee nodded and glanced back down the aisle. Bruce and John had stopped in the middle and were talking as the group filed past.

China sauntered close to the two. Her gaze settled on John, but, though their conversation halted, neither man looked up. They waited until she passed. Bruce said something to John, who glanced at Sharee and frowned.

The church emptied, parents grabbing children's hands and hustling them to the door. The teens trailed after them, laughing and talking. A few adults lingered, conversing among themselves.

Her focus returned to John, smiling when he thrust a hand through his dark hair, liking the way his hair, deep-set eyes, and angled chin combined for a rugged look.

She turned at the sound of someone clearing their throat. China stood in the aisle next to her. The girl's hair was pulled back into a long ponytail. The tiny silver stud in her nose was highlighted by soft make-up. She wore black, form-fitting pants with a wide, white and silver belt. Her white running shoes appeared spotless. A short, zippered, gray sweatshirt complemented the outfit. Accented with a silver locket, the sweatshirt's zipper stopped about two-thirds the way to the top, making it obvious there was no shirt underneath.

Sharee straightened, not being able to stop a comparison between her plain jeans and t-shirt and the girl's obvious sexiness. When China spoke, her voice had a slight edge. "You two have a hard time keeping your eyes off each other. He seems completely, well, in love."

Something in the words caught Sharee's attention. She tried to identify what bothered her about them. "Well, hopefully, he is, since we're engaged."

"Some women might see that as a challenge."

Sharee studied her and rose to her feet. China stood three or four inches taller, but Sharee met her stare. She'd like to tell the girl to stay away from John and to zip up her sweatshirt, but it would make her sound as insecure as she felt. Instead, she crossed her arms over her chest and lifted her chin. "They might."

China smiled and walked off.

Sharee stared after her. Was the girl really...

"Sharee?" John's hand caught her elbow, turning her his way. His voice sounded impatient. He glanced past her, watching China's exit. "I need to talk to China. Meet me at Alan's office in a few minutes."

She put a hand on his chest, and he glanced down, a line creasing his brow. She bit her lip. Why did he want to talk to China?

"Bruce wants the three of us to meet with Alan." His gaze shifted back to where China had disappeared through the doors. "Let me catch her before she leaves. I'll meet you in the office."

He walked off, and she dropped her head, hoping the feelings rising in her did not show on her face.

Bruce's wheelchair stopped beside her. "You stood up. That was good. Now get your head up."

Her head did rise but in surprise.

He smiled. "Don't worry about China. That man loves you."

She looked down at her ring. "I know."

"Okay, then. Let's go to the office." He rolled the wheelchair forward but stopped. "What were you looking at?"

She showed him the ring, thinking how John had rubbed it the other day also saying she had no reason to worry about China. She needed to remember that.

Bruce nodded. "About time. He had the ring sent to me, and I dropped it at his place while he was still overseas."

Sharee felt her eyes widen. How many people knew he'd planned to ask her before she did?

The corner of Bruce's eyes crinkled. "You weren't sure, but he was. He said he knew before Christmas, but he didn't want to scare you off. As it happened, he almost did, anyway, didn't he?"

Sharee shook her head. "I was just confused."

"Not now?"

"Definitely not." She hesitated a minute, and he seemed to be waiting. "I love him. I know that. And more than that, I know God put us together."

Bruce nodded, smiled again, and rolled forward.

Pastor Alan cast tired eyes at them as they came into the office. "It's late, guys. Where's John?"

"He'll be here," Bruce said.

"Okay. Coffee?" They shook their heads, but Alan stepped to the coffee maker and pulled a filter and the coffee from a cabinet. "I need it. John likes coffee, too, doesn't he?"

Share sat back in one of the chairs, distracted by her thoughts. Bruce and Alan bantered back and forth about different things. She looked at her watch. What could he possibly be talking with China about? Minutes ticked by.

The door opened, and John came through. "Sorry to keep you waiting. Just something I needed to take care of."

He glanced Sharee's way, but she dropped her head, looking down at her hands.

Bruce's hand covered hers for a moment. "Hey, head up." He squeezed her hand.

Sharee raised her head, gave him a quick smile, and looked back at John. His eyes were on Bruce. He frowned and raised an eyebrow. She glanced back and forth between them. Bruce grinned.

Alan cleared his throat, holding out a cup toward John. John took it and shifted a chair next to Sharee's.

Pastor Alan settled in his. "Let's get started, Bruce. What's up?"

Bruce's nod indicated Sharee. "Sharee might want to start."

"Me? What? You mean about Ted?"

"Yes, I believe it's something both John and Alan need to hear."

"But it's—"

"What about Ted?" John set his cup on the desk, eyeing her.

She shrugged and described her confrontation with him.

"He'd obviously come to the church to confront her," Bruce said. When John started to say something, Bruce interrupted. "Wait. Let Alan tell you about his run-in with Ted."

"I'm not sure that's for publication," the pastor said.

"I understand, except I did overhear it; and it says a lot about what's going on inside him. It could give an indication of whether or not he was capable of causing Sharee's accident."

John straightened. "In that case, I want to hear it."

The pastor said nothing for a minute then also placed his cup on the desk. "All right. I tackled Ted on his relationship with Marci. During our discussion, he made references to how things happened to people who got in his way."

"He threatened you?" John's voice thickened.

"And those in the congregation." His head inclined Sharee's way. "He mentioned you by name and others by inference."

"You've got to be kidding." John turned and put a hand on Sharee's knee. "You're hearing this, right?"

A breath of cold air moved up her spine. She nodded.

"I told Ted he was not welcome on the church grounds again. I'm surprised he showed up this evening. We need to love him as Christ would, but I have to protect the congregation, too." He turned toward Sharee. "And you. You saw Ted with Marci, and you and Ted argued about that, right?"

"It wasn't an argument. Just words."

"To you, Sharee. Ted took it as a challenge, I think."

John raised a brow. "Do I know about this or is this a separate incident?"

"You know about this." She heard him give a sigh of relief and smiled.

Bruce rolled his wheelchair closer. "Maybe we should talk to the police about these threats. As you said, there are people to protect. He could have caused Sharee's accident. Although I have a hard time seeing how that would fit with John's accident. Whatever the case…"

Sharee leaned forward. "Maybe he just said that to scare me. I can't see Ted doing this. He's just talking."

The crease in John's brow deepened. He rose from his chair. "Ted is like a kid with a handful of cherry bombs and matches, just waiting for a time and place to set them off." He began to pace. "Cherry bombs are not the right analogy. The man is dangerous, Alan."

"I've already talked with the police."

"You have? Good. Are they going to question him?"

"Yes, but he moved out of his apartment. They haven't found him to talk to him, yet." His gaze shifted to Bruce. "I will report what happened tonight, too. He was told to stay off church property."

John's jaw clenched. "I'd like to talk to him myself."

Pastor Alan focused on him. "I think we'd better let the police handle this. Once I've reported what happened tonight, perhaps the police will investigate both your accidents more thoroughly. But first, we'll pray. John, sit down. God knows more about this than the police, than any of us. We need His wisdom."

John glared but lowered himself into the chair and took Sharee's hand.

She squeezed his. "You know, God kept us safe through these accidents. It could have been much worse, and Bruce was there tonight. Whatever's going on, we need to trust God to lead us."

"I suppose that means you don't want me to punch Ted out the next time I see him?"

Bruce laughed. Sharee shook her head.

The concern still showed in his eyes, but a corner of his mouth lifted, "Okay. Let's pray."

Chapter 8

Lynn's text message caused Sharee to drop her Kindle. "Bruce will be singing in tonight's service," it read. "You coming?"

Her thumbs flew in response. "What? You're sure? He hasn't sung since his accident."

"I know. Just heard from Daneen."

"Yeah! John and I will be there."

She texted John. He'd be as thrilled as she was. The Sunday afternoon had dragged so far. John had needed extra time after this morning's service to finish mowing the church grounds. April in Florida never failed to bring rain and, with it, high grass. But after the week working at home, Sharee chaffed at the forced solitude. But now...

She curled up with her book, thinking about this evening's service. Bruce's singing used to bring not only the youth but also the adults to their feet—or their knees.

After an hour, when she hadn't heard back from John, she tried calling him. No response. He always returned her messages or answered her calls. What if something was wrong? What if...

Feeling foolish, she texted Daneen. Had she seen John this afternoon? Yes, came the answer, out in the field on the mower.

Sharee stared at the screen. Just like he'd said. What was the problem then? Even on the riding mower, he would have his phone with him—on vibrate so he could feel it. She chewed her lip. He'd broken enough belt clips, though. Maybe he'd lost it or left it inside.

He'd be there tonight. No problem, but he wouldn't know to come by for her. She'd begged off tonight's service wanting to prepare to go back to work tomorrow and get to bed early.

As time for the service drew near, she found herself pacing back and forth in her apartment. John should be getting ready for church now. So, why hadn't he returned her call?

When the clock showed fifteen minutes before the start of service, she decided to drive herself. John wouldn't like it, but where was he? She took the back roads. Her grip on the steering wheel caused the muscles across her shoulders to tighten. A headache had started by the time she arrived.

She pulled into the parking lot and saw John standing by China's car. Her heart squeezed, jumped, and then fire flicked inside and rose in her face. *This* was why he hadn't answered her calls?

John's head raised and his eyes widened. He said something to China and strode to Sharee's car. Grabbing the driver's door handle, he jerked the door open.

"What are you doing?" The accent on each syllable and his clenched jaw left no doubt about his mood.

"Coming to church. Looking for you." Her tone rose to match his.

"You're not supposed to be driving."

"I had no other way."

"You knew I'd come get you. Why didn't you call?"

"I did call." Her eyes went past him. "But perhaps you were busy."

He glanced at China and back to her. "I told you…"

"In fact, I texted and called."

"I never got it. I couldn't find—"

"As I said, perhaps you were busy."

"I told you that you had nothing to worry about in that area. Get over it, will you?"

Get over it? As she climbed from the car, other people went past them heading for the church.

He took her arm. "What were you thinking, driving yourself here?"

She snatched it free. "I wasn't thinking anything. I came to hear Bruce sing."

"Bruce? What's going on with you two, anyway?"

"Nothing's going on, *Mr. Get-Over-it*. He hasn't sung since before the accident. You know that. I just wanted to be here for him." She looked past his shoulder, and China smiled at her. "And you're embarrassing me. Everyone can see we're arguing."

John's brow wrinkled. He glanced around. With her smile hovering still, China started up the church steps. Another couple glanced their way as they mounted the steps after China.

"Oh, for heaven's sake," John said.

Hearing his impatience, tears sprung to her eyes. What was wrong with her? She wasn't going to cry about this.

John growled something she couldn't understand and caught both her arms. "Come here." He pulled her to him and kissed her hard on the mouth.

Someone giggled behind her. Sharee yanked free. Out of the corner of her eye, she saw Ryann and a friend walk past. Heat singed her face.

"What are you doing?" she hissed.

"You're so worried about everyone knowing we're fighting, that I thought I'd do something about it."

"Don't ever do that again."

"What? Kiss you?"

"You know what I mean."

"You embarrass too easy." His tone was dismissive. "I couldn't believe you weren't home when I…"

"I might embarrass too easy," she cut across him, "but do you always have to act on the first thought that comes to your mind?"

"Better than being ten years late."

"Ten years early is just as bad."

They stood glaring at each other until John's face changed. Amusement lit his eyes, and his mouth curved upwards.

"This is not funny." She punched him in the chest and walked past him.

"Hey!" His voice followed her. "You almost broke my collar bone, woman."

Sharee ran up the steps and ducked into the ladies' room. Four or five women stood before a large mirror, fussing with their hair and make-up. Her eyes filled with tears. Why couldn't the bathroom be empty?

Someone swung the door open behind her. "Okay, everybody out. Now. But you, Sharee." Lynn pointed her finger at her. "Ladies, you're going to have male company any minute. You'd better hurry."

The others sent a glance Sharee's way as they filed out.

"He wouldn't dare."

Lynn nodded at her. "Oh, I think he would. I barely stopped him just now. I told him I'd bring you out."

"No. Tell him to leave me alone."

"Yeh, that would work. He'd be in here in half a second. You've got to come out."

"You don't know—"

"No, I don't, and I don't want to know. You'll work it out." Hard knocking made them both jump. "Give us another minute, please."

"Tell him to go sit in the sanctuary," Sharee said. "Then I'll slip out the back."

"No way." Lynn shook her head. "Didn't you come to hear Bruce? You're not slipping out anywhere. Go sit with John and talk to him after the service." Sharee scowled at her, but Lynn waited until she jerked her head in agreement. "Okay. I'll tell him to find a seat, and that you'll come out in a minute." She went out the door.

Left alone, Sharee dried her eyes, and stood silent, dredging up the courage to walk into the sanctuary. She heard the music start and gritted her teeth. Lifting her head, she went out the door and walked down the aisle.

Everyone stood in front of their chairs, singing. No heads turned her way, but she imagined their eyes settling on her when she passed each row. She grumbled under her breath when she saw that John had picked a place near the front.

Stopping next to him, Sharee sent a glance his way. He moved back so she could slide past. She had to touch him to get in place, but when she turned to face forward, she left a large space between them. And the singing continued forever. Would it ever end?

Pastor Alan finally moved to the podium. "Bruce came to me yesterday and said it was time he sang again." Clapping interrupted him. "Yes, we've missed the anointing God has placed on him. He told me he had a special song on his heart. It's a familiar one. 'It Is Well with My Soul.'"

John tilted his head in her direction. "I went to your place, and you weren't there."

The words barely reached her. Sharee stiffened. She didn't want to talk to him. "I'm trying to listen to Pastor Alan."

John muttered something she couldn't make out but leaned closer. "You told me you weren't coming tonight, but when I couldn't find my phone, I decided to drive over to make sure. I was running late, but when I got there, your car wasn't there." She shifted in the seat but didn't respond. "Have you any idea what I thought?"

"As some of you know," Pastor Alan continued, "the song was written by Horatio Spafford in the late 1800's. Two tragic events happened to him during that time."

"I tried to call you and text," Sharee said under her breath. "I left a couple of messages but never heard from you. It was getting late, and you still hadn't called, so I just decided to drive. Is that okay with you?"

"No. You're not supposed to be driving. How was I to know where you'd gone? I raced back here to find my phone in case you'd called, and…"

Pastor Alan's eyes focused on them. "First, Spafford lost his fortune in the Great Chicago Fire of 1871. He was ruined financially."

"Ssshh," Sharee whispered, wishing they'd sat farther back.

"China was the first person I saw," John continued. "I asked if she'd seen you, but then you drove up. I couldn't believe…" He cut short the words as Pastor Alan again turned their way.

"The second tragedy in Spafford's life," the pastor said, "happened when his four daughters were killed in a ship collision a few years later."

John touched her arm. "After what's happened, can you understand what I felt when you weren't home?"

Sharee started to snap back at him when his question registered. What had he thought when he couldn't find her? The same anxiety that had crawled through her must have assailed him, too. No wonder he'd lost his temper.

She covered his fingers with hers. "I'm sorry. I didn't…" She stopped. Pastor Alan's gaze slid their way again.

"Later," he said, "when Spafford himself took a ship across the same area, he wrote this song that we all know so well. Afterward, he and his wife went on to become missionaries in Israel. The song bears listening to again." When he emphasized the last sentence, Sharee felt heat rise in her face. He moved off the stage as Bruce rolled forward.

Sharee tilted her head in John's direction. "I'm sorry. I was so annoyed that I couldn't get in touch with you that I didn't think."

His eyes came her way, and his face relaxed. His hand circled hers.

The music started. Bruce glanced their way and then over the rest of the congregation before he closed his eyes and began to sing. His rich, deep voice filled the church.

"When peace, like a river, attendeth my way,

"When sorrows like sea billows roll;

"Whatever my lot, thou hast taught me to say

"It is well… it is well…with my soul."

As Bruce sang the chorus again, the words hung over the sanctuary, permeating the air like warm, moist liquid.

"It is well… with my soul,

"It is well; it is well, with my soul.

"Though Satan should buffet, though trials shall come

"Let this blessed assurance control

"That Christ has regarded my helpless estate,

"And has shed His own blood for my soul."

Sharee felt the presence and anointing of God descend across the congregation. John's fingers intertwined hers, and she closed her eyes, listening to the words. Everything else dropped away. Bruce's voice and an overwhelming sense of God's presence filled her.

"It is well… It is well…with my soul…with my soul.

"It is well, it is well… with my soul."

Tears formed behind her eyelids. She wasn't sure why. Perhaps for Bruce, for others she knew that had been through hard times, and because God was so good. Why had she been so impatient with John? *God, why would you visit us? Me? What am I that you are mindful of me?* She felt humbled, like she wanted to kneel, to lie on her face.

"My sin, oh, the bliss of this glorious thought!

"My sin, not in part, but the whole,

"Is nailed to the cross, and I bear it no more.

"Praise the Lord, Praise the Lord, Oh my soul.

"It is well…It is well…with my soul…with my soul.

"It is well, it is well with my soul."

As Bruce sang the chorus again, John's whispered words of prayer came her way. Sharee's heart swelled. The tears wet her cheeks now. Bruce's voice changed as he began the last stanza.

"And, Lord, haste the day when my faith shall be sight,

"The clouds be rolled back as a scroll.

"The trump shall resound, and the Lord shall descend.

"Even so, it is well…with my soul.

"It is well…It is well…with my soul…with my soul.

"It is well, it is well… with my soul."

The richness of his voice drew out and as the music ended, no one moved. Sharee bowed her head. *Lord God, nothing compares with the beauty of your presence.*

When the service ended, John enclosed her hand in his, and they walked through the doors toward the field. The peace that filled the sanctuary hovered close. The night sky stretched high overhead, and stars pricked its darkness. Wind stroked cool fingers across her skin, lifting her hair.

They stopped at the pond's edge, and he drew her against him, her back to him. "Sharee, did you ever think God could be so personal? So real?" His voice was a whisper. "It was like this overseas. His presence…so thick."

She said nothing, not wanting to break the awe that surrounded them. Across the water, the cypress trees swayed against the inky sky.

"The daily things don't seem at all important when you feel His Spirit like we just did."

"It puts things in perspective."

John sighed. "It does."

"I'm sorry."

He turned her around. "No, I'm sorry."

"I was so upset when I couldn't get you—"

"And I panicked when I couldn't find you."

"Then seeing you with China—"

"Seeing *you* drive up." He enfolded her in his arms. "I lost my temper."

She leaned her head against his chest and sighed. "I love you. God is good to us."

"He is." He rubbed the roughness of his chin over the top of her head. "But please…don't disappear again without warning."

"Don't misplace your phone."

He chuckled. "I'll try. Look up here."

"What?" She lifted her head, and he covered her mouth with his.

When he pulled back, he traced a line along her jaw. The smell of night jasmine circled them.

"I love you, too."

"Umm." Sharee snuggled close.

"Come on. I showered this afternoon after mowing, and I bet I set my phone down there." They walked to the parking lot. "Wait here, why don't you? I'll check the shower stall in the tool building, and then I'll drive you home."

"But I've got my car."

"The doctor said—"

"If you drive me home, one of our cars will be here."

He said nothing, but she sensed his hesitation.

"John?"

"I want to take you home. Let me get my phone."

As he turned away, she said, "You can't protect me 24/7."

He stopped. "I know that."

"Can't you just follow me home? Get your phone and follow me in the truck? I'll be okay."

He hesitated longer, this time, ran a hand through his hair and then exhaled. "Okay. I'll follow you. Wait for me."

Sharee climbed into her Honda and watched him disappear into one of the buildings. She leaned back against the seat, and the pain in her back told her she'd been up too long.

It rankled when he acted like she needed taking care of. She'd been on her own for eight years. But she had to admit, at other times, having someone look out for her was like a warm fuzzy.

Sharee glanced across the parking lot and saw John walk from the building. Alan followed and turned to lock the door.

She backed out of her parking space, passed his truck and looked his way again. The two men stood close together. John's head tilted toward his cousin's.

"Come on, babe." She yawned and eased her Honda CR-V forward, around the fellowship hall and down the driveway toward the road. Braking at the six-lane highway, she waited and smiled. He'd be in overdrive if she went on without him.

A few seconds later, lights swung around the building and headed up the drive.

All right. She pulled onto the highway. The trip to her apartment would take ten, maybe fifteen minutes. Her eyes focused on the rearview mirror. She frowned. That looked more like a car than John's truck. As the other vehicle passed a street light, Sharee shook her head. It was a car. She'd pulled out in front of someone else.

The car's lights brightened, approaching fast. Sharee pulled into the outside lane. Which one of their law-abiding congregation was this? She smiled. All right. Pass me. You're obviously in a hurry.

But the car swung in behind her, the lights swelling as it drew close. Sharee straightened. The rearview mirror glowed now, the car almost on top of her. She yanked the steering wheel and swung back into the middle lane. The car behind her swerved, too, then closed the area between them in a burst of speed.

What... Sharee jerked the Honda back to the right, but it was too late. The other car slammed into hers. The impact flung her head back then forward and sent the SUV sliding out of control.

Moments later, the car slowed. She shoved herself upright and gripped the wheel. What had just happened? Was the person drunk? On drugs? A glimpse at the rearview mirror gave her an instant of warning. The other car jumped forward again. The collision, this time, snapped the seat belt tight, cutting into her neck and spun the SUV across the roadway. She clung to the wheel. The side of the road flew at her, and the Honda CR-V shot over the dirt and grass, bucking hard before crashing into the ditch. The airbag exploded.

Sharee sat still, stunned. The car had filled with smoke. Someone had just run her off the road. Her hands began to shake. She unlatched her seatbelt and threw open the door. As she stepped from her SUV, her peripheral vision caught the other car's lights making a wide turn. She twisted in its direction even as it barreled her way.

Run.

The car's engine sounded louder. Headlights hit her; the motor revved.

Run.

Sharee scrambled up the other side of the ditch toward a stand of trees. The vacant lot offered cover. Behind her, the car squealed to a stop. The door slammed. She heard someone clamber up the ditch just as she entered the shelter of the trees.

She ran. A group of pine trees loomed, and she darted behind them then around a stand of palmettos. Anything that might hide her. Her foot slipped on the leaves and dirt, and she grabbed a small pine to right herself. Darkness closed around her. She could see nothing ahead of her. She blinked and glanced back the way she'd come. Streetlights barely penetrated the darkness. She dropped behind the palmettos, making herself as small as possible.

Lord, please.

Her hands shook. She wiped her sweaty palms on her jeans, gulped shallow breaths and tried to hear. Nothing. Was the person standing still, too? Listening for her? She glanced at her dark clothes. *Thank you, Lord.* Her hand tightened on the small tree. She didn't dare move. Close by, a twig snapped then another.

On the other side of the palmettos, leaves rustled. She held her breath as her pursuer moved past. Quiet steps echoed in the darkness. The muscles in her legs screamed at her. Would she be able to get up if needed? Desperate for air, she sucked in a shallow breath. The noise sounded loud in her ears. Time crept as slow as the wait for morning. She struggled to hear what her pursuer was doing but heard nothing. A cricket chirped, then another.

From a distance away, a car door slammed, an engine started. The noise rumbled over her hiding place, filled the night, and died. She exhaled a long, slow breath. Whoever it was had gone.

Her body relaxed, her breathing became natural, and she straightened on unsteady legs. Silence filled the night.

Striving to see, she put her hands out to feel her way through the trees. The darkness confused her, but the street must be close. Noise from a car passing nearby gave her direction. Lights flickered through the trees. She stopped. Had the person come back? She waited again, but the car sped past. Another car, going fast, zoomed by the vacant lot. Good. She was headed in the right direction.

The third engine sounded deeper than the others. It moved fast, also, but the sudden squeal of brakes brought her to a standstill. The screech of wheels followed. Lights flashed through the trees. She leaped back from their glare.

A car door opened.

"Sharee!" John's voice echoed loud and strong and anxious.

The truck's lights sent yellow beams through the darkness. She ran toward them. He shouted her name again. Relief washed over her.

"John." She could see him now, next to her Honda. "John!"

He spun in the direction of her voice, scrambling out of the ditch toward her. She ran from the trees.

"Sharee, what…" He reached her, caught her waist, and pulled her hard against him. "What are you doing? Why didn't you wait for me?"

She clung to him, fighting to get her breath. Sirens sounded in the distance.

"Someone ran me off the road."

"Ran you—"

"And chased me through the woods." She threw her hand toward the trees. Her body began to shake.

He hugged her close. "But you—"

"I heard him leave. He…" Her voice cracked. The trembling grew.

"It's okay, babe. I'm here. You're okay."

She buried her head against his shoulder. His hand stroked her hair. After a moment, he moved back and looked down at her. "You are okay?"

"Yes. I…I'm fine."

"Come on." He turned them toward the street, toward the noise of the sirens.

Two Sheriff's cruisers ran up onto the grass, lights flashing. Sharee put her hands to her ears, closing her eyes against the sporadic bursts of color. When the night went black and silent, she lowered her hands. John led her forward. Two deputies, dappled by the streetlights, made their way around the cruisers and moved toward them.

"We received a report of an accident and two people running into the woods," said the taller of the two.

Sharee recounted what had happened, and the deputy jotted notes as she explained. Her body felt cold and sweaty still. She huddled closer to John's warmth.

"Did you see the make of the car?"

"No. I just knew that it wasn't a truck."

Both deputies glanced at John's truck.

"I wish you'd waited for me," John said, his voice low.

"I thought it was you. I was waiting in the drive, and I saw it swing out from behind the church. So I thought it was you."

The first deputy jotted in his book. "You mean the car came from behind the church?"

"Yes. There's a parking lot there, and a back entrance that leads to the neighborhood behind it."

"I'll check the car." The other deputy walked past them, circled the SUV and glanced at the damage on the bumper and the trunk.

"We've got tire tracks and paint." He walked toward the ditch and studied it. "You ran up this way?"

"Yes," Sharee answered.

"There will be some prints. Ground's messed up. I'll secure the perimeter."

Sharee turned back to the other deputy. John was filling him in on the other two accidents.

"I heard something about a parishioner threatening the pastor there."

Sharee raised her head to meet John's look. "Do you think Ted...?"

"He did threaten you."

The deputy flipped to another page in his book. "You were threatened?"

"Yes, but...but I don't think Ted..."

"Ted's last name?"

"Hogan."

"That should have been reported," John interrupted, "a couple of days ago."

The other deputy reappeared. "We're going to need forensics to take paint samples and tire casts. Also, footprints." He eyed Sharee's shoes and then John's. "Did you go into the ditch, too?"

John nodded. "I ran from her car to the other side of the ditch."

The officer gave a snort. "Of course. We're going to need both your shoes."

Almost midnight, John noticed, as he helped Sharee into his truck. They'd pick up her car whenever the Sheriff's office released it. He studied her a moment in the cab's light. The tightness in her face and jaw told him all he needed to know. She was fighting exhaustion and nerves. They rode in silence.

She tucked her bare feet under her and laid her head back against the leather seat. He'd had another pair of shoes in the truck, but she had nothing.

He directed his anger at himself. Why had he agreed to her desire to drive home? He fixed next on Ted. If Ted had run her off the road, chased her through that vacant lot...

"John."

The tenuousness in her voice captured his attention. "I'm here."

"I don't know whether to cry or scream."

"Neither will help. But I could make a target with Ted's face on it, and you could throw darts." Her head rose. He forced a grin.

"But what if it wasn't him? I can see why he might want to run me down, but why you? And you were first—before I saw him with Marci."

"You're right, but let's leave it to the Sheriff, right now. They get paid for this."

"I won't be able to sleep. What if he shows up at my place?"

"You mean if it is Ted?"

"Yes. I'm sorry. I'm going back and forth, aren't I?"

"Perfectly normal."

She lowered her head. He could feel the emotions swirl through her, and he slid his arm around her shoulders and drew her as close as possible.

When they reached her apartment, he drove around the building, checking everything, before he parked. In the light from the antique lampposts, he inspected her. How could he leave?

"Sharee." His voice was a rough whisper. "I'm going to stay tonight." When her eyes met his, he added, "I'll sleep on the couch, but if you need me, I'll be here."

She straightened and pulled free. "I'll be okay." But her voice underlined her uncertainty.

"I'll sleep on the couch," he said again.

"What about Cooper? Don't you—"

"He'll be okay for the night. In fact, maybe I should bring him over tomorrow." He gave a half smile. "He's good protection, and you two might as well get used to each other. He's part of the package, you know."

"Part of the…Oh." She tried to smile, didn't succeed, but punched him. "I knew that."

He grabbed her hands, holding them. "You know you almost decked me earlier."

"I did not."

"You threw a punch like a guy." He made his voice light.

"Right. So good that you were only a step behind me. Trying to get into the ladies' room."

He tugged her back into his arms. "I should never have let you drive."

"It wasn't your fault. I wanted to drive. Remember?" In a minute, her voice rose, "None of this makes sense. Who would do this? I can't see Ted doing it, but who would? What do they hope to gain?"

"Sssh." He put a finger against her mouth. "Don't get upset. We can't do anything, but the police will now. Let's go in."

"John, you can't stay."

He heard her uncertainty again. "Why not? Do you want to be alone?"

"I…" her voice trailed off. "No."

"I don't want you alone either. Come on." He climbed down and scrutinized the parking lot before putting a hand out to help her. The motion light he'd installed a week earlier came on.

He stopped. "Your back? You haven't said a thing about your back."

"I know. It hasn't bothered me since I ran into the woods."

"No? That doesn't make sense, but sometimes…God does miracles."

"He did do a miracle. He kept me safe." She took her keys out, opened the door, and flipped on the lights.

John locked the door, set the bolts, and turned to see her dump her purse on an end table. She kept her head down. He remained quiet.

"I don't know why anyone would do this." Her voice caught.

He'd expected the break and knew when it came, he'd be in trouble. He moved next to her, holding his body and his own emotions in check. He was here to help her feel secure, nothing else. She looked up at him, and he bent to kiss her—a quick, butterfly kiss.

"I don't know any more than you, babe, but we're going to be okay."

"I know. I…it's just…thank you for being here."

Her eyes seemed bigger than ever and her hair wild, curling in a hundred directions. She looked beautiful and fragile, and he wanted to make love to her. He dropped his hands to his side and took a step back.

"I don't know if I can sleep," she said.

For a minute, he made no response, swallowing every thought that rose. He cleared his throat. "I'll be here. You won't be alone." His fists tightened. "Try to get some sleep. I'll be on the couch." He looked over her head to the bedroom. "Go to bed. Lock the door."

"Lock the…" She tilted her head and frowned. "Lock the door?" Then her eyes rounded, and a smile touched her features. "Do I need to?"

"The way I'm feeling?" He forced a grin. "It would be wise."

Chapter 9

The cell phone's bouncing melody thrust its way into John's consciousness. He shook himself awake and took a moment to orient himself. Sharee's apartment. Okay. The hard couch. Okay.

The phone fell silent.

He stretched to see the clock. 8:00 A.M. He hadn't slept long, and he'd tossed and turned most of that time. He stretched his neck, releasing the kinks. The first thing they needed when they married was a comfortable couch. Yeah. A comfortable couch. In case, he had to sleep on it for another reason.

The phone's melody began once more. Sharee's purse still sat on the end table. He reached, grabbed it, and fumbled the phone out of it, pushing the button that showed an incoming call.

"Yeah?" The roughness of sleep sounded in his voice, and he cleared his throat. "Yeah? Hello?"

On the other end, another throat cleared. "Hel...lo?" Sharee's father's voice lifted the last syllable.

John jerked upright. His feet hit the floor. Why had he answered her phone? "Uh...sir?"

"Hello, John. Just calling to...that is, just wondering how my little girl was doing this morning."

Little girl. John remembered the way she'd looked last night and forked a hand through his hair. Right.

"Sharee's fine, sir. She's still asleep. I mean I'm sure she's fine. She's in bed...I ..." He stopped and closed his eyes. *What am I saying?* Silence filled the phone line. He sent a look heavenward, took a deep breath, and started over. "Look, I'm on the couch. She's in her bedroom. There was an accident last night, and I didn't want her to be alone."

The quiet this time lasted three long seconds. "I think," Brian Jones said in an even tone, "that at a later date, we'll have a good laugh about this, but right now...I just received a call that said she was run off the road last night and chased through a field."

"That is correct."

"I'm assuming, since you're both there, and not at the hospital, that she's okay."

"Yes. She was scared, of course, but okay."

"You want to tell me about it?"

John gave the details of what happened. "My fault. I let her talk me into driving herself home. I didn't feel right about it, but I gave in."

"I thought she wasn't supposed to be driving, anyway."

"Well, sir..."

"You can drop the sir."

John grinned to himself. "I'm trying to, believe me."

Brian Jones chuckled. "I understand. I appreciate you staying the night—on the couch. Sharee means a lot to me, to both her mother and me, as she does to you. Why was she driving, or do I need to ask?"

"I think you realize your daughter is a...an independent young woman. She couldn't get in touch with me and felt the need to drive to church on her own. And then, of course, she wanted to drive home."

"I understand." The smile in his voice changed to a serious note. "My friends in the Sheriff's office here have made contact with the detective assigned to this case—a Detective Shepherd. He should be contacting Sharee today. What can you tell me about Ted Hogan?"

"You do have good information." John gave a short rundown on Ted Hogan. "What have you heard about my neighbor, George?"

"You'll be glad to know that he seems to be just what he says he is. He does, however, have some friends that could bear watching. We will be giving that information to your detective. It will be part of his investigation, I understand."

"I'm glad that we're be taken seriously."

"Yes, they might make some headway at this point. Well, John, it's been nice talking with you this morning. My wife is waiting at my elbow to hear what all this is about, so I think I'm in for some explaining, too. I'll ring off. Please have Sharee call us when she gets up."

"I will, si—" John stopped, biting short the word. On the other end, he heard Brian Jones laugh. "I will," he said again and pushed the "end' button.

Yeah, one day we'll laugh about this.

❧

Sharee pushed John toward the door. Daylight had brought courage. "Go home. Feed your dog. Take a shower. Let *me* take a shower and get some work done."

He frowned. "I don't…"

"I heard you tell dad I was fine."

"It's one thing to tell your dad you're okay, another to leave you by yourself."

"Nothing's going to happen to me. Not here, anyway. Besides, you can't stay forever." She gave him a smile that teased. "At least, not yet."

He growled and slid his arms around her. "Don't go anywhere."

"Certainly, sir." She saluted, mocking, remembering with amusement his own use of "sir" a short time ago. She'd stood in her doorway listening to his conversation. "Whatever you say, sir."

"Stop that. I mean it."

She laughed and tipped her head back, taking in the intense darkness of his eyes, the line of his mouth. He bent his head, his lips finding hers, kissing her roughly as if imprinting his claim on her.

She watched from the window a few minutes later as his truck backed from its parking space, and she raised her hand to her lips. That's what it had felt like. As if in claiming her, he could keep her safe. She didn't know what losing someone she loved would do to her, but she knew what it had done to him.

Lord, give him peace. Give me peace. Protect us.

She went to the refrigerator and took out the soft ice pack. Crazy back. It hadn't bothered her until this morning. If she iced it for a while, maybe she'd feel like doing something around the apartment. She stopped and smiled. Well, maybe not too much unless she wanted another lecture.

He hadn't wanted to leave. It wouldn't surprise her if he turned around and came back. She leaned against the counter, treasuring the warmth of his concern for her.

Knocking sounded from the front door.

She straightened and almost laughed. "I knew it."

The knocking sounded again, quick, hard raps. She walked to the door.

"Wait a minute, Mr. Impatient. You know I've got three sets of locks here." She flipped the bolt near the handle. The knob shook, and the door jiggled. "Hold on, I'm not through. You're the one that added all these locks." She took the chain off.

The door handle shook once more. She stopped, hesitating with her hand raised toward the last lock.

"John?"

No answer.

Her stomach tightened. The deadlock held against another

shaking. She moved to the peephole. Why hadn't she done that first?

She put one eye to the hole then jerked away. *No.* She fumbled with the chain lock, hands shaking, trying to get it back in place.

"Look, open the door." Dean Strasburg's voice assaulted her ears. "I've been here all night waiting for the boyfriend to leave." A moment's pause, and he said in a softer tone, "Come on, Sharee. I just want to talk to you. We never talked."

He'd waited all night? Then perhaps Ted hadn't caused the accidents. Dean fit the profile much better. And he would never believe that John had slept on the couch. She'd stopped Dean's sexual advances just as she had others, and he'd waited longer than most to push that agenda. As their relationship progressed, his frustration grew. Frustrations, she emphasized to herself, frustrations that included her close relationship with her parents and with God.

"We're in the 21st Century, for pity's sake," he'd said one day. "You need to throw half this religious stuff out the window."

It had shocked her. He'd presented himself as a passionate Christian, attending church with her numerous times. The passion, she realized later, centered on the physical, even if he'd waited to express it. His words that day had begun to open her eyes to who he really was.

The pounding increased. "Open the door."

She backed away. How many times had he lost his temper? How many times had she been afraid? But not until she challenged him about his relationship with God had he actually hit her.

Now his voice lowered in a way she remembered, cajoling. "Come on, Sharee, I'm worried about you. It was hard seeing you in the hospital. Let me in, please."

She said nothing but stepped to the end table near the sofa. Her purse and phone lay on it, sprawled there from last night. She grabbed the phone.

"Sharee." Dean's voice lowered, but she heard the change. "The boyfriend spent the night." His quick, harsh laugh followed. "What happened to all that self-righteous purity of yours?" The door handle shook once more.

She punched in John's number.

"Sharee?" John's voice came quick and warm.

"He's here, John." She tried to keep her words even.

"Who's there?"

"He's pounding on the door. He wants me to let him in."

"Who?" His voice changed. "Don't open the door."

"No."

"Where are you?"

"At home. In the living room." Her voice shook along with the door. The pounding grew. "Do you hear him?"

"Yes." The decimal level of John's voice jumped. "Sharee, there's no way he can get in, but get into the bedroom, lock that door, hang up, and call 911. I'm on my way."

Sharee sucked in her breath. Dean stood at the wide living room window now, watching her.

"What is it?"

"He's at the window."

"Can he see you? What's he doing?"

"He's just standing there. Watching."

"Okay. Get into the bedroom where he can't see you. Close the door. Lock it. Call 911."

She took a step backward. Dean's eyes never left hers. "John…"

"I'm on the way. Get into the bedroom. Are you there yet?"

"Yes," she whispered, watching Dean's eyes, feeling as she had before—almost hypnotized by their magnetism. She shivered.

"Okay. Close the door; lock it." When she didn't respond, he said, "Close the door."

Her hand shot out, shutting it against Dean's gaze. She stumbled backward, hitting the bed, dropping hard onto the mattress.

"Sharee?

"Yes?"

"Is the door closed? Locked?"

"There is no lock."

"Put something in front of it."

Her gaze flew around the room. Nothing she could handle without some effort.

"Who is it?" John asked.

"It's Dean."

"The guy at the hospital?"

"Yes."

"Put something in front of the door. I'm hanging up. I'm calling 911."

"John…"

"Wait for the police. For me. Do not come out of that room for anyone else."

The phone went dead. Silence settled over her. The pounding had ceased. What was he doing? Fear traced its finger up her spine. She stood.

A moment later, she pulled her desk and chair in front of the door. A box of things she had for The Salvation Army, her books, pillows from the bed—all went on top of the desk—anything to stop him and buy time if needed.

John had said he couldn't get in, but she'd flipped the bolt and hadn't locked it again. She knew people said the chain locks were pretty easy to get past. That left the deadbolt John had installed.

Lord, let it hold. She looked for a weapon, picked up the tall lamp from the bedside table, unplugged it, took off the shade, hefted it in her hand. Then she sat back on the bed and twirled the cord around the lamp, holding it like a club...and waited.

"He can't get in," she said aloud. The window was up to code. Only a hurricane with 130 MPH winds could break it.

Her phone rang. She grabbed it and fumbled it open, shaking. So much for having no fear.

"Did you call the police, Sharee?" Dean asked. "Like before? Did you?"

She punched the end button. It rang again immediately. She jumped and backed away. The phone continued to ring. She inched forward, looked down and snatched it up.

"John, he called!"

"Who? Dean?"

"Yes. He called my phone."

John muttered something.

"What?"

"Are you okay?"

"Yes."

"I'm almost there."

"Someone's trying to get in."

"Into the bedroom?"

"No, the phone."

"It could be 911—calling you. Or him. Don't answer. One of your neighbors had already called 911. Thank God."

"How did he get my number?"

"It doesn't matter. You can have it changed. Do you hear anything now?"

"No."

"He probably left. But stay there. I'm turning into your street."

Silence filled the room. Her hand tightened on the phone.

"Do you know his car?" John asked, breaking the silence.

"He did have a black Ford Explorer."

"I'm making a circuit. I don't see an Explorer nor anyone in front of your place. Nothing looks suspicious." The quiet stretched. "Nothing in back. Sharee, I told them you had a restraining order against him at one time, that he had assaulted you physically once before. But I didn't know for sure."

"He did." She heard him curse under his breath. "John!"

"Go on. What did he do?"

"He…he hit me, and I ran. Slapped me, actually. But so hard he knocked me down." Silence filled the line. "John?"

"You don't want to hear what I'm thinking. Okay, I'm parked out front. I hear sirens. I'm going to wait for the police. Stay there."

"I will."

"They're pulling up now."

A few minutes later, her phone rang again. "It's okay. He must have left. No one's here. I've got the key. I'll let us in."

She looked at everything piled in front of the bedroom door and felt the fear drain out of her. "Okay, but it will take me a minute to come out. I've got to move all this stuff." Better safe than sorry, her dad always said. She set down the phone and began to drag things away from the door.

Voices sounded in the living area.

"Sharee?"

"I'm almost out." In a minute, she opened the door. John gave her a quick hug and a searching look. "I'm fine."

A deputy sheriff stood just behind him. She waved at the chairs and sofa and dropped onto the sofa. John sat beside her, his arm circling her shoulders.

The deputy took a chair across from them. "Let me get your name and some other information, and you can tell me what happened."

Sharee described the previous events with Dean, the restraining order, the car accidents, and then his visit to the hospital.

After a few more questions about today's incident, the deputy flipped his book closed. "You might have felt threatened today, but, from what you've said, there was no actual threat made."

Beside her, John stiffened.

"There is history, however. You had a restraining order—for a reason. We can question him, but we can't charge him with anything. And the questioning might make things worse." He walked to the door and inspected the locks before glancing at John. "You've got some decent locks and bolts here I see."

"John installed them after I came back from the hospital."

John sat forward. "How do we stop this guy if all you can do is talk to him?"

"It might make him think twice if we corner him at work. You both stay alert." He tipped his head in Sharee's direction. "You want to make sure these bolts are always fastened. Be careful coming and going, getting in and out of your car. Use the peephole like you did today. Don't walk into a situation. If you see him, walk away, drive away. Don't wait. Don't talk."

When they were alone, John began to pace the room. "What else needs to happen before they take this seriously?"

"At this point, I think their hands are tied."

"Ours, too." He swung around. "How did you get involved with someone like that?"

She frowned, feeling defensive, not sure if the anger in his voice was aimed at Dean or at her.

He stepped around the trunk she used as a coffee table. "You always hear that women in abusive relationships have low self-esteem or have been abused at home, so, they're looking for someone to fill that gap. But you're not like that. You and your family are close. You have friends at church. Why did you go out with him?"

"You sound like it's my fault."

"No, I'm not saying that."

"Aren't you?" Emotion rocketed through her. She couldn't keep the hard edge out of her own words. "The reasons you just lined up are all the woman's fault."

"I was just repeating what others have said."

"And these are all experts, right?" Did he think the abuse was her fault? She stood and walked past him. "You're judging me. Blaming what Dean did on me."

He frowned. "No. I didn't mean…"

"What did you mean?"

"I meant that…"

"Well?" The word snapped, challenged.

He studied her. "You know, I'm not sure."

"Dean always made me feel that whatever went wrong was my fault. That's what abusive men do. That's what you're doing."

His whole body stiffened. "What?" The word came sharp and startled.

"I think that was clear."

"Yeah, it was, and it was a low blow."

She stared. He stared back. Emotions tugged each way. She needed to get hold of them. He wasn't Dean. She knew that. But she wanted to make things clear. She wasn't taking blame for another man's abusive behavior.

"All right, that was as low as yours—blaming me for something that's not my fault."

"I did not mean to do that. I'm angry at Dean and at what happened when you dated him. And confused." He paused. "What I said a few moments ago is all I know. I can't grasp why or how you—or any woman—would become involved with an abusive man or stay with him."

Sharee walked back to the couch and sat down. She couldn't blame him for that. She hadn't understood it herself. She'd become entwined—walked into the spider's web—before she knew where she was. Lynn had joked about her being desperate, and maybe she had been.

"Can we talk about this?" His question interrupted her thoughts.

She'd told him no before because she didn't want to talk about it, didn't want to go through it again, but he should know. He deserved to know. He had asked her to marry him and that meant sharing herself at a deep level. Could she extract the emotions and memories she'd hidden?

Hidden? Something sharp jolted her upright. Hadn't she given this to the Lord and forgiven Dean? Why the sudden resistance?

"Sharee?"

She nodded, and he lowered himself beside her.

"Give me a minute."

His hand covered hers. "As many as you need." His voice had changed, softened.

The words and the tone sliced through her fear, her anger. What was she afraid of? John wasn't Dean. How many times did she need to tell herself that? The difference between the two men rivaled the Grand Canyon in size.

She inhaled and slipped her fingers through his. "Okay."

"Take another breath."

She slid him a smile. "I can tell you about me. Not everyone is the same, but there are similarities. First, I didn't know the warning signs. I believed what he said, what he presented. He acted protective and attentive." She stopped and gave him a meaningful look.

"You're saying I'm like him?" His voice grated in a way that told her he didn't like the comparison.

"No, I'm not saying that. Dean's attention and protection had a whole different meaning than yours does. And I've seen you angry." She smiled. "More than once."

"I'm working on that."

"But you've never threatened me. Well," she smiled again, "there was that caveman thing the other day."

"Sharee."

"But you're not manipulative. In fact, you're just right out there about what you want from me. You are strong with it, but I'm not afraid you'll hit me. You're tender, too."

"Okay, but—"

"That attentive, protective treatment that Dean presented looked a lot like love—like the real thing—especially when he did it for months. I didn't know the other signs and had no way to judge whether it was real or not." She stopped and stared across the room.

His thumb rubbed across her hand. "What other signs?"

"Wanting a quick commitment. And even that felt good—after…rejection by others. But then he began to try to keep me away from my friends. We always did things together, just the two of us. Something always came up when we made plans that included others. Even my family. And, of course, he was jealous. He began checking up on me—where I'd been, whom I talked to. I caught him checking my phone once, and although I had this red flag waving in front of me, I still didn't get it."

"You think there was a reason you didn't see it? You said you didn't know the signs, but wasn't God speaking to you?"

"Oh, he was speaking—through my parents, through Marci, through his Spirit. I just wasn't listening." She gave a half-smile. The heat ran up to her face. "I wanted someone. I was tired of being alone, and I'd dated so many 'nice Christian boys' who only wanted one thing."

"So, you've dated a lot of sleazebags? Why didn't I know this?"

She scowled at him. "I gave up dating. I told God if he had anyone for me, he'd have to drop that man right in front of me and have him carrying a sign showing God's approval."

"I was right in front of you, anyway." John squeezed her hand. "Go on."

"Today, girls—or women—can feel like outcasts if they don't buy into the sexual culture. If they do, they often become just a commodity, something to be used. I had friends in high school, and later in college, who hooked up with guys one day only to be ignored the next day during classes. The guy got what he wanted, but she didn't. She wanted a relationship."

"There are women out there who only want a casual hookup, too."

"You're right. It's sad. There's more to life than just hopping from bed to bed."

His thumb caressed again. "I know."

"One of few."

"I think there's more than a few. It's hard, though. Hard when some women offer themselves so freely these days, not realizing that what they have is…"

Sharee cocked her head. "Is what?"

"Valuable, something to be prized. Not to get rid of, but to bestow in love."

She stared but didn't say anything. *Wow, Lord.* Her throat tightened, and she swallowed hard. *How did you bless me with someone like this?*

"And I'm not saying that men have an excuse for their actions. I'm just saying…it's hard. And that lifestyle is everywhere, on every TV program, the movies, most of the music." A trace of a smile. "Sorry. Go on."

"Okay, but I understand what you're saying. Well, Dean acted different from others, like he cared, and didn't push for sex—not right away. Later, things changed. The verbal abuse started—everything being my fault. And he would have these sudden mood swings. The eggshells people talk about? I was skating on them."

His brow creased. "You didn't see that as a problem?"

"You get so far in that you can't see it. And then he hit me."

John's eyes darkened. "Sharee—"

"It's okay, John. You know—"

"It's not okay."

"No, I didn't mean that, but you know how God will use everything for good? Not that he causes everything. God doesn't tempt people to do evil. God didn't tempt or direct Dean to hit me. But what He did do was use it as a wake-up call. I realized I had to get away, to break it off. Then. Not later."

John stood once more and paced. Sharee gave him time, directing her concentration to what was happening inside her. *Lord, you're helping me again, aren't you? When Dean showed up at the hospital and then today, it threw me. It can't be like that forever. Thank you for giving me the courage to talk to John.*

John came back to the sofa, took her hand again. "I'm sorry you had to go through that. I'm sorry that men—especially Christian men—have mistreated you."

"Thank you."

He kissed her gently then looked down at his hands. "I wish I could get hold of a few of them."

"John."

One side of his mouth lifted. "Tell me why women stay with men like that. Why they go back to them."

"I don't know for sure, but for some, it's easier than being alone.

You have someone. Or he supports you and your children. Without him, you would be on the streets. A lot of the women need help these days—a place to stay, transportation, an education, child care, food. When they don't have that, a man—even an abusive man—looks good."

"It's beginning to sound like your homeless ministry."

"Well, the abusive man or husband often does keep them from becoming homeless. That's not a small thing, especially if they have children. And some women are kept by fear—fear of what he might do, especially if they try to leave. Women are beaten, hospitalized, even killed when they try to escape."

John's gaze went past her. A minute later, his expression changed, and his eyes focused on her again. "I know this is hard for you. Thank you for sharing."

Sharee studied her hands, noting how his fingers, larger and darker than her own, surrounded hers. "No, thank you for being who you are, for not being a jerk."

He chuckled and kissed the top of her head. Sharee felt a lump in her throat. What was the problem? She wasn't going to cry here, but before she could control them, tears pooled and spilled. She tried to catch hold of the emotions, tried to make sense of them.

"Hey." He brushed the tears from her face. "It's okay. Everything's okay now."

She pulled his head down to hers, wanting to forget everything that had happened. John's arm slid down her back, tugging her close, meeting her kiss. A fire ignited deep inside her, the flame igniting dry timber.

Lord...

John pulled away. "Sharee..."

She drew him back. His arms tightened around her, and he groaned as he met her kiss again. Its intensity warmed and scared her.

Lord, I love him so much. I want him, and I have no control here. Please help me.

As she moved within his embrace, pain, like a bolt of lightning, shot up her back. She cried out.

His head jerked away. "What is it?"

"My back." Her breath caught as the pain sharpened. She laid her head back against the sofa, her breathing ragged. The swirling emotions, the flames that had started, died. A moment later, she started to laugh then gasped as pain shot through her again.

She giggled at his confused expression. "I think I just received an answer to prayer, but it's not at all what I expected."

Chapter 10

The next morning, as she pulled on her jeans, she stopped and drew a breath against the pain. Instead of leaning over to get her t-shirt, she bent her knees and lowered herself the few inches needed to lift it from the lower drawer of the dresser. She let out a long sigh, slipped it over her head, and looked in the mirror.

You asked for help, girl. She shook her head and sent a look upward.

Her eyes came back to the mirror, and she ran her fingers through her hair. No combing this mess. She took a pick from the dresser and picked at her mass of curls. Wild, John had said. He liked wild? She shook her head. Well, today he'd have what he liked.

As she finished her makeup, Sharee pondered the different ways that prayers are answered. She'd been saved from her own desires by a return of pain. And this morning, as if in reminder, the pain hung close to each move.

Tentative knocking came from the apartment door. She walked to the door and glanced through the peephole. Ryann Byrd grinned at her. She smiled and opened the door. Ryann, Abbey Somers, and Matthew Thornton entered.

"We've brought food!" Ryann's grin stretched wide.

Sharee hugged her. No denying this teenager had been a favorite in the Bible study she'd taught two years ago. A bond had formed then that warmed her heart today. Abbey, her Goth look done to perfection, scooted past them.

"It's good to see you three. Since Ryann started college, I don't see much of any of you."

"That's what I told her," Matthew said.

Sharee allowed the high school senior to slip past. His size and ruggedness gave him a much older look. He, like Abbey, had not reached the hugging stage yet.

"Lots of studying." Ryann's grimace followed a toss of her long hair. She handed Sharee a large bag. "We made the food ourselves. Didn't we, Abbey?"

Abbey nodded and moved with quick grace into the living area, glancing around. Her all black outfit contrasted with the other girl's multi-colored layered tops. She slipped over to the large TV and grinned. "Hey, pretty good. When did you get this?"

"Christmas. Mom and Dad. Nice to have parents, huh?"

"Yeah, sometimes." Matthew handed Sharee a second bag. He brushed curly blonde hair from his eyes and headed for the sofa.

Ryann met his quick gaze before turning to Sharee. "Ms. J, how are you? We've heard a lot of stuff on the grapevine lately."

Sharee headed to the kitchen table with the bags. "You did, did you?" She lifted Tupperware dishes and other cookware from the bags. "Wow, you guys, thanks a lot. It smells delicious. Are you going to eat with me?"

"Naw," Matthew said. "We made it for you. Try the chocolate chip cookies. I made those."

She looked at each dish, then pulled the foil off a plate of cookies and brought them over. "So, Ryann, what did you hear?" She passed the cookies around.

Abbey bit one, took her phone from a small purse and began to text, but she glanced at Sharee. "We heard someone's trying to kill you." Her thumbs stopped. No one spoke, but three pairs of eyes focused on her.

Sharee straightened in her chair and glanced from one to the other of them. No one seemed surprised but her.

"Well, the church gossip line's working well, isn't it? Where did you hear that?"

They all looked away and then at each other.

"Oh, just around." Matt pulled at his t-shirt, still not meeting her eyes.

Sharee assessed the situation, wondering how much she should say. "Well... you must have heard that a car almost ran me down, and I was in the hospital a few days. It happened again after church last Sunday evening." She hesitated. *All right. Lord, I am not going to lie to these kids, but you will have to take over and make good use of whatever I say.*

"Someone did run me off the road."

"But why?" Ryann asked.

"I haven't any idea."

"I heard Mr. Jergenson talking with Pastor Alan today." An embarrassed pause followed. "They were outside the fellowship hall, and I was inside, getting some of this stuff ready. They were talking about that guy named Dean. The one you dated." Her eyes were a little wide.

Sharee compressed her lips. *I am going to trounce them both. And they say women gossip.* She picked up the plate of cookies and passed them around again. "Well, do you remember when I talked that Wednesday night to the youth group? About a year ago? I talked about abusive relationships." She glanced at their faces. "I'm not sure who all was there. Anyway, I have to admit that a lot I talked about came from my relationship with Dean."

"I told you." Ryann looked around at the others. "Mr. Jergenson said Dean came here yesterday, and you had to call the police."

Do these men ever think to see if anyone is around when they are talking?

"Well, Dean did come here yesterday. He even came to the hospital to see me when I was there. But when he showed up yesterday, he sounded angry. He scared me. I called John, and John called the police."

"Did he and Mr. Jergenson get into a fight?"

"No, they didn't get into a fight. Dean was gone before he got here."

"You don't have to worry with Mr. Jergenson around. He'll protect you." Matthew's voice had deepened.

Sharee stared at him. Realization hit her. As much as she fought against John's protectiveness, it was for that exact reason that she'd called him. *Lord, help me to appreciate what you've given John even as I want him to appreciate the gifts You've given me.*

"Okay, guys, let's talk about something else. How are things at school?"

She listened to an abbreviated summary of tests and homework and tough teachers. In a few minutes, they turned the subject to the new things planned for the youth group.

Ryann rose when they finished. "We gotta get back. College has a lot of homework." Her eyes went to Matthew. "Much more homework than high school."

"Yeah, yeah." His tone indicated they'd discussed this before. "She thinks she's hot now, going to college." He brushed against her with his leg.

Abbey pulled the band from her long hair before running her fingers through it but didn't rise.

"Come on, Ab, we've got to go."

The teen pocketed her phone and stood. "Well, Ms. J, I'm glad you're okay. You and Mr. J set a date yet?"

Startled remembrance went through her. What was wrong with

them? They hadn't. "You know what, we haven't. But it's going to be soon, I think."

"How soon?"

"In about three months."

The three of them looked at each other, and she saw slow smiles pull each face.

Abbey grabbed Ryann. "Well, okay, let's go. Will that car of yours get us home?"

"Hey," Ryann pulled the keys from her jeans. "It got you here, didn't it?" They went out the door elbowing each other, laughing.

"Matthew," Sharee called after them. He came back as the others went to the car.

"Yeah?"

"You and Ryann going out?"

He crossed his arms across his chest. "Yeah."

Sharee nodded. "Okay. I just wondered." Let it go, she told herself.

"Yeah, I know. Everybody's against it. Mom and Dad have been all over me."

"Matt, it's not that everybody is against it...it's just..."

"Yeah, she's older and she has a rep. I know all that." His voice was a mixture of anger and resignation.

"The only rep she has with me is a good one. She's always trying to help people. Just like bringing the food over for me. Just treat her with the respect that she deserves."

"I do. Other people don't."

"I'm sorry to hear that. I care for you both."

Something moved across his face. The line of his mouth tightened. "Everybody is so interested in us. But what about my mom? What about that guy that keeps calling her?"

"Huh?"

"She thinks we don't know because we're kids. But we're not blind. We hear things. We see things. My dad's the one that's blind. I ought to wake him up."

"Ted is calling your mom?"

"Yeah, and I heard that Pastor Alan asked him to leave the church."

Lord, how do they know everything?

"And yet," Matthew continued, "he called my mom again. I heard her talking to him." Raw pain filled his voice.

Sharee shoved a curl from her face. Why is it adults think their children are deaf and blind? "Matthew, I don't know what to say."

He spun away from her. "Well, why don't you say something to my mom?" He turned at the door. "And you know what? Ryann and I both believe what Mr. Jergenson said. Despite what happened before. So you can tell everybody that they ain't got nothing to worry about!"

The door didn't slam after him, but she felt sure that's what he wanted. One thought after another flooded her mind. A minute later, she walked to the door and slid the locks, set the bolts. She went back to the couch and curled up.

A lot had happened last year, everything seeming to lead up to the Christmas program. What was Matthew trying to get across to her? That he and Ryann would be okay, but he wasn't sure about his mother—or in the long run then about his whole family. Sharee bowed her head and prayed.

A few minutes later, she tugged a blank sheet of paper from her printer and began to review the times and dates of the accidents, including Dean's appearance at the hospital and then again at her apartment. She jotted down the times and then wrote a list of suspects—Dean, Ted, George's friends, and a question mark for any persons unknown.

Another list included motives. Greed, passion, self-preservation… No one could think they had any money, could they? Nothing worth killing for, anyway. Could they, in any way, be stopping someone else from obtaining money? No inheritance. Both their parents were alive. What about passion? That would include jealousy, revenge, hate, and other things. Her mind shifted to Ted. She had pointed out that his relationship with Marci was wrong, and he resented that. He had threatened Pastor Alan and the church. She had to consider him a serious threat. And what about Dean? She knew his anger and his jealousy from the past. A definite threat. And George's friends? She couldn't dismiss them.

Her head ached. She rubbed her forehead with both hands. Self-preservation? Were she and John a threat to anyone? How could they be? Something they didn't know? After a few minutes, she jotted down another question mark for unknown motives.

She threw the pen down, went to get an ice pack, and lay down on the couch. She let out a long breath and closed her eyes. The phone rang.

Groaning, she reached for her cell, glanced at the screen. The Sheriff's Department? "Hello?"

"Ms. Jones?"

"Yes."

"This is Detective Shepherd. How are you doing today?"

"Good today."

"I'm glad to hear that. I talked to the deputy who was there yesterday. I thought it might be a good idea for us to meet—for coffee or something—so I could hear your story first-hand."

"If you've read the other report, perhaps you know I was in the hospital for a few days?"

"Yes."

"I'm supposed to be resting and icing my back, and I've been up a lot today already. I know that sounds like an invalid, but could we do this by phone?"

"I like doing a face-to-face, but if you want, I'll get a few things down today. Can I give you a call tomorrow and see how you're feeling?"

"Yes."

"Okay. When Strasburg came to the hospital, was that the first time you'd seen or heard from him since the restraining order?"

"Yes."

"How long ago was that?"

"Almost two years. A little over a year since it was in effect. I don't see why after all this time…" She let it trail off.

"How long have you and John Jergenson been engaged?"

"A week."

"Was there an announcement in the paper?"

"No."

"Who knew about the engagement?

"No one that I know of. I mean, John told my parents at the hospital, but no one else knew until we told my friend Lynn. Dean came to the hospital before that."

"Strasburg came to the hospital before anyone knew about your engagement?"

"Yes, well…John sent the engagement ring from Indonesia to a friend."

"The friend's name?"

"Bruce Tomlin. But he's in a wheelchair, and I'm sure it has nothing to do with him."

"I'll check with him. He might have mentioned it to someone else."

"You think Dean heard about it and attacked John?"

"Let's just say we need to check all possibilities. Then I might have a talk with Mr. Strasburg. What about your work?"

"My work?"

"Yes. Is there anyone at your work who might have something

against you? Is there anyone…that you have been involved with or anyone who might think there is some kind of relationship between you and him? I am talking about other employees or clients."

"Employees?"

"Or clients. Is there anyone or anything you can think of? Take your time."

"I've worked there for eight years." Sharee threw her mind back and brought it forward. "No relationship stuff. There's always someone along the way who doesn't think we do enough for them. Right now, though, I only remember one over-the-top person. He had definite expectations that we could not meet."

"Who was this?"

"A family came in—man, wife, two kids. He became upset because…well, because he wanted more than we could give him. They were living in their car at the time. I was a first contact, and he was upset that I couldn't find a place for them right away, a place for free, until he could get a job. A very loud, angry person."

"Did he threaten you?"

"Not that I remember. We keep files at Downtown Ministries. That would be in it if he did."

"When was this?"

About two months ago."

"Do you remember the name?"

"Paul…Paul Jenkins." Her work? Why hadn't she thought of that? She stood up, went to the kitchen table, and pulled over her list of suspects.

"Okay."

"Detective?"

"Yes. I've been getting anonymous phone calls for about a month or longer."

The tone of the questions changed as he took in this new information. It was almost twenty minutes later when she hung up.

She made a few notes before resting on the sofa again. If Dean knew about the engagement before she did, or if Paul Jenkins had decided to get even with her for some imagined offense then either could have attacked John. She bit her lip. If that was the case, she had increased the danger to him by accepting his proposal, not the other way around as he thought.

No wonder John had thought about breaking their engagement after talking with his neighbor George. She felt the same way now.

And what about George's friends? Or Ted? Perhaps whoever attacked John was different from the person who attacked her.

And what about Ted? Shepherd said they still had not found him. But Ted had nothing to do with John. Did he? She huffed. None of this made sense.

Her body ached, and she closed her eyes. Sleep had come off and on last night. If she could rest now then maybe…

The phone's ringtone woke her. She reached over the couch to the end table and fumbled for her phone. "Hello?"

"Sharee, you called the police." Dean's voice filled the line. "Do you know the trouble you've caused? Again? Having the police come to my business?"

Her hand shook as she held the phone. "Be strong and very courageous," the words came back. She took a deep breath and cut across his cursing.

"You came to my place. You waited all night. That's not normal." Why was she talking to him?

"So now I'm not normal?" The words whispered over the line. "You self-righteous little…"

"Dean!" How could she have been so stupid? "Don't call me again. Do you hear? Don't call again." Her fingers moved to disconnect him, and she heard him laugh.

"Oh, I won't call, sweetheart. I won't call."

She shut the phone off and fought the unease those last words had initiated. She took a long breath and blew it out. Dean would not cause her to feel like a rabbit that needed a hole to hide in. He was a bully that was all.

Running her fingers through her hair, she stood and started for the kitchen.

Knock! Knock!

Her head jerked toward the sound, and her stomach tightened. She grabbed her phone again. She'd call 911 first this time.

"Hey, Sharee, you there?" Bruce's voice came through the door. He knocked again.

Thank you, Lord! She ran to the door, stopped, stared through the peephole, then unlocked and unbolted the door.

"Hey. John told me about the other night, so I thought I'd come…" his voice trailed off. "What's wrong?"

Her eyes ran over the parking lot. "Quick. Come inside."

He rolled his wheelchair forward. She closed and locked the door. "What is it?"

"It's Dean. He called again. Do you know about yesterday?" She backed up and sat down on the sofa. "I thought it was Dean when you knocked."

"Why would you think that?" When she didn't answer, he rolled his wheelchair next to her. "John and I talked this morning. He told me about Dean, and about your car being shoved off the road, and someone chasing you. But that's all I know."

"Dean just called again. He threatened me."

Bruce's face hardened. "Don't talk to him. Don't listen. Just hang-up."

"I know. I don't know why I did…I…just did."

"Well, stop it." The roughness of his voice surprised her. "The man is dangerous."

"I know."

"It seems to me that since God has put his finger on you and John to do ministry together, you've come under attack. So pray and ask God for that discernment and then stand against the enemy. Identify the areas where he is attacking and begin to pray for help and power there."

"You're right. I don't pray as much since John came home."

"Well, it's good he's here, but prayer is your weapon against the enemy. You need to pray in advance. Think about what it will be like in Indonesia."

"You're right. I've never had to face physical threats before, and it's scared me." She walked over to the table and picked up the papers laying there. "Here's my list of suspects. Tell me what you think."

He took his time, going over the different lists, and moving back and forth between them. "Not bad. What is this note you made that says 'work' with a question mark?"

She told him about Detective Shepherd's call. "I felt like such a fool after he called. He knows what he's doing."

"Let's hope so. What are the E's by each person's name and then the A's? What do you mean by that?"

"Well, at first, I eliminated them all—one by one—for different reasons, but after thinking about it again, I added them all back on."

He laughed but sobered a minute later. "You should tell the police about Dean's phone call. And when John gets here, make sure you tell him, too."

"He'll be upset."

"Yeah, well, he's protective of you and wants to keep you safe. It's driving him crazy that he can't quite do it himself." The amusement showed. "He and God are still working through a few things there. At some point, he'll have to hand you over to God."

Sharee smiled. "You think that's a problem?"

"A major issue, I would say." He studied her. "That

protectiveness and "get things done" attitude is like your dad, I bet."

"You know, that's something I've never thought about. He is like my father that way."

"Probably what attracted you to Dean, too. In that case, however, he kept a lot of things from you. Don't blame yourself. We all thought he was Mr. Nice Guy." He moved his hands to the wheels of his chair. "I'll be going. Just wanted to stop by and see how things were."

"Thank you for coming by and for being concerned."

He nodded. "We'll work on that list of yours another time. Keep the doors locked. Don't talk to strangers. All that stuff."

She grinned. "You and John."

"And your father and the police. Wisdom, as they say."

"I'm listening."

"Good." He rolled to the door.

The white sands glistened in the late afternoon sun, and the waves reflected liquid gold with an intensity that proved impossible to watch. Sharee shielded her eyes and looked away from the brightness. John's arm circled her waist.

"You should have hung up." The mixture of roughness and concern in his voice made her smile.

"I know."

"I'm glad Bruce stopped by. It's possible Dean was watching you."

Sharee shuttered. "I don't want to think about that."

"Me, either, but we have to. Sharee—"

"I'll keep the doors locked. I'll be careful. Don't worry." She touched his hand as he let out an impatient breath. "You've done everything possible. Now, we have to trust God."

They walked in silence. She could almost feel his struggle. Let go and let God. How many times had she heard that? Acting on that was proving hard for them both.

The salt smell and the woosh-woosh of the Gulf waves surrounded them. The last time they'd been here, confusion had ruled her thoughts. She lifted her head. His gaze met hers.

"John, I'm sorry I hurt you."

His chin roughened her hair. "It's okay. That's why we came. I wanted to cancel out the negative. Maybe I was too sure of myself that day."

She pulled her head back to see him better, feeling the pain he'd gone through.

One side of his mouth hitched upward. "Can't have our favorite jogging spot filled with bad memories."

They watched three pelicans glide past just over the water. Small sea birds ran back and forth following the waves that licked up the shoreline.

"Are you up to this meeting?"

"With Janice's parents?"

He nodded.

She didn't reply for a minute. "I still don't understand why they want to meet me."

He took a deep breath. "Maybe it will bring a type of closure for them—to Janice's death. I know when she died that they couldn't let go, and you know I'm still in communication with them. I've tried to break that tie since I came back from Indonesia, in the midst of everything else. I think I'm beginning to understand that as long as I've stayed around, they haven't had to deal fully with Janice's death. Our marriage will make a huge difference in their lives."

"They will hate me."

"I don't think so, Sharee. I think it will be a step toward acceptance. But you don't have to do this."

"I'll do it if you think it will help."

"We'll keep it short."

"When did you first tell them?"

"About us? At Christmas. When I went to meet your parents. Afterward, I went home, but usually, I go see them first. Spend Christmas Eve with them, then drive home. My parents understood. But this time, I went to your home, so I didn't see them until a few days after Christmas."

"And you told them you were going to ask me to marry you? You knew then?"

His eyes lit. "Yes, I knew, but it wasn't until the day before I left for Indonesia that I told them. I thought it would give them time to deal with it while I was gone."

Wisps of hair blew across her eyes. She shoved them aside. "This will be hard for you?" How much had he loved this woman to keep in touch with her parents? What if she didn't measure up? What if, after they were married, he regretted it? Her insides iced.

"Hard? In a way." He broke into her thoughts. "Closure—for all of us."

He still needs closure? *Show me what to do here, Lord. I'm feeling threatened—by his love for this woman who passed away.*

Don't let me get lost in my own insecurities.

They turned, walking back the way they had come, across the causeway to the other side of the park. The sun warmed their backs, and their shadows stretched long and distorted in front of them. The Gulf waters rippled and winked. People sunned themselves on towels on the asphalt or on the backs of cars. Fishermen were thigh-deep in the water, casting into the fading sky.

Laughter and music and snatches of conversation floated on the air. Sharee inhaled the smell of grilling food. When they slipped onto the tree-covered path on the other side, palm trees and twisted oaks closed in around them.

"I'll be starving before we leave this place," John said.

"Uh huh. And you'll probably grab the first rolls they set in front of us at the deli." Sharee glanced down. "You're limping."

"Longer walk than I remembered. I'll rest when I get home."

Fading sunlight threw shadows across the path. "Ryann, Matthew, and Abbey came over today. They brought some food they had cooked themselves. We talked for a while. Matthew told me Marci is still getting calls from Ted."

John's eyebrows lifted. "Is she? You mean she's accepting them?"

"That's what it sounded like. I wonder if she realizes what's happening—what could happen. Breaking up her family? The pain to the kids, Stephen, herself?"

"People have an idea it won't happen to them. Perhaps she thinks she can have her marriage and Ted, too." He shook his head. "It won't work that way. The devil won't let it."

They were quiet for a while. "It's sad and frustrating. I wish I could open that head of hers and pour some sense into her."

"We tried. That's all we can do. And pray."

"I know." She waited a beat before changing the subject. "Did you know that Ryann overheard your conversation with Pastor Alan this morning?"

He said nothing right away, but before long, his eyes widened. "What did she hear?"

"She and Abbey and Matthew asked me about Dean, and they asked if someone was trying to kill me."

"I had no idea anyone was around. Not that early. It was about 8:30. What teenagers are up at that time?"

"They were. Using the kitchen, I think, to make the food for me."

"We were working outside the fellowship hall. I don't remember everything we talked about, but... Neither of us would have brought that subject up if we'd known anyone was around."

"Yeah, well. Be careful next time." More bothered her than that. "There's something else we need to talk about."

"What?"

She cocked her head. "Perhaps you'd better tell me what you said to the youth the night you spoke to them. I keep getting these funny looks."

"You do?"

"Uh huh."

"All right. It concerns you, anyway."

"I thought so."

He took her hand and led her through the pines and dappled shade to the water. They stopped at the last group of trees at a small, isolated portion of the beach. The setting sun had just touched the water. Wisps of clouds burned shades of pink, peach, and apricot across the turquoise sky.

He squeezed her hand. "It's beautiful here."

"Yes, it is." The wind tugged at her hair. "But I'm more concerned about what you said."

He stepped between her and the sun, shading her eyes. "I guess I'll confess. Don called at the hospital. Do you remember? He'd just heard about your accident and about our engagement." He gave her a wicked grin. "You did tell Lynn, after all. His call couldn't have been more than two hours later. Anyway, after asking about you, he asked me to speak to the youth on purity and abstinence."

"Really? Was that out of the blue?"

"It was. But it sounded like God's timing to me." He ran a finger down her cheek. "Just when I was struggling with...those same things. Don needed a fill-in. His speaker couldn't make it, so I was the substitute."

"But..."

"I talked that night about how things are today—how things are portrayed on TV, in the movies, all that I said to you the other day. Then I explained how God has given us the best way, which is to wait to have sexual relations until marriage. I used scripture and statistics about marriage and divorce, and how today's culture of couples living together has a higher divorce rate than those that don't.

"It's amazing how little they know. They think that what they've learned from TV and the movies is how it is. When I pointed out that TV shows and movies show no consequences with recreational sex, they understood that. On TV, you just rebound from anything by finding another partner and go on. But that's not real life. Real life hurts, and there are things like pregnancy, abortion, STD's, broken families, and even the poverty single mom's live with when the dads leave."

"You went into all that?"

"Uh huh. I told them about how many girls—and boys, too— come out of a relationship with broken hearts and feelings of worthlessness."

"But..."

He caught her wrists. "Wait. I haven't told you everything. They asked about us. Don knew he was putting me on the spot. He knew it would make things real to them if he could get someone to talk about purity, about abstinence, that was actually living it.

"He questioned me about that before he asked me to share. And it was the first question the teens asked when I finished. Were you and I planning to wait until we married? I told them, yes, we were. You should have seen them trying to get their heads around that. We're old, you see, in their eyes. And I've been married before. Why should we wait? I had to explain our commitment to God, our belief that what he tells us is right and for our good—and the rules don't change with age or circumstances."

Sharee tried to hide her smile. "I didn't think you were always so determined about it."

"Well, let's put it this way. I know what's right, and it certainly helps when you have a partner who feels the same way. Makes my 'want to' into a 'surety.'"

"So that's why I got those looks afterward."

He dropped her wrists to circle her with his arms. "I hadn't expected you to be at church that night, so when you asked to be there—well, I knew I should have talked to you beforehand, but it was too late. And I didn't want to embarrass you in front of the group. Anyway, I have many excuses, but I did ask them not to talk to you that evening. I wanted time to tell you myself."

"Which you didn't."

"Guilty conscience." His voice held an apology. "And as much as I thought I knew them, I hadn't expected the way the questions and comments would go afterward."

She huffed. "I don't know whether to be angry or not. I'm glad you did it—because young people today need to hear that—but you talked about personal things without asking me." She squirmed to get free of his hold, and his arms tightened.

"You're right. I should have consulted you."

"You'd better remember that next time."

"Yes, ma'am." He grinned but chuckled a moment later. "What?"

"They did ask if it was difficult."

"Difficult?"

"Yes, abstinence. I told them I do a lot of jogging."

She laughed. "I bet your foot limits that these days."

"You think it's funny?" He growled into her hair. "Just watch yourself."

"You jog. I do a lot of praying."

"Do you?" His fingers moved with butterfly touches over her cheek and neck, and then he leaned down and kissed her. She let her body melt into his. His kiss changed, the gentleness deepening until the fire started inside again.

She pushed away, breathing deeply. "Don't start something you can't finish, Mr. Abstinence."

"You make it hard."

"Me? You're the one with the electric kisses."

"Electric?" The grin returned but he sobered a moment later. "Talking about purity and walking it out are two different things."

"Yes, they are."

Chapter 11

As they walked into the Lucky Dill, past the display of desserts, a rumble of voices and laughter met them. The smell of fresh-baked bread, of garlic, and warm soup filled the air. Sharee glanced around the large room, eyeing the bar, the large seating areas, and especially area by the windows. Outside, patrons filled the tables. People talked and laughed and ate. To the right another room with an array of bakery items enticed. A waitress hustled past them, then another. She moved aside to give room for the large tray one woman carried. The plates on it were piled high with sandwiches, salads, and bread.

Sharee glanced at John and followed his gaze to the back left corner. An older man stood and gave a low wave. Sharee's stomach contracted as the man's eyes rested on her. She saw something cross his face, and he bent down to the woman next to him. The woman looked up, and their eyes met. The woman's face stilled. Sharee bit her lip, and her hand went to John's arm.

He folded her hand in his and led the way through the tables. "You had no trouble finding it?" John asked the older man.

"No. We came straight here."

John nodded and glanced at Sharee. "Well, this is Sharee. Sharee, this is Tom and Lorraine Wicker."

"It's nice to meet you." Sharee swallowed and tightened her fingers on John's.

Lorraine Wicker stood, too. Sharee felt dwarfed when she did. Tom Wicker's height came with a solidness that outweighed John's, but Lorraine's tallness was accentuated by her thinness. Realization hit her. Janice must have been tall, too. No wonder John had teased her about her height when they first dated.

The man indicated the chairs across from them. He smiled at Sharee. "John has told us a lot about you. Have a seat. We're glad you came."

John pulled out a chair for her. She lowered herself into it, glancing across at Lorraine once more. What could she say to these people?

Lorraine, her caramel-colored eyes smiling now, leaned over as John sat down. She reached out and touched his hand. "It's so good to see you. It's been too long." Her eyes shifted to Sharee. "You've kept him busy."

"I…We've had a lot going on since he came back."

"I hope you don't feel too awkward." Lorraine's focus shifted from her to John again. "John has been a part of our family for so long that we felt we had to meet you."

"Thank you."

John's hand gave hers a reassuring squeeze. "Was it a long drive from Orlando?"

"Well, you know how I-4 is," Lorraine said. "Always harrowing. Whether afternoon, evening, or night, I still think it's a nightmare. Of course, Thomas drove today. He's much more patient than I am."

"We didn't mind the drive." Tom Wicker leaned forward. "We're just glad to see you. And to meet Sharee. You told us about the accident—someone trying to run you down. That seems incredible. You've recovered from that? And Sharee from hers?"

"We're both doing better," John said. "Sharee's back has improved. I still have an air cast and the crutches, although I don't use them as I should. I do some walking, but I'll be glad to start jogging again. Cooper misses the jogging."

"You still have that dog?" Lorraine smiled. "I remember when you and Janice got him from the SPCA. He was so cute and wiggly. So little at the time." She stopped, blinked, and glanced at Sharee.

Sharee bit her lip and fought to keep her face expressionless. She'd never thought about when or where John had acquired Cooper. So many things she didn't know about him. His former in-laws knew him better than she did. These three had shared life and death together. What was she was doing here? Did she belong at all?

"Yes, Cooper is doing well. He's big these days. Not that squirming puppy you remember."

The waitress stepped forward, setting menus down in front of them, along with an assortment of soft rolls in a basket.

"What would you like to drink?" The waitress asked. After they gave their drink orders, quiet settled over the table.

"What do you recommend?" Tom asked.

"I've always liked their sandwiches, and the Greek salad is a favorite." John focused on Lorraine. "You like pastrami on rye. It's very good here." He took a roll from the basket, tore it in half, and handed half to Sharee.

She nibbled on it but couldn't quite get it down. Glancing up, she caught Lorraine watching her and managed a smile. Sharee lifted the basket of bread and offered it to her.

"Did you look at their desserts as you came in? They're so delicious, but there's never enough room for them after you eat."

The woman shook her head but didn't answer. Great, Sharee. Can't you think of anything better to say?

She heard John question Tom about his work. Quiet stretched between the two women.

Sharee couldn't get past the thing that was on her mind. "This must be really hard for you. I'm so sorry about...your daughter."

Lorraine had been looking down at the table. She didn't move.

Lord, please help. Now I've really upset her.

After a minute, the older woman raised her head. Her expression was blank, her eyes darker than before. "It is hard," she said. "Thomas felt this was something we had to do."

Sharee reminded herself of what John said about closure. Lorraine stared past her then turned to John.

"Are you going to continue working at the church or are you planning on something else?"

John paused a moment before he said, "I've thought about going for more schooling."

"Have you? To USF?"

"No, I've got my BA, and what I need is not at the university."

"Such as?"

"I'm thinking of a private technical school."

"A technical school?" Lorraine's brow wrinkled. "Didn't you do that before? Why go four years to college and then to a tech school? What do you want to study?"

"Mechanics."

"Mechanics?" She tilted her head to the side. "Why would you want to take mechanics?"

John hesitated. Sharee turned her head to look at him, questioning. Lorraine shifted in her seat. "You mean aircraft mechanics."

"Yes." His assent dropped into dead air.

Lorraine's eyes went to Sharee. "You want to make sure it doesn't happen again."

"Yes." His voice sounded as forced as Lorraine's, but he went on. "I have to know how to fix the plane in case there are problems overseas."

Sharee sat, not understanding the undertones for a full ten seconds. Then the knowledge of what they were discussing hit her. They were discussing Janice's death.

Tom turned to her, pain evident in his eyes. "So you and John are planning on going overseas after you marry?"

"Yes, we…" She glanced at John. "We both want to do ministry, and this seems to be how God is leading us."

Again, the awkward pause and Sharee remembered John telling her how he and Janice planned to do ministry work together. Heat rose in her face and fanned her body. *Why do I keep saying the wrong things? I've got to have a few minutes, and they need a few minutes— without me.* She pushed back her chair and started to rise. John's hand went to her arm. She hesitated but didn't look at him.

"Sharee?"

His phone rang, startling them all, breaking the tension. John gave a gentle tug on her arm, and Sharee lowered herself back into her chair. He pulled the phone loose from its belt clip.

"Sorry. I forgot to change it to vibrate." He glanced at it and frowned. "I need to take this. Give me just a minute."

"Alan?" he questioned and turned away from the table. "What's up? What? Mark? You're at the church? Where's Alan?" He listened a moment. "And Don's not there either? Okay. Is there a problem? An alligator?"

Sharee leaned forward. John's expression changed to amusement.

"Well, how big is it? That sounds pretty large for that pond. Look, he's not going to bother anyone if you leave him alone. Who else is there? Well, tell everyone to stay away. What? Her new one? Tell her to keep that pup away from the edge of the pond. He'd look like dinner to a gator."

He lowered the phone and glanced from Sharee to Tom and Lorraine. "Mark Thornton with the youth group. They've seen a gator in the pond."

He moved the phone. "What are you all doing there today? Waiting for Bruce? Okay. But where's your brother?" John's smile changed, and he straightened. "Ted's there? Are there any other adults around? Okay, look, I'm on my way. Do me a favor. Get everyone away from the pond. See if the fellowship hall is open. I'll be there ASAP." He powered the phone off and looked at Sharee.

"Matthew is talking to Ted. Don's not there, and Bruce is running late."

"Ted's at the church?"

John's glance jumped from her to Tom and Lorraine. "I'm sorry. I have to get out there." He rose. Sharee picked up her purse and rose, too.

"Where?" Lorraine asked.

"The church. An alligator is one thing; Ted Hogan is another. There might be trouble between him and Matt. I need to go. I'm sorry."

"Go on," Lorraine said. "We have a GPS system. We can find our way to the church later if everything is okay."

"That might work. I'll call you. Sharee?"

"I'm ready."

They slipped out the door and ran to the truck. Sharee strapped herself in as John backed out and sped down the road.

"Why is Ted there?"

"Who knows? Mark said Matthew spotted Ted and went to talk to him. I don't like the sound of that—after the threats Ted made. I wonder why he's there. Usually, no one's there on a Thursday evening. I wonder… Call Alan and Detective Shepherd, will you?"

Sharee dialed Pastor Alan's number. No answer. She left a voice mail. The call to Detective Shepherd had the same response. She left another message.

"Should we call the police for a patrol car to be sent out? Something?"

"I wish I knew. Call Bruce and see what his story is. Mark said he's taking Don's place tonight, but he's running late."

She punched in the number. The voicemail came on. Frustrated, she tried again.

"Yeah?"

"Bruce?"

"Yeah. Is John with you? We've got a couple of problems, and I could use him."

"We're on our way."

"Good." His voice was even. "Ted's here."

"Do we need to call 911?"

He didn't respond.

"Bruce?"

"Wait. I think he's leaving. Okay, yeah, he's leaving. I'm glad I got here when I did. Matthew lit into him about his mom, I think. It looked pretty heated when I drove up. Look, I've got to check on the rest of the kids. Someone said something about a gator."

"Okay. We're coming." She clicked off her phone and glanced at John. "Ted's leaving. Evidently, Matthew had words with him."

John's jaw tightened. "I wonder where he's been hiding. If the police haven't been able to find him…"

When they pulled into the back parking lot, Bruce and the youth were by the pond. They scrambled from the truck and strode down the cement path.

The path ran from the parking lot around the field, past the pond and back. Sharee hadn't liked John's proposal for it back in January, but once it was complete, many in the congregation used it for jogging. Bruce practiced racing his wheelchair on it.

"I'm glad you got here," Bruce said, rolling toward them. "Matthew mentioned a few moments ago that he'd seen Ted in the office and then in the fellowship hall, which is where he was when Matthew confronted him. No one knows why the office was open. Mark called you from there, right?"

John nodded. "Yes. I thought it was Alan at first. So you've talked with Matt?"

"He thinks Ted must have a key to some of the buildings."

"Well, if so, we'll do something about that. We can get the locks changed, but I need to talk to Alan first. Perhaps he left the office open by mistake, and a lot of people have keys to the fellowship hall. They're not always careful about locking up. What else did Matt say?"

Bruce's face lightened. "He told him to stay away from his mom."

"Well, good for him. But Matthew shouldn't have tackled him on that—it could be dangerous. In fact, this whole thing with Ted is volatile."

"I agree."

"Sharee left a message for Detective Shepherd. We'll see what he has to say when he calls. I'll get in touch with Alan and see what he wants to do." They all turned as the voices of the teens climbed louder.

"Gator," Bruce remarked, shaking his head. "Well, let me get back over there before we have one of them wading into the pond trying to wrestle it."

Sharee slipped her hand in John's. They fell behind as Bruce sailed his wheelchair up the path. She gasped as he braked on the edge of the concrete walk right before it dropped into the pond.

John chuckled. "Don't worry. He's got a disc brake that really grabs."

"Disc brake or not, he might be wrestling that gator himself if he flies off the path."

John squeezed her hand. As they neared the group, Sharee could feel their excitement.

"Seen him yet?" John asked. "Mark says he's, at least, eight feet."

Bruce grinned. "If he's five feet, I'll be surprised."

Behind them, they heard a car's engine. Sharee glanced around. A blue Ford Focus pulled into a parking space. Tom and Lorraine Wicker climbed from the car.

"Oh." The one syllable came with surprising emotion. Why had they come? John had said he'd call.

John glanced her way. "Listen, stay with Bruce. I'll talk to them." He made an about-face and limped back to the parking lot.

Sharee bit her lip. His foot must be hurting. Bruce's head turned her way, but he said nothing. Then the teenagers circled them, laughing and pointing and talking over each other.

"We were going to feed it Ryann's dog, but she wouldn't let us..."

"You are so full of it, Mark. I can't believe...."

"Hey, Ms. J, you come to see the gator?"

"I don't think it's any eight feet..."

"It isn't! Mark couldn't tell the size of a..."

Bruce held up his hand. "Wait. Wait a minute. Just where is Ryann's dog?"

"Matthew's got it now. He and Mark almost had a fight over it." Laughter from the group.

"Can't you two keep a lid on it for two minutes?" Bruce questioned the brothers in mock severity.

"Do you see it, Ms. J? It's on the other side of the pond, near the trees."

Sharee felt their infectious laughter and smiled. "Yeah, I see it. But its head is pretty small. Sure it's not just three feet?"

"Ah, Ms. J, you gotta be joking." Mark's expression made her laugh. "It's, at least, six feet."

"Well, it certainly ain't no eight, bro." Matthew stepped up. He held Ryann's puppy in his arms.

"Keep a good hold on that mutt," Bruce said. "One gator took a dog off its leash the other day. You hear about that?"

"I did!" Ryann popped her head forward from the back of the group. "I told Matt, too. Ms. J, you going to help Bruce tonight? I think he's going to need it. I've got the dog to watch, and China's not here."

Sharee laughed again. "Well, I hadn't planned on it."

"We have another church's youth group coming in about two hours. They've planned a mini-concert. Don had something hold him up, so he called me." Bruce looked at her. "I could use your help until he gets here. Yours and John's both."

"I can't speak for John, but I'll be glad to help."

"Good, come on then. We'll head to the fellowship hall and order pizza for everyone."

Sharee turned. Lorraine Wicker stood just behind her. "Oh. Hello."

Lorraine smiled. "The men were talking, so I came over to see the alligator."

The students were walking past her. Bruce halted and turned his wheelchair back toward the pond. "Don't worry, Sharee, if you can't do it."

"Oh, no, I..." She hesitated for a minute. "This is Lorraine Wicker, Bruce. Lorraine, this is Bruce Tomlin. He's working with the young people tonight."

A questioning look passed over Bruce's face. He gave a push on the wheels and rolled toward them.

Lorraine stared across the pond. The gator's head and a ridge of tail rose just above the water. "It doesn't look that big. But this pond's not deep either, right?"

"Not right here," Bruce said, "but a few feet out it drops off to about eight feet. And the muck on the bottom is like quicksand. But the gator will find lots to eat. See that black bird on the tree limb? With its wings spread? Well, that's an anhinga, like a cormorant. It dives into the water for fish. There are lots of fish here...little brim. Some people call them sunfish. Lots of turtles, too. That gator will find enough to satisfy him before he moves on."

"Well," Lorraine said, "we've been in Orlando for a while, on the north side, away from Disney. The area has numerous ponds and lakes, but I never learned to swim, so I stay away from them. I can do without gators and snakes."

Bruce grinned. "I can understand that. Well, I can't leave those kids for long." He turned his wheelchair around, waving. "When you can, Sharee..." He almost ran into Tom and John, who were walking their way, engrossed in conversation. He swerved, and with another wave of his hand, went toward the fellowship hall.

John was smiling at something Tom said as he came up to Sharee. He planted a kiss on top of her head. She turned to look up at him, glad to see his smile return. He gave her a brief hug and turned to glance over the pond. "Oh, yeah," he said with his customary amusement, "eight feet long. Not quite. What do you think, Tom, more like five?"

"If that. Well, you know what boys are." His tone was amused, too.

"The kids are a handful, but I appreciate all the energy they have."

"You would be good with kids, John," Tom observed.

"Oh, he's good with them, all right," Sharee said. "Sometimes he forgets he's not one himself."

Tom laughed. "Yes, I could see that. Well, Lorraine, we'd better go."

Sharee turned to find Lorraine studying her.

The older woman dropped her gaze. "Yes, we left the restaurant without eating. Is there somewhere near here where we can eat?"

John focused a look on Sharee before replying. "Yes, just down the road. I'll go with you."

Sharee squeezed his hand. He'd read her uneasiness with Janice's parents. "I just told Bruce I would help him with the teens. They have about two hours here before a group from another church comes. For a concert."

"That's okay," said Tom. "We understand." His eyes held an apologetic look. "I'm sorry this was awkward for us all. Lorraine wanted…" He let it tail off. "Well, I'm glad, though, to have met you. You know you're getting a good man…and I'm sure he's getting a good woman."

Lorraine began to walk back. Tom looked after her. "It's still hard for both of us, but we have to get past the pain at some point. And not just for ourselves, but for our son. He's what we live for now."

They all turned and began to follow Lorraine back up the path. At the parking lot, John climbed into his truck. "Follow me, Tom. There's a nice place to eat just down the road." Then he glanced at Sharee. "I'll be back to get you in a couple of hours."

"I might want to stay for the concert."

"That's good with me."

♺

Sharee rested her head against the back of the truck seat and inhaled the night air. The concert had lasted later than either of them expected, but the feeling inside—washed, cleansed—still filled her. The music team had interspersed the worship with times of prayer and repentance.

Thank you, Lord, for emptying me of all the junk—the worry, the fear. She looked at John. *Even the struggle to be pure. I'm having trouble, you know that; and if I'm having this battle, he is, too. We need your help.*

John's hand tightened on hers, and he sent a brief glance her way. "The concert was good."

She made a small sound to indicate consent. He seemed free during the concert. She assumed he'd made his peace with Janice's parents or a break—whatever he needed—and that he'd come into the sanctuary with a lighter heart than usual. Whatever it was, his praise and worship had been unselfconscious.

"Sharee," he said a few minutes later, "we need some time apart."

She straightened. "As in…?"

"As in…if we want this purity thing to work, we can't be together—alone—this often."

Wow. That's a quick answer to prayer. "I know."

His eyes slid her way, "You understand what I'm saying?"

"I believe so."

"It's not that I don't want to spend time with you. It's just…physically, you are…" His voice trailed off.

She touched his hand. "I understand, John. It's okay. We both need it."

He expelled his breath. "As easy as that?"

"You thought I'd argue?"

"That you might not understand."

She smiled. "Oh, I understand."

He put his arm around her shoulders, drawing her close. "Three months, darling. We need a date."

"Yes."

He turned into her apartment complex and circled the building. Sharee noticed the glance he threw over the darkened cars.

"Do you think they might try again?"

"I have no idea, but better to be careful. I don't see anyone suspicious sitting in a parked car. I guess the only person you need protection from is me." He squeezed her and parked the truck. They sat for a minute in silence, neither moving.

"This is not going to be easy. Climb down, girl."

She waited a couple of seconds. It wasn't easy. She opened the door and slid her feet to the ground. "You're not going to walk me to the door?"

"I love you, but you'd better walk yourself to the door tonight."

"A date for the wedding?"

"I'll call you when I get home. We'll discuss it then."

"I love you, too." She closed the door, bit her lip and stared at him through the window.

He moved his hand and the window rolled down. Leaning across the seat, he pulled her lip free. "Go." His voice sounded husky.

She nodded and walked to her apartment. The motion light blinked on as she neared it. When she unlocked the door, she turned to wave. He gave her a thumbs-up then backed out of the parking space.

When she'd locked the door, she stood in the darkness, feeling alone, fighting her own battle with desire. God, how quickly temptation comes. No wonder he didn't kiss me goodnight. It's right there, isn't it? Satan trying to steal what we just agreed upon.

She tossed her purse at the end table. In the dim light from the window, she watched it slide across the surface and fall off the other side. Shaking her head, she walked to the opposite wall and switched on the table lamp. Half of the items in her purse had scattered across the floor. She knelt to retrieve them.

A sound came from behind her. Sharee jerked around. A figure stood by the door. She leaped to her feet.

"Dean?"

"Surprise, sweetheart."

"What are you doing here?"

"I came to see you."

"But—" She fought to keep her voice calm. "How did you get in?"

"The key, of course. Remember the key you gave me once? To bring something up for you? I had a copy made. Just in case."

Cold alarm dropped into her stomach. She glanced at the door.

"Oh, he's gone." Dean smiled. "I heard the truck leave. No kiss tonight? Is that why you threw your purse?"

"What if he'd come in?"

"I was prepared, but he hasn't stayed since the other night."

She gaped at him. "You've been watching me?"

"Did you think I'd go away? Like before?" His eyes narrowed. "Or that you could continue to embarrass me and get away with it?"

"I didn't—"

"Or that my job isn't important?"

"What are you talking about?"

"Sending the cops to my work—as you did two years ago. My boss was hot last time."

"I didn't send them."

"Oh, yes, you did." He crossed the space between them. His hand shot out.

Sharee flinched backward, but his fingers dug into her arm. She clawed at his hand. He snatched it back, and she vaulted for the door, fumbling with the locks.

Dean grabbed both her arms. "Where do you think you're going?"

She bit the hand that held her. He jerked free and thrust her away from the door. She slipped and hit the wooden floor face first.

The sound of the blinds closing brought her head up. She pushed herself to her knees. Something hard pressed into her hip. Her phone.

Dean stepped next to her. "Get up!"

She turned away from him and thrust her hand into her pocket. It closed over the hard rectangle.

"I said get up!"

Dean caught her arm, pulling her to her feet. Her hand tore free from her pocket, but she held tight to the phone.

He thrust his face close to hers. "Don't try that again. Do you hear me?"

Sharee swallowed and nodded, hiding the phone behind her back. He laughed, loosened his hold and let his eyes drift over her.

She shuddered. She had to get away. If she could use her phone for one minute...

"You and I have some unfinished business. You know that, don't you?" He raised his hand to her chin. She drew back, and his fingers tightened. "What's wrong, sweetheart? Doesn't my touch entice you anymore?"

Sharee wrenched her chin free then brought her hand up and slammed the phone against his head. Dean yelped and jumped back, but the next instant, he sent an uppercut to her jaw. Pain exploded through her head. She stumbled backward, knees buckling, and fell.

Blackness pulsed in and out before her eyes. Dean stepped next to her, cursing. He reached down and grabbed her arm, but her phone had fallen under her. She grabbed for it and crashed against Dean's leg as she did. He stumbled backward, tripped over her foot and went down. Sharee scrambled to her feet and ran for the bathroom.

Dean's yell followed her.

She rammed the door shut and locked it just as he hit it. Gripping the phone in shaking hands, she tried to punch 911 but hit the wrong numbers. She tried again. Something crashed into the door. It splintered, and she leaped back staring down at the phone.

"Hello? Hello?" No one answered. Had she hit the wrong number again? A second crash came. She stabbed the speed dial for John's number.

A third crash came, and the lock gave way. The door flung open.

Dean sprung at her. "Give me the phone."

"No!" She twisted away and hunched over it.

He grabbed both arms and yanked them behind her. The phone fell, sliding across the tile floor. Sharee screamed.

"Shut up!" His hand slapped over her mouth. She bit into his fingers and snatched her face from his grip.

"Let go!"

He swung her around and shoved her toward the doorway. Sharee stuck her feet out, jamming them against the wall on either side. Dean cursed and pounded a fist against her leg until it dropped.

"Who would have thought you'd turn into such a spitfire?"

"Leave me alone, Dean. You'll end up in jail. Is that what you want?"

His hand cupped her chin, squeezing hard. "If I do, it will be for something worthwhile." He pulled her to the door. "We were just going to have a nice talk and maybe I'd give you a little something to remember me by, but now…You owe me, sweetheart, and I'll enjoy collecting."

Icicles formed inside her. "Someone heard the door crash in. They'll call the police."

Dean laughed. "Oh, we're not staying."

"They'll come after you."

"Your concern is touching." His arm tightened around her waist. "I have a place where no one will find us."

He hauled her to the front door and fumbled with the locks. When she fought him, he twisted one arm behind her until she yelped with pain.

"If you're not quiet, there will be more pain. I'll do what I have to do to get out of here. You can live or sign your death warrant. Your choice."

"Let me go, Dean. Please."

"Shut up." He opened the door and looked back and forth before pushing her into the cold. The motion light came on. He jerked to a stop then dragged her into the shadows and along the sidewalk.

Sharee tried to see into the blackness, into the parking lot. Was anyone out there? If she screamed… Pain surged up her arm as Dean twisted it again. She gasped.

"Don't make any noise."

An apartment door opened. Dean whirled, bringing her around. Through a whirlpool of pain, Sharee saw a gray head and a woman's apron.

"I've got a gun," Dean growled. "Get back inside."

The door slammed shut, its light extinguished.

A gun? He was lying. Wasn't he? He would have said something or she would have felt it.

"Call the police!" Sharee yelled.

"I told you to shut up!" He shoved her in front of him.

Sharee grabbed onto the next door handle. No light showed in the window, but she yelled anyway. "Help! Please, help me!"

He shook her free. She stomped on his instep, and they fell against the wall. His hand found her neck and squeezed. Blackness threatened, strobing in and out.

She clawed at his hand, panic shooting through her. *Lord, help me, please.*

"If you yell again, you're dead." His face was in hers; his grip loosened. "Do you hear me?"

Sharee gagged and nodded.

His hand dropped to her arm. "Get going!"

The squeal of breaks broke the night. Lights hit the building and flashed over them. Dean whirled, yanking her around with him.

The truck's door flung open, and John jumped from the cab.

"Stop!" Dean commanded. "Now!"

John stopped. His gaze fastened on Sharee. Hope fingered its way into her heart.

"Don't come closer," Dean said as he backed away. "She's dead if you do. I have a gun."

"He's lying! He doesn't have a gun."

Another apartment door opened. Dean whirled, yanking Sharee around with him. Pain surged up her arm. She screamed, and John lunged forward. Dean shoved her at him, and she crashed into his chest.

John caught her and held her close. "Are you okay? Are you hurt?"

"No, I'm fine. I—"

"You're sure?"

"Yes, I—"

"Stay here." He dropped his hands and raced past her. A moment later, he vanished past the corner of the building.

She ran after him. Somewhere ahead of her, a motor revved. She rounded the corner just as a black SUV shot out of a nearby parking space.

John skidded to a stop and jumped clear as the SUV roared past, almost hitting him. Sharee caught sight of Dean at the wheel. The vehicle disappeared around the next block.

John stared after the disappearing vehicle then turned. His gaze met hers, and he held out his arms.

✥

The small hospital room in the ER overflowed with people. John sat on the corner of Sharee's gurney and fought to keep his temper under control. Who had allowed all these people back here? He'd called Sharee's dad, Pastor Alan, and Detective Shepherd on the way to the hospital. Now he questioned the wisdom of those calls.

Sharee hadn't wanted to come, but a mass of bruises marred her face, and she held her arm as if Dean had broken it. Twisted it behind her, she said, but he wanted a doctor to check it. He glanced at his foot. The throbbing there began as soon as he found out Sharee would be all right. He grimaced. It would take care of itself.

During the call to Alan, he'd heard Lynn's voice in the background. The alarm that flew through him proved correct. Lynn's information highway had moved with NASCAR-like speed. Sharee's small partitioned area in the ER was now crammed with visitors.

He studied Sharee's face, and the surge of adrenaline hit once more. God wouldn't approve, but he wanted to pound Dean into the pavement. The fact that the man had escaped added additional fuel to the fire inside him. He took a deep breath and unclenched his fists.

Sharee sat tight-faced and stiff against the pillows, the bruises like smeared mud on her cheeks and along her chin. After telling her story to the hospital staff, then the police, she now had to retell it to her friends. John marveled at her control.

Ryann and Abbey had arrived a few minutes after Alan, Daneen, and Lynn. He couldn't believe Lynn had actually told the girls. Sharee's father had appeared a while later, making amazing time from Ocala. John shifted in his chair and watched Abbey's fervent texting with growing concern. Who was she telling?

"I can't believe you used to date this guy," Abbey said, putting her phone aside for a minute.

A flush started at Sharee's neck and climbed to her cheeks. It highlighted the bruises and mottled her skin. After all the questions, the comments from the two girls seemed hardest for her to answer. She tried to smile but failed, and tears filled her eyes.

"Oh, Sharee..." Lynn's voice broke. She stepped next to the bed.

That was it. John surged to his feet. The room full of people leaned away from him like a school of fish fleeing a predator. Good. He sent a scowl in Lynn's direction.

"All right, that's enough. Everybody out."

"John..." Sharee said, struggling to protest.

"I mean it. You've been through enough." His gaze circled the room. "Everyone out."

Sharee's father rose from his chair in a corner of the room. "I think you're right, John."

"Dad..."

John glanced his way. Legally, the man had more right here than John. "Please stay. I wasn't including you in this."

Pastor Alan leaned forward. "He's right, Sharee. You don't need all of us. Just our prayers."

Daneen leaned over and gave her a hug. Everyone, except Lynn, said goodbye and filed out the door.

Pastor Alan's head reappeared. "Give us a call tomorrow, John. Let us know how she's doing."

"Okay. I'll call. You inform everyone else. Tell them no calls or visits for the next twenty-four hours."

The pastor grinned. "I'll let them know."

Lynn hovered near the bed. She gave Sharee a hug and John a belligerent look.

He scowled. "Those girls—"

"I did not tell those girls. Marci must have, or they were there when I called."

"No one should have been told about this."

"Sharee doesn't mind Marci knowing."

"I mind. She doesn't need—"

"John Jergenson, you need a marriage license before you can take control here."

He tightened his jaw, and Lynn narrowed her eyes before turning and leaving. A marriage license. That was exactly what he needed and wanted.

He turned back to Sharee. Her eyes had widened.

John crossed his arms over his chest. "You didn't need a circus. The police had enough questions, but your friends..." He bit off the rest of what he wanted to say.

Brian laughed. "I was feeling the same way. Thank you. And it's a good thing Marilyn's visiting her mother in Georgia. Seeing her daughter like this..." He dropped his gaze to Sharee, his look softening. "They said they were going to let you go home tonight."

"They have to finish the paperwork."

"Come home with me until this man is found."

Sharee hesitated. "No, Dad. I'm not going to let Dean run me out of my apartment. John can come and make sure that...no one's there. No one could get in after I lock and bolt everything. And he can change the locks tomorrow. Dean won't come back, anyway. Not now."

John cleared his throat. "I'll go back with you and sleep on the couch again. Tomorrow, you call Lynn or someone to come over—for a day or two. I don't want you alone. Just to be sure."

Sharee's gaze held his. "But I..."

"Not up for debate."

"I..."

"*Not* up for debate."

Her gaze didn't move but, finally, she nodded. "Okay."

He let his breath out. "Good."

❧

Quiet enveloped the truck's cab as they headed for her apartment. John fought his own exhaustion and thought about the calm her dad had brought into the hospital room. He wished he had that ability. His mind went to Dean, and he gritted his teeth. He should have gone after him. He should have...

"I think Dad wanted to stay." Sharee sat close beside him in the darkness, and he kept one arm around her. The sound of the truck's tires on the road provided a soothing white noise.

"I'm sure he did." His hand tightened on the wheel. *Revenge is mine, says the Lord. How do I give this to you, God? I want my own revenge.*

He needed to get his mind off Dean and onto Sharee. She deserved to be out of harm's way. Perhaps instead of taking her home, he should take her to his condominium. His place would be safe.

"My place might be safer than yours."

"What?"

"My place. Dean won't think of looking for you there."

She was silent a minute. "I'd need to get all my stuff. My clothes and everything."

"You can stay a few days."

"A few days?" Surprise showed in her voice. "John, I...don't think...it wouldn't look right. Besides—"

"You need someplace where Dean won't think to look."

"But...there would be other problems."

He squelched the exasperation. She didn't need to receive the bite of the emotions he'd rode after hearing her scream over the phone, after hearing Dean's threat against her, after the hospital fiasco. He steeled himself against a need to lash out at someone.

"I think it's a good solution."

"No."

"Why not?"

"No."

"You're being stubborn." The words jumped out before he could stop them. "It's a good idea."

Quiet filled the truck again. She turned her head away, brought her hands to her face. In the streetlights flashing past, he saw tears run out between her fingers. *Idiot. She's been mistreated enough without your badgering.*

"I don't…want to fight." Her words came halting and stifled.

When he pulled into her apartment complex, he turned and gathered her into his arms. "I'm sorry, babe. It's okay."

He ran his fingers through her hair, twisting the soft curls and feeling her warmth against him. Yeah, she was right. There'd be other problems. He kissed the middle of her forehead, remembering that her whole face seemed bruised.

She sniffed. "I'm glad you got there. He…He was crazy."

"Don't think about it. You're safe now." He leaned down to find her mouth. She clung to him, her mouth answering his. His fingers trailed down her throat, and he tightened his hold, intensified the kiss.

He wanted her, more than ever. "I love you."

"I love you, too." Her words sounded as ragged as his.

"Let's go in."

She drew back a little, trying to see his face.

He bent his head again, his mouth searching hers. "Let's go in. Let me help you forget this." His hand touched her cheek, feather-light, hesitant.

"John, no, I…" She was shaking. "We can't."

"I love you. You know that. You—" He stopped, fighting the desire, halting the thoughts that accompanied it. The temptation surprised him with its force.

She prayed under her breath. *"Lord, help us."*

His mouth twisted. She was safe, he'd said. Obviously not. Earlier this evening, she'd agreed they needed time apart. How easy it seemed to get her agreement, and he'd been deceived by that. Satan had a plan all the time.

He mixed his prayer with hers. *Lord, help us.*

It took another minute before he set her away from him. A long pause followed. "I'll go check your apartment. Stay here."

She put a hand on his arm. "John, your place would be more of a temptation. Do you understand?"

"Anywhere with you would be a temptation right now. I won't stay. I'll go in and check your place. Once you're inside, lock and bolt the door. I'll stay in the truck tonight."

"What if Dean comes back?"

"He won't. I'll be fine." It would be a struggle to leave her inside by herself, but much more if he was on the couch. His labored breathing sounded loud in the night.

God will make a way of escape… The words swept over him, and he reached for the truck keys, saying, "Look, this is not going to work. I'm taking you to Alan and Daneen's."

Car lights swept the parking lot, and a car pulled in next to them. Sharee jumped, twisting in her seat. John wrenched his head around. The car lights went out. He stared through the window and chuckled. "Your father."

"Thank God."

"Yes." His voice held as much relief as hers. He put his arm across her shoulders. They sat in silence.

Sharee's dad climbed from the car and came over. John rolled the window down. Brian glanced from him to Sharee.

"Well, I was on the way home but couldn't make it." He smiled at John. "She is my daughter, after all, and I thought I'd probably do better on the couch tonight than you."

John met his eyes, and he nodded. "Yes..." he agreed on a long note. "Yes, you will."

Chapter 12

Still groggy from sleep, Sharee opened her bedroom door. She heard voices and stared across the living area at her dad and John, who sat at her small kitchenette.

"Honey," her father said and pushed himself up from the table.

Her eyes opened. "Oh!" She awoke with a start and jumped back into the bedroom, slamming the door. What was John doing here this early? She'd let her dad have it next time they were alone. The extra-large T-shirt she wore most nights covered her in a modest way, but she still felt embarrassed to be caught off-guard.

Running her hands through her hair, she went to her bureau and pulled clean jeans, underclothes, and another T-shirt from it. Well, John had seen her at her worst in the hospital. A few minutes later, she took a deep breath and opened the door.

Both men glanced her way and stared. John's chair scraped the floor as he started to rise.

She held up a hand then pointed to the bathroom. "Just let me clean up, please."

Closing the door after her, she pulled out her toothbrush and toothpaste and began brushing. Her eyes lifted to the mirror, and a strangled cry escaped her lips. The toothbrush clattered to the counter and into the sink.

"Sharee?" Her dad's voice sounded concerned. "Are you okay?"

She didn't trust her voice. She didn't trust her eyes. She rinsed the toothbrush off, setting it on the sink, and picked up the mouthwash, rinsing it through her mouth. She did not look in the mirror again.

"Sharee?"

"I'm...okay." Picking up the hairbrush, she ran it through her hair, keeping her eyes downcast. When she set it down, she took a long, slow breath and raised her eyes. Black and blue patches spread across both sides of her face. Her bottom lip was swollen. Tears spilled over her eyelids and down her cheeks.

I look horrible. Worse than last night!

She heard quiet talking, and chairs moving and then the door to the apartment open and close.

"Sharee." John's voice came from just outside the door.

"Give me another couple of minutes, please." Steps moved away from the door. Her shoulders relaxed. What she wanted most was to crawl back in bed and hide.

A few minutes later, John's voice came through the door again. "Please come out."

She drew it open, keeping her head averted. He took her hand and drew her over to the sofa, pulling her down beside him.

"It's okay. You're okay. The doctor said…"

"I look terrible."

"Who cares? You'll look fine in a few days…well, maybe in a week… or ten days…"

She buried her head into his shoulder. Tears pooled behind her closed eyes. His hand stroked her hair. When she pulled away, she stared at the wet spot on his shirt, keeping her head down.

"Where's Daddy?"

"He went to get lunch."

"Lunch? What time is it?"

"After 1:00. You slept late." His hand touched her cheek. "Sharee, look at me."

She swallowed but slowly raised her head.

His lips compressed, and his eyes darkened. "I'd like to get my hands on the man. If I'd walked you to the door last night…"

"Don't even say that. It's not your fault."

"What I'd like to say would earn me a bolt from heaven."

She tried to smile, but it hurt her broken lip. "He was inside, anyway. And you came back. I don't know how you heard…"

"When I heard you scream, I made a U-turn in the middle of the road." He stared out the window. "Probably a few drivers still recovering from that."

"John?"

He shifted and took a deep breath. "Your dad and I had a long talk while you were asleep. He can relate to what I'm feeling. He's…a godly man. You're blessed to have him."

"I know."

"Someone needs to be here, Sharee. You'll feel better if you're not alone. I'll feel better."

"I know. I'll ask Lynn like you said. Mother, can come in a day or two. You'll change my lock?"

"Yes. Today."

"They'll find him." She made it a statement but heard her own nervousness.

"They will. He can't go back to his own place or to his work, but he'll need money." John frowned. "He must have been watching you for some time."

"Then you think he's the one who's been doing this?"

"Detective Shepherd thinks so. We talked early this morning."

"But Dean said he saw mom and dad leave the hospital. That's how he knew I was there."

"Probably lying. Shepherd wants to talk to you again."

She drew in a weary breath. "All right. You know, I hate to think of Dean following me, stalking me for a while. And that I didn't know. But what set him off?"

"Maybe he was just keeping tabs on you and then we started to date. When I left for Indonesia, he might have assumed we broke up. How was he to know where I went? Then I came back. That could have triggered it. It was that day that I was run over. Right after dropping you off."

"He did tell me the night that you stayed here that he'd waited all night for you to leave and that he'd been watching me since."

"He said that?" His look became distant once more. "You could go home with your dad for a few days. That wasn't a bad idea."

"And miss more work? When I went in for a short time the other day, they teased me about needing reliable help. I need to be there, you know that. I have work to do. I have clients to see, classes to teach... "

"Okay, okay." He held up his hand and grinned.

"And I have bills to pay."

"We can work something out about that."

"I'm not taking money from you. We're not married yet."

"I keep hearing that. How long does it take to get a license in this town?"

"John, be realistic."

"I am. Why wait three months if we don't have to?"

"If you think I'm getting married looking like this, you just think again."

One side of his mouth lifted. "You looked pretty cute in your T-shirt awhile ago."

She punched his arm but twisted toward the door when a sharp rap sounded.

A key turned in the lock, and her dad's voice preceded him into the room. "Look who I found outside."

Lynn came in, carrying a sleeping bag and an overnight case. "Hope you don't mind putting up with me for a few days, but I'm tired of having my best friend beat up." Then she stared at Sharee and put her hand to her mouth, gasping. Her eyes rounded. "Oh, Sharee, you are beat up! I'm sorry."

She dropped her bags, crossed the room in two steps, and elbowed John aside.

Tears filled Sharee's eyes. "Oh, Lynn." Two words were all she managed.

‿

"Forgive him?" John's lowered brow and voice carried their own message. He wasn't happy with her pronouncement. "I'd like to do a lot of things to him, but forgiving him is not one of them."

"We don't have a choice, John."

"You might not have a choice, but—"

"If you two don't mind," Lynn stood with her hands on her hips, "I think I'll run home. It's wonderful that the police found Dean and arrested him. You don't need me anymore. I'm going to scoot home and get ready for church." She gave them both a huge smile. "You two can finish fighting without me."

Sharee grabbed a few of her friend's things and helped her pack. "We're not fighting."

"Oh, sure. Sorry." Lynn stuffed a number of make-up items in a designer bag. "That's just what it sounds like."

Sharee hugged her. "You're the best friend ever. I'd forgotten how much fun you were."

"That's because you spend all your time with John. I just get left out."

John looked up from knotting the tie on her sleeping bag. "Is there a competition?"

Lynn sent him a look from narrowed eyes, "You know, I really could use a wedding date. You're not dragging your feet, are you?"

"Me? If anything, I'm trying to move it up. The bride-to-be can't find a good time for us to talk about it. I told her to just pick a date. I'm free any weekend."

"Any weekend?" Lynn's eyes rolled. "Aren't you going to have a honeymoon?"

"Oh, we'll have a honeymoon."

Sharee handed Lynn her purse. "Now that Dean is in jail, and all this craziness is over, maybe we can pick a date."

John's face changed. "A few years in prison would be good for him."

"I never said he shouldn't go to jail." Sharee's voice sharpened. "I only said that God loves him, and we need to have compassion..."

Lynn held up her hand. "The church service starts in less than an hour. I'm glad you came, John, so you can take Sharee. I'll run home, and I'll see you two there." She gave them a mocking smile, lifted her bags, and went toward the door.

John opened it, and Lynn left, shaking her head. He closed the door behind her and made a slow turn. "So, you've forgiven him already?"

"John, he hasn't got what we have. We have God. We have each other."

"And I'm supposed to forgive him, too, now that you have?"

She bit her lip but said nothing. The relief, the elation, she'd felt—that they'd both felt—at Detective Shepherd's call had vanished. Those jubilant emotions, for her, had only lasted a few minutes. The turn Dean's life had taken was heartbreaking. John's reaction was a hundred and eighty degrees different.

Sharee dug her nails into her palms. "He's in jail. I feel sorry for him."

"You what?"

"Feel sorry for him."

"That's ridiculous. I don't understand that. He hurt you."

"I don't understand you. How can you be like this?"

"Me? Look what he did to you. What he tried to do to us both."

"He denied trying to run us down. He said he didn't do that. Or chase me into the woods."

"And you believe him?"

"I don't know what to believe."

"But you forgive him?"

"John, yes. It's just there."

"He doesn't deserve your forgiveness."

"We don't deserve God's forgiveness either."

❧

Here they were again. Standing in church, singing praises to God, with this hardness between them. Was she a hypocrite when she answered Lynn's question a few moments ago in the affirmative? Yes, she and John had argued, but did that mean she wasn't fine? She listened to the words of the song. God was real, He was alive, and He was in control. She could put her trust in Him. And she would. Once more. Sharee slipped her hand into John's as they stood together, singing.

No, she wasn't a hypocrite because she didn't tell everyone her problems. She was fine because of God.

John's head turned, his gaze dropping to her.

"I love you," she mouthed.

He gave a brief nod, but his hand tightened around hers. When they sat to listen to Pastor Alan's sermon, his arm slipped around her shoulders. At the end of the service, he indicated the side door with a move of his head. She nodded, and they slipped outside and walked across the field to the pond.

The dark water reflected the image of the tall cypress, Spanish moss and hanging fern. As they came near, a turtle scurried from the bank and hit the water, sending ever-widening rings to break the reflection. John pointed to the opposite bank.

Sharee tilted her head, checking the abundance of fern and cypress knees. "What? Oh." The alligator lay half hidden among the foliage. The sun's rays had dried his dark hide to gray.

"The anhinga's in the tree above him."

"I wonder who steals fish from whom."

"That would be good to get on an animal webcam."

"The service was good."

He slid a glance her way. "Guess I needed it."

"We both did. Amazing how Alan preaches right to our needs."

"God knows. Alan listens to Him."

"Yes."

"Sharee…"

She heard the change in his voice and raised her head.

"I'm sorry about losing my temper this morning. When your dad and I talked the other day, he told me how he felt the first time Dean hit you, and he told me what God had done in his life so that he could forgive him. I should be able to do the same, but every time I look at your face, the anger builds. When you said you felt sorry for him, I wanted to explode. I couldn't imagine forgiveness coming that fast. It's going to take me longer."

"It's okay."

"No, it's not, but I'll get there. One day. What was not okay was asking if I could come in the other night."

"I said no, but I didn't want to."

He dropped his head and smiled down at her. "And so you prayed."

"Yes."

"That was humbling when I heard it. And put me on the right track. Along with your father showing up." He gave her a squeeze.

"Our culture today doesn't understand purity, doesn't understand yet what has been unleashed on us because we've let it slip. I thought I wouldn't have a problem. But things started getting out of hand at the hospital, as you know. Still, I felt I could handle it. I didn't see that as pride, but it was. As well as underestimating the enemy. I was blindsided by what happened to you."

"It's okay, John."

"No, it's not okay. It wasn't right. I wanted you, you know that, but I also wanted our love as revenge for what he'd done to you. Does that make sense?"

"Like you wanted to erase the bad memories at the beach?"

"In a way." A splash came from the pond as he studied her. "Every time I turn around, something happens to you. I'd like to take you to my place and lock you up so no one could get in."

"I think you've threatened me with that before." She put a hand to his face. "You can't protect me from everything. Only God can do that, and He doesn't sometimes—or doesn't seem to. I can't explain that, but we do what we can and trust God with the rest."

He held her tight against his chest. "I'm having trouble with that. I don't like the way He's looking out for you, and to trust Him completely means I have to let you go completely."

"If something were to happen to me, if I were to die for some reason, I'd want you to go on serving Him. God's called you. And the God we serve is worthy of that kind of love and devotion."

His eyes closed. "How you challenge me."

A loud splash came from the pond. They both glanced in that directions. The alligator and the anhinga had disappeared.

John gave a wry smile. "Well, we need National Geographic here to film whatever's going on under water. Sharee…"

"What?"

"Let's get married."

She tilted her head and smiled. "I already said yes."

"Today."

"What?"

"I checked online. We can get a license and get married the same day."

Chapter 13

Sharee hefted the water balloon and bounced it gently in her hand. He'd been serious, but she'd broken that bubble for him. "It's Sunday. We can't get a license today."

His face had changed. "Tomorrow. They have someone that will perform the ceremony right there."

"You're crazy."

"Crazy is waiting any longer than we have to."

"Lynn would kill us."

"Now that may be a possibility." He had hugged her to him. "I love you. I know you want a beautiful wedding. We could have a church wedding later."

She'd laughed and pointed to the riding mower sitting near the office. "Don't you have to mow or something? If you do that today, we can talk about this tomorrow—after I've had some time to think and pray."

John had agreed and left her to wonder what her parents and her friends would say if they did go ahead and get married. Yeah, Lynn would kill her.

Now, she glanced from her hiding place behind a pile of sand and waved at Matthew and Ryann. Crouched at the back of a wheelbarrow, they raised their hands in reply. A few yards over, Mark used a thick pine tree as cover. His face radiated excitement.

John had called after he finished mowing the property, little knowing what she'd planned. They needed some laughter more than a quick marriage.

She glanced at her watch—only twenty minutes before the evening service. Matthew had spied out the work building a few minutes ago to make sure John was inside. Not just there, he reported, but he'd heard the shower. John was getting ready for this evening's service. So, the four of them had taken up positions outside.

Nervous excitement ran through her. The teens had only needed a little encouragement before agreeing to help. Their added enthusiasm bumped hers to another level.

She juggled the balloon back and forth in her hands. One of four they each had. That should be enough to soak him. She held back a chuckle. From her right came Ryann's high giggle.

"Shh!"

The door of the work building opened, and John stepped out. Sharee jumped to her feet and threw the first balloon. From her right, other balloons flew in quick succession. All four of them slapped the building behind John. He jumped, twisting his head to see the wall then spun back around.

Mark's second balloon hit him square in the chest. Matthew's sailed after it, breaking on one leg. Sharee tossed hers, hitting the building again, and Ryan's flew wide. John dashed for the corner of the building. More balloons sailed after him. One caught his right shoulder, another two breaking against his back. Hers hit the ground just as he vanished from sight. Ryann was laughing so hard she dropped her last one.

"Got him!" Matthew gave a whoop, grabbed Ryann's hand, and they ran for the church. Mark did the same.

Sharee shook her head. Deserted in a minute. She bent to pick up the two balloons she had left and stepped out from the sand pile. Where was he? She looked from one side of the building to the other. His head emerged from the edge of the building where he'd disappeared.

"Gotcha!" she said, grinning.

He narrowed a look at her then glanced back and forth. "Where are the others? They left you?"

"Guess so." She bounced on her toes, still smiling.

"Well, you should have left with them." Stepping from the side of the building, he raised a thick hose in her direction.

As the realization of what he held hit her, she spun around; but the water slammed her back before she could run. She stumbled from the onslaught, her back soaked from head to foot.

John laughed. "So, you were going to get me, were you?"

Turning and dropping her head, she ran at him. The rush of water hit her again, almost knocking her to the ground. His laughter mixed with the "whoosh" as it came at her. When she reached him, Sharee threw her arms around him, breaking the two balloons against his back. His body jerked, and he dropped the hose to enclose her in his arms.

"What was this for?"

"Just a little levity."

"At my expense? You're in trouble, girl."

"Worth it."

He tightened his arms. "You're not getting away lightly. Where are the others? Who were they?"

She stuck her tongue out at him. "If you didn't see, I'm not going to tell you."

His eyes narrowed. "Perhaps some time under the shower might change your mind." He turned her toward the building from which he'd come.

"Don't you dare!" She dug in her heels. "I'm already soaked!"

"So you are." He chuckled, bent down and kissed her. "But you'll have to pay for this, you know."

"Will I?" She made her voice light, leaning back against his arms.

"Yeah."

Sharee twisted, broke free of his hold and dropped to the ground. Grabbing the hose, she straightened and blasted him full in the chest. When his hands jerked upward for protection, she dropped the hose and ran.

Twenty minutes later, Sharee stood among the teenagers as they milled around the front of the church. She'd changed into dry clothes, finger-combed her wet curls and come out on the porch to wait for John. She glanced at Matthew. He and Mark had spread the word, and the other teens were waiting, too.

John came around the last building and walked toward them. Sharee narrowed her eyes. Not just his clothes but even his hair looked dry. How did he do that? She watched his eyes run over the whole group. He was inspecting them as much as they were inspecting him.

"He's not wet at all," Abbey whispered. "You sure you got him?"

"Oh, we got him," Sharee answered.

John's eyes moved over the teens one by one. Ryann ducked her head and slid behind one of the other girls. Sharee flinched. *Oh no, Ryann. Not a good move.*

A smile played across John's face. His eyes slid to Matthew, but Matt stood still and stared back. John's gaze flicked over the others, resting on Mark. Mark twisted away and began an animated conversation with the girl next to him.

John's head gave a slight inclination as he mounted the steps. The group of students shuffled backward. His look bounced over them and settled on Sharee. She stood at the back of the crowd and grinned at him, rocking back and forth on her feet. The line of his mouth straightened, and his eyes narrowed before he stepped forward.

The teens scattered, jumping off the steps and disappearing around the corner of the building or into the sanctuary. John stopped in front of her, cornering her between the cement wall and a railing leading down the side steps. His height blocked her view of anything else.

Her heart did a quick flip in her chest. Was he angry, after all?

He picked up a wet curl next to her face and twirled it around his finger. A mocking smile started at the corners of his mouth.

Sharee straightened. "If you're trying to intimidate me…" Amusement sprang to his eyes, and she paused. "If you are, it will take a lot more…ouch!"

"A lot more what?" He questioned, tugging on her hair once again.

She grabbed his hand. "Stop that! A lot more than—" His finger tightened on the strand, and she tried to loosen his grip.

"What was that for?"

"Just because." She couldn't help the big smile. Sticking her tongue out at him occurred to her, but she didn't want to push him too far.

He smiled, too. "You said once you get even. Well, girl, I do, too. More than even. Be forewarned."

"And just how do you plan on doing that?"

"What's going on here?" Pastor Alan mounted the steps. He glanced at both of them. "I don't know whom I'm saving from what, but I think church started a few minutes ago."

John's hand dropped to Sharee's arm. "We're having a short discussion."

"Ah." He waited a moment. When they remained quiet, he said, "Okay…. Well, I'm late. Had a counseling session that ran over. Good thing the worship group can carry on without me." He glanced again at John's hand on her arm and raised his brows. She saw him notice her wet head. "Hum. Well, are you two coming in?"

"Of course," Sharee said.

"In a minute," John stated.

Pastor Alan nodded, looked them both up and down once more. "Don't be too long." The door closed behind him.

John's arm slipped around her waist. "The shower is close by. Did you bring another set of dry clothes?"

"Don't even think about it."

His eyes danced, but he opened the door for her. "Oh, I'll be thinking about it, all right, but it would be much more fun if we were married."

๛

The service ended, and people began to file out. Sharee smiled and nodded as some passed by. Neither she nor John moved but watched as the church emptied. Marci and Stephen went by. Marci carried the baby. Three of their youngest children followed.

Lynn stepped next to them as the Thornton's passed. "I have a couple of wedding questions, not even having to do with a date—although that would be a milestone for my planning. Let me ask the bride a few questions, and you can take her home." She waved her hand at John, indicating she wanted him to leave.

John eyed Sharee then stood. "Go ahead. She's the boss. Of weddings."

Lynn shook her head. "I heard that qualifier."

John grinned.

"Hey, Mr. J, how ya doin'?" A voice asked.

Sharee glanced up and saw a number of young people walking past, Mark and Matthew in their midst. Six pairs of eyes looked their way.

"Totally fine, Josh. What's up?"

"Oh, I'm just chillin', Mr. J, just wet and chillin'." Josh's head bobbed up and down, his eyes laughing.

The group went on, and John's gaze slid her way. She held a hand to her mouth to stifle a giggle.

John leaned over and whispered in her ear. "Paybacks can come at any time, babe. Beware." He stood up, smiled at Lynn and walked down the aisle toward the side door.

Fifteen minutes later, Sharee shoved the sanctuary door open, and she and Lynn walked out onto the wide porch. She'd hated not telling Lynn of John's words earlier, but what could she do? Nothing was decided.

The porch and back parking lot were empty. A lone light shone in the pastor's office.

"You don't think John left you, do you?" Lynn asked.

"No, he wouldn't do that. He must be with Pastor Alan."

"Ms. J!" Ryann dashed up the steps, skidding to a stop in front of them. "He's got that big round cooler. And it's full!"

"Who's got a cooler? What—"

"Mr. Jergenson! I saw him filling it up in the fellowship hall! The cooler we use when we camp. Ms. J, you know he's coming to get you!"

Sharee felt her heart jump. He hadn't wasted any time. "Me?

What about you? He knows you helped me."

Ryann squealed. "You think so?"

"Oh, yeah. When did you see him? Right now?"

"Just a minute ago. Abbey is keeping an eye on him through the window. Ms. J, you know he's gonna get you back. You better run."

"You better, too." Sharee looked at Lynn, whose Cheshire grin spread large across her face. "You've got to take me home, girlfriend. Quick."

Lynn nodded. "Let's go before he gets here."

"Ryann, will you ask Abbey to tell him I went home with Lynn?"

"Yeah, sure, as long as he doesn't see me."

"Where's Matthew and Mark?"

"They left just after their parents."

Abbey skidded around the corner and jumped onto the top step. "He's coming!"

"Already?" Ryann's voice jumped two decimals.

"Oh, no!" Sharee grabbed Lynn's arm. "Come on, girlfriend."

"My car's that way." She pointed back the way Abbey had come.

"We'll have to go the other way." Lynn didn't move. Sharee shook her. "Come on, girlfriend."

Sharee ran down the steps, out of the light into the darkness. Footsteps followed. They rounded the edge of the building.

Something moved ahead of her, and she skidded to a stop. What—

The other three ran past her.

"No! Wait!" She grabbed for Lynn but missed her.

From the deep shadows next to the building someone shifted forward, and the light from the streetlamp caught a flood of silver just above the girls' heads. Sharee heard them scream. He'd gone around the other way. He must have seen Abbey.

Sharee twisted around and ran back the way they had come, across the front of the church, and into the darkness on the other side. She sprinted away from the fellowship hall toward the work buildings, skidding to a stop as she remembered the shower inside. It would not do to get caught here.

She changed directions, gasping from nervousness and laughing at the thought of Lynn, Ryann, and Abbey. They would be soaked! Completely! And John had missed her! He'd come looking, no doubt about that.

Sharee slid to a halt. The office lights glowed. Pastor Alan must be there. If she could make it to the office, she'd be safe. She stepped into the shadows and crept toward the building. With a final glance at the sanctuary, she flew across the empty ground, grabbed the door handle and bolted inside.

Two people jumped and spun around. Sharee gawked, her heart plummeting. Ted and Marci stood on the other side of the room. *Lord, not again.*

Marci stepped forward. "Now, Sharee."

"I thought you left with your family, Marci."

"No, I—"

Sharee held up her hand. "I don't want to know. I'm leaving." She reached for the door.

The knob turned in her hand, and John stepped in, an imitation of Lynn's Cheshire grin on his face.

"You think you're safe here? Let me..." His voice trailed off as he caught sight of Marci and Ted. A moment of silence followed.

"I know what you're both thinking," Ted said, "and it's wrong."

"It is. Really." Marci reiterated.

"What are you doing here, Ted?" The roughness in John's voice was clear. "You were asked not to come back."

"Pastor Alan knows I'm here. We talked before church. Marci's just here to say goodbye."

"Alan knows you're here?"

Ted nodded. "Yes, and I'm leaving for a while."

John's eyes narrowed. "You are? Where're you going?"

"I have family near Pensacola. I'm going there." His eyes focused on Marci before moving to Sharee. "I've caused some problems. I...I guess I should apologize." The words were low.

John slipped his arm around Sharee, drawing her close. "Yeah, you have. You should."

Ted shuffled his feet and looked at Sharee. "I wouldn't have hurt you. I was just angry. You were in my face. Preaching at me. I talked with Pastor Alan about it. He understands. He...helped me see some things differently." His chin rose, his eyes meeting John's. "I would never hurt anyone. I just wanted...well..." He shot a glance at Marci, and the words trailed off.

Sharee studied Ted. He seemed contrite. Were his words sincere? "Your apology's accepted, Ted."

John cocked his head. "When are you leaving?"

"Tomorrow. I asked Pastor Alan to let Marci know. She's just here to say goodbye."

"Hmm." John's gaze settled on Marci a moment before jumping back to Ted. "What are you going to do when you get there?"

"My family owns a factory. I can work there for a while. My job here is gone, anyway."

"What about your stuff here?"

"I'm giving it to the church. That way Pastor Alan said he could legally get it from my apartment and bring it to me later. I can't go back there. I haven't been back home since Pastor Alan and I had that blow-up. I knew he might call the cops. I wasn't really thinking straight. I just hid out."

"Where?" John asked.

"In the woods." He nodded in the direction of the vacant lot next door with its large stand of trees. "I snuck out to clean up and use the bathroom here one evening, and Pastor Alan caught me. We talked. I told him I wouldn't hurt anyone." His eyes narrowed. "I thought he'd know that. Know that I was just talking. Anyway, he said he would leave the work building with the bathroom open at night and not report me to the police if I would come each evening for counseling. He left the office open sometimes too, in case I needed to use the phone."

John's jaw clenched. Silence settled in the room. "What happens now?"

"Pastor Alan bought me a ticket—an airplane ticket to Pensacola."

John nodded. "If Alan gives the okay, we'll load your stuff in my truck and bring it to you in a week or so."

Ted's face changed. "That would be a help."

Sharee glanced at Marci. Too many questions tumbled through her mind. She couldn't ask any of them.

Marci stared back at her. "Stephen is waiting for me in the car."

John's jerk of surprise matched her own. *Lord, protect Stephen. Protect Marci. Protect their marriage. And help Ted.*

John slipped his hand down to catch Sharee's and glanced again at Ted. "You can sleep at my place tonight if you want. It might be better than sleeping in the woods. I'll take you to the airport in the morning."

Sharee wrenched her gaze from Marci to John.

Ted cleared his throat. "That would be real nice. Thanks."

"All right. You know my truck. We'll be waiting." He turned to Marci. "Your husband is a good man."

Marci straightened. "I know."

John drew Sharee out the door. They walked in silence. He opened the door of his truck, and they climbed into the cab. Neither spoke.

Sharee's heart danced. *Thank you, Lord. Thank you for working in that situation for good.*

Her breath halted a minute—but if Ted hadn't chased her through the woods, and Dean said he hadn't, who had?

Chapter 14

"Two weeks?" Lynn nearly shrieked. "You've got to be kidding! You are kidding, right?"

"Well, actually, no."

"Sharee, there is no way possible."

"Can't we just simplify some things?"

"*Simplify?* Do you know all the planning I've already done? All the time I spent searching for and working with the colors we discussed, the materials, and decorations? You still have no invitations yet, no caterer, and no flowers! You haven't okayed anything."

"But Lynn, we could call around and find out who has what and just go with what we can get. Besides, you know everyone in the church will bring food. And we have white tablecloths for the fellowship hall. Maybe we could have The Lucky Dill cater or something like that."

The phone went silent. "Lynn?"

"Just call around...just go with what we can get...or something like that? No, I'm not doing this. You cannot be serious."

Sharee remembered John's words. "She'll either have a heart attack or kill you."

"Sharee." Lynn's voice wobbled. "This was John's idea, wasn't it? How did he talk you into it?"

"He didn't have to."

"But a wedding is special. It's holy. I can't believe you just want to rush into it." She stopped abruptly. "Sharee, you're not...not..."

"No, I'm not pregnant."

"Sharee..."

"John told me everyone would think that."

"You mean he tried to talk you out of this?"

"Well, no. He just told me there would be some...problems."

"Problems? Oh, there will be problems, all right, and the first one is that the wedding planner quits!"

"Lynn, no. I told John if that's how you felt then...then we would wait."

"What do your parents think? What about John's parents?"

"Well, we're talking with everyone today. He's talking to his parents, and I'll talk to mine later."

"Why do you want to rush into this?"

Another question she'd have to face again and again. "So much has gone on. We've both been beaten, battered physically, emotionally, spiritually. I just want to be with him…without any more battles."

The pause lasted ten full seconds. "But two weeks?"

"It was John's idea. He suggested, you know, just running off and getting married first. Today, in fact. And having a reception or something when we got back."

"He's crazy."

"Yeah, well, that man thing, you know. Always a little crazy."

"And they say we are."

"He feels like I do, Lynn. Tired of all this and ready to get on with our lives."

"But two months—that's all it is now—is not long."

"I suppose not… just longer than two weeks and much longer than today."

ی

Sharee's mom let out a shriek. "You're not serious!"

"I am. We—"

"Brian!"

"Mom? Mom?" Sharee heard a muffled reply, and then her mom talking to her dad.

His voice came on the line a minute later. "Your mother went to lie down. Sharee…you want to get married in two weeks?"

"Yes."

"Can I ask why?"

"I am not pregnant." She wondered how many times she'd have to say that, and how many times John would.

"Then why?"

She explained as she had to Lynn.

"You and John have certainly been through a lot. Why don't you just run off and get married and tell us when you get back?"

"You sound like John."

"Do I? Well, I knew that had crossed his mind. He seems the type of young man that doesn't want to wait once his mind is made up." He paused then said, "Of course, that outlook has many good points about it."

"Yes, it does."

"I like him, honey. But a wedding in two weeks…your mother…"

"I know, Daddy, but it's what we want." She heard him sigh.

৵

At midnight, her phone rang. She needed the deep breath she took.

"John?"

"I wanted to see how you were doing."

"Horribly."

"As bad as that?"

"I only got to half my list, and I am so tired of saying I'm not pregnant." His chuckle sounded in her ear. "It's not funny! How many did you call?"

"All of them."

"You talked to everyone on your list?" Her voice jumped.

"Yes. Guys take less time, you know. My parents, of course, were the longest. My sister, next."

"John, I think you were right. We should have run off and got married. Daddy said the same thing." Quiet filled the air. "Go ahead, say it."

"What?"

"You know what."

"You mean, 'I told you so?'" He chuckled again. "Is that your teeth I hear grinding?"

"No!"

"I bet. Well, lady love, get some sleep. Finish calling tomorrow, and I'll take you out for a quiet dinner someplace."

"That will be nice, if Lynn lets me go. She is taking me shopping tomorrow. We've got to get flowers, a dress, and invitations she says. Tomorrow!" She needed the second deep breath, too. "John?"

"Yes?"

"Is it too late to run off and get married?"

He laughed.

৵

They had been to three bridal shops before 1:00 PM. Leaving the third empty-handed had her muttering under her breath. "Lynn, this is the third bridal shop, and it's…" Sharee dropped her head to see her watch, "It's one o'clock!"

Lynn stopped in front of Sharee's SUV. "And?"

"And I've tried on every decent dress there is! Every shop will probably have the same styles. Who knew it would be impossible to find the right one?"

Lynn's "I told you so," proved more irritating than John's. To Sharee, the day's emotional highs and lows had created a wave chart of exceptional scope.

Lynn climbed into the car and snapped her seatbelt closed. "And we're going to run into a flower shop. It's on the way to the next bridal shop."

"Ahhh. What are you doing to me?"

"Making you responsible for this wedding. Did you think you were going to just drop this on me with only two weeks to go? You and I are going to pick out flowers!"

At two o'clock, Sharee walked slump-shouldered to the car, and they drove to another flower shop. An hour later, she skipped out, Lynn skipping beside her.

"Such nice people." She was gushing but couldn't help it. Something accomplished. Finally! "And a great deal on the flowers." She grabbed Lynn. They danced and hugged.

"Next, the card shop." Lynn said as she pulled onto US 19.

"What? You didn't say anything about a card shop."

"Invitations. Whatever am I going to do with you? And don't think we've finished dress shopping." Lynn tossed her blonde hair. "I know of three more shops in the Tampa Bay area—and I'm sure there are ones I don't know. We'll find something."

"Now you sound like me! Something. I don't want just something."

"Ha! I knew you'd come to your senses. You want to be beautiful just like every other bride." She patted her own stylish clothing. "You have to have something chic, Sharee. You want to look great. For John. For the Lord."

"But is it out there? I'm too short, Lynn, and you know it. There's nothing made for five foot two brides."

"We'll find something beautiful. Don't worry."

Sharee sat back and closed her eyes against the lights of the fourth bridal shop. Her arms and legs melted into the chair. Even with the euphoria of ordering the invitations and being assured they would be ready by the end of the week—she would hand most of them out in church Sunday, others Monday at work—the problem with the dress overshadowed all.

Lynn and the bridal assistant were scouring the store for anything in the style she wanted, anything that could be altered in the short amount of time they had.

Lord, lead us to the right dress. She offered up the hundredth prayer today.

Her phone's melody sounded, and she fumbled in her purse. John hadn't called since early this morning, but he'd be wondering how the shopping was going. She glanced at the phone's display, and her heart skittered. No name. Was this starting again?

"Hello?"

"Hello, Sharee? This is Lorraine."

Sharee frowned. "Who? Oh. Mrs. Wicker. Hello." The woman had her phone number? John must have given it to her, but why...

Lynn peered at her from a rack of dresses. She lifted a manicured brow.

"It's Lorraine," the woman on the other end said. "Call me Lorraine."

Sharee straightened in the chair. "Of course. Lorraine."

"I wanted to talk to you. Can we meet today for a short time, possibly this afternoon?"

"This afternoon?" Sharee stared at Lynn, who put a dress back on the rack and walked to her side. "I'm sorry, Mrs... Lorraine. Today is very full. Perhaps if—"

"But I'm in town today. I can't make it back anytime soon. Don't you have some time later today?"

Sharee hesitated. "I really am busy, but...You're in town, you say?"

"If you have a half hour."

"A half hour?"

Lynn scowled and mouthed. "Not before 5:00."

Sharee raised her hands and shrugged. The woman was being insistent. What could she do?

"Could you wait until 5:30? Like I said, it's a hectic day."

"That's fine. 5:30 will work. Please don't tell John. I'd like to keep this between us."

"Mrs. Wicker, I don't keep things from John. We..."

"I know you're planning the wedding, and he shouldn't have to worry about me or how I'm doing. So please, can't you keep this between us? At least, until after we talk. Then you can decide."

Sharee put her hands to her head. So, Lorraine didn't want to upset John. The subject then would not be an easy one. *This is not what I need right now, Lord.* Guilt curled around her like a snake. How could she deny this woman a few minutes?

"Okay. He's picking me up at 7:30 for dinner. I'll need to get back in time to dress."

"Thank you. You don't know how much this means to me."

"I know a café where we could meet."

"Oh, no. I thought we could meet at the church. I know where that is. At the parking lot in the back."

"The church? Well, okay. That will be on my way home."

Lynn pointed to her watch.

"I'll see you at 5:30, Lorraine. Goodbye." Sharee ended the call and tilted her head at Lynn. "What do you think she wants?"

"Who knows? Do you suppose John told them about the new wedding plans?"

"Yes, she knew; and they were on his list to call, anyway. But I can't imagine what she wants to talk about. I wish I didn't have to go." Sharee dropped her gaze.

"What's wrong now?"

"That's pretty selfish, isn't it? Here am I planning my wedding, while she…"

Lynn touched her arm. "Don't feel guilty. You came into John's life long after Janice died. Lorraine can't blame you for anything. Don't blame yourself."

"I know. I'm sure they feel like I'm taking John away, though."

"In a sense, you are; but it's time—time for them to move on, as hard as that is. And time for them to let go of John."

Sharee turned off US 19, feeling the tightness across her shoulders. What could Lorraine want? She started to call John but stopped. No, she'd given her word. No matter what the woman wanted, they'd both be on their way in a half hour. She would give that much time.

Jesus, you know I need your help with this.

Sharee eased into a parking place at the back of the church and climbed from the SUV. Her gaze drifted over the lot, the office, the fellowship hall behind her. No one was here, which made sense. Pastor Alan left at five, and some days he wasn't in the office at all. He and Daneen visited individuals at the hospital or worked with other non-profits helping the indigent and doing counseling.

The hum of a car engine caught her attention. Lorraine's blue Ford rounded the corner. Sharee straightened and waved.

The car swung her way, picking up speed. It took two full seconds before the warning surfaced. Had the woman not seen her? Had she hit the accelerator by mistake?

Sharee scooted sideways. The car swerved and sped straight for her. Behind the windshield, Lorraine's face knotted into an ugly mask.

Sharee jumped farther from the car's path, but it veered in her direction again. The blue hood filled her vision. She dove sideways, hitting the grass and rolling out of the way. Brakes squealed, and Sharee climbed to her feet. She jerked her head around.

Lorraine had stopped right before slamming into the fellowship hall. Now, the car jerked into reverse. Sharee gaped at her. What was happening?

The Ford lurched forward again. Heart thudding, Sharee jumped for the small tree near the entry way. The car skidded past her, missing her by inches. Brakes shrieked. She didn't wait this time but ran the other way, across the parking lot toward the field.

The screech of tires reached her. The woman was trying to kill her! She needed cover. Fast. The large pine and the bleachers offered the only hope. She raced past the tree and rounded the bleachers. The engine's roar grew. She bounded onto the steps and ran up them.

The car slammed the side of the bleachers and knocked her sideways onto the seats. She tried to break her fall, but her hands shot uselessly between the seats. Her head slammed against the metal. Pain seared her head and body. She drew in deep breaths and didn't move.

The bleachers rocked and sang. Panic shot through her, and she shoved herself upright. Lorraine stood on the bottom step. Behind her, the car door stood open.

Sharee rocketed to her feet and swayed as her head spun. "What are you doing?"

"You're not marrying John. Do you hear me? He loves Janice. He always has." Lorraine jumped over the next step.

Sharee backed away, along the bleacher seat. "You're crazy."

The woman jumped the next seat and dove at her. A hand clawed at Sharee's arm, but Sharee twisted out of her reach, and Lorraine grasped air. The woman's foot shot between the seats, and she fell.

Silence settled around them. Lorraine groaned and tried to roll over. Sharee eased around her and ran down the steps. At the last step, she glanced over her shoulder and saw Lorraine pull her leg free and push to a standing position. Leaping down, she raced past the blue car. The engine still ran. She stopped.

Behind her, the metal stairs screeched. Sharee whipped into the driver's seat, slammed and locked the doors. Her hands shook as she pulled the phone from her pocket. She punched 911. Her hands shook, her sight was fuzzy.

Help, Lord.

The door locks clicked, and the door flew open. Lorraine grabbed her arm and the back of her shirt, yanking her out of the car. The phone flew from Sharee's hand. Her feet hit the ground, and the woman pummeled her over the head.

Sharee threw her arms up for protection. "Stop! What are you doing? Stop!" She dropped to her knees.

"You'll never marry him! You hear me?"

The pounding slowed, and Sharee thrust herself away and shot to her feet. Lorraine charged her. Sharee sidestepped, ducking under the woman's grasping arms, and Lorraine slipped on the ground.

Sharee's eyes darted toward the office. She had to get away; she'd never win a battle with this woman. "Janice is dead. You can't bring her back."

Lorraine's face skewed. "But you won't take her place! You're not marrying John. You're not going to Indonesia. That was their plan."

"John and Janice never planned to go to Indonesia. They…."

"Shut-up! Don't tell me what they planned." Her eyes flicked over Sharee with disgust. "I don't know why John picked you. You're nothing like Janice. She was gorgeous and tall and blonde. You're nothing."

Sharee sucked in her breath, but her eyes went past the other woman. *The pond.* If she could get to the pond. Lorraine couldn't swim. The pond, the cypress trees, the road behind them all offered avenues of escape.

"Does Mr. Wicker know you're here?"

"Of course not. He thinks it's good John is remarrying." Her face screwed into an ugly sneer. "John told us before he left for Indonesia. I wanted to kill him. I tried when he got home. I told Tom I was going to see a friend, but I drove over here from Orlando. With the GPS, it was easy to find his place; but then I realized *you* were the real problem. So I found out where you lived and tried again. But I barely hit you." She stopped and eyed Sharee. "You escaped the next time, too. You've been lucky until now."

Sharee straightened. "I haven't been lucky. God has protected me."

"Don't talk about God. Janice believed in God and look what happened."

"Things are not perfect just because you believe. This world is messed up, and—"

"You think I care about that?" Lorraine's eyes blazed. "I stopped caring three years ago! When John called last night, I knew I couldn't wait any longer."

"This won't help. This won't bring Janice back. It will just—"

Lorraine lunged forward.

Sharee ducked beneath her outstretched hand and dashed for the pond. Could she make it? Would she—A hand grabbed her shoulder and spun her around. Her foot slipped and she fell.

The woman sprang on top of her, straddling her, battering her around the head and shoulders. Sharee tried to heave her off, but Lorraine was too big, too heavy. She tucked her head away from the pounding fists, reached out and grabbed Lorraine's waist. The woman fought to keep her balance, but Sharee yanked harder, and Lorraine toppled forward.

Sharee scrambled to her feet. Her breathing ratcheted, but the pond's closeness generated a surge of energy. She ran. Pounding feet let her know of Lorraine's approach. She swerved right around a small oak and several bushes.

The cement path and the pond's edge dropped right into the water. If she didn't want to break a leg, she'd have to jump out as far as possible. She heard Lorraine shout behind her and leaped into the watery darkness.

&

Sharee hit the water and her feet slammed into the mucky bottom. Her legs buckled. She sat down hard, the water—barely two feet deep—lapping at her chin. Had she broken a leg?

Lorraine skidded to a stop. To her right, on the bank, an alligator rose and hissed. Lorraine jerked in its direction, emitted a squeal, stepped backward and plunged into the pond. The gator scrambled forward and dove into the water, also.

Sharee's heart jumped. Would it swim away or attack one of them? It was small—about four feet. It shouldn't hurt them, but something hard lodged in her throat. She didn't want to swim into the deep and chance it.

Lorraine rose on all fours then struggled to her feet. Her head jerked back and forth. The green pond water ran down both sides of her head. Sharee stood up. They were feet apart, and the inky water washed against their knees. Lorraine's face drew into a sneer, and she threw herself at Sharee.

Sharee screamed and tumbled back into the water. The woman

was on top of her, grabbing her head, forcing it down. Tearing at the claw-like hands, Sharee tried to push free, but her feet slid in the mud, and her head plunged beneath the surface.

The woman's weight held Sharee down. She ripped at the woman's hands, bucked up, and tried to dislodge her.

Something hard slammed her side, and the woman's weight fell away. Sharee jerked her head up and gasped for breath. She twisted her head around. What...? A wheelchair lay on its side in the water.

A wheel and Bruce's head showed just above the surface. She staggered to her feet.

"Bruce!"

Her feet slipped in the mud, but she stumbled to the wheelchair. It had fallen on its side, and Bruce held tightly to the wheel, holding his head above water. She grabbed the chair's arms and tried to right it, but its weight combined with Bruce's held it down.

Her heart double-timed. "I can't get this up, Bruce. Can you get out?"

"My leg's caught, but I'm okay. Get Lorraine." He jerked his head toward the deeper water.

Sharee glanced in that direction. Lorraine's arms thrashed in the water, her eyes wide and panic-ridden. She shifted her focus back to Bruce and shoved at the chair again.

"Sharee, get her."

"She can stand up."

"No, it drops off."

Sharee's feet sank deeper in the mud. She fought with the wheelchair, her breath hammering.

"I can hold myself up." Bruce used one arm to push against the muck. "She can't swim. Get her."

Sharee planted her foot against the side of the chair and tried to lift it, but her foot slipped beneath the wheel, burying in the mud. Her heart thudded. They'd both drown this way. She fought to pull her foot free.

"Help!" Lorraine's cry pierced her concentration.

"Sharee!" Bruce's voice came impatient and edgy. "She'll die. She doesn't know the Lord."

Sharee threw another look at Lorraine. The woman slapped the water in panic and disappeared beneath the surface.

"Sharee! Go! Save her!"

She dropped the wheelchair, threw herself past him and into the deeper water. She dove into the murky blackness, feeling around. Nothing. She forced her eyes open. There. She grabbed a handful of clothes and kicked upward.

When she broke the surface, she gasped for air. Lorraine hung limp beside her. She found an arm and slipped hers under it, lifting the woman's head from the water. She'd never taken life-saving courses but knew enough to keep the woman's back to her. They both dropped below the surface again, and a surge of panic overtook her. She kicked harder, broke the surface again and struggled toward the embankment.

Someone reached past her and helped pull Lorraine from her grasp. Spitting dirt and water from her own mouth, Sharee climbed from the pond and collapsed onto the grass. Pastor Alan slipped down next to her.

"Are you okay?"

"Yes. But get Bruce. Help Bruce." She waved back toward the pond, heaving, trying to catch her breath.

Pastor Alan scrambled to his feet, stepping over both women. Sharee rose to her knees looking at Lorraine. Was she breathing? She put her ear to her mouth but heard nothing. She looked at her chest. Nothing.

Do CPR.

CPR? How long had it been? Compression or mouth to mouth? Her own breathing was ragged. She leaned forward, put one hand on top of the other and began chest compressions.

Daneen dropped down beside her. "Is she breathing?"

"I...I don't think so."

"Okay. You're exhausted. Let me do this." She nudged Sharee out of the way.

Sharee staggered to her feet, turned and watched in horror as Pastor Alan wrestled to pull the wheelchair from the mud and the water. Only the wheel remained above the surface. He grabbed Bruce's shoulder and lifted it and his head out of the water.

"No!" Sharee ran forward and splashed into the water. They fought the weight and the water until another set of hands joined theirs. The three lifted the chair and pulled Bruce's body free.

"Bruce!" Her voice was high and uneven. "Bruce!"

John and Alan staggered back to shore and laid him on the ground. Pastor Alan bent over him. He listened for his breathing then started chest compressions.

John pulled her away. His arms encircled her as they watched. Behind them, they heard coughing, someone spitting up...and, in the distance, sirens.

Chapter 15

Hundreds came for Bruce's funeral. The road to the cemetery narrowed as cars parked and lined each side. Family and friends stood close to the grave. Others, drawn by the media coverage that highlighted Bruce's wheelchair race to save Sharee's life, circled the area.

The bright May morning, with its singing and preaching and talk of resurrection, reminded Sharee of Easter mornings as a child. She stood next to Bruce's parents. They had come to stand beside her—as if they would support her.

An impossible scenario. The worst grief in the world, she'd always heard, was to lose a child, no matter the age. Yet, the comfort of God, the presence of the Holy Spirit, surrounded the Tomlin family. She could see it in their faces.

A fog had surrounded her every day since Bruce had died, and now it settled more heavily, graying the sunlit service.

She'd let Bruce die.

Pain spread through every cell in her body. She couldn't talk about it. The guilt, the pain. Not to John or her parents or to God.

Bruce's friends and relatives stepped forward to tell how much Bruce had meant to them— emphasizing the funny, touching, and compassionate things he had done in their lives.

Her thoughts drifted. The woman had planned to kill her, and now she was alive while Bruce… Sharee closed her eyes. The world swam. She swayed.

John's arm came around her, but she straightened, stiffening before he could say anything. Tears threatened every time she let his concern or his tenderness touch her. But it was because of her that he'd lost someone else for whom he cared, and she wondered if he blamed her as much as she blamed herself.

Pastor Alan stepped forward and took the microphone. Behind him, the sun radiated, shooting out fingers of light around his head as if he were an angel. Sharee lowered hers. Angels and demons and God—did she believe anymore? Did she want to?

They all listened to Pastor Alan's sermon. From behind, Marci Thornton touched her arm. Sharee glanced her way. Stephen stood beside her, holding Elizabeth. Marci neither smiled nor said anything, but for one instant Sharee thought, she knows.

The second thought came as quick. Of course, she knows. That boy in the accident three years ago. She closed her eyes again. Love and pain. Life and death.

When she opened them, Miss Eleanor smiled at her—a concerned smile. Yesterday, she had come with Pastor Alan to Sharee's apartment; and in the midst of turmoil and numerous visitors, she sat on Sharee's couch and quietly prayed.

"You know," Pastor Alan's voice broke into her thoughts, "I don't believe this happened to Bruce without—without Bruce having an idea that it might. A few weeks ago, he asked if he could sing again. He hadn't sung since his accident. That night he sang, 'It is Well with My Soul.' The power of God was strong that night. Later, Bruce talked with me about what it would be like to actually be in God's presence…about being in heaven…as if he knew…"

Mrs. Tomlin's soft cry broke across the gravesite. Pastor Alan looked at her, his eyes filled with compassion. He glanced around at all those standing close then studied the many others behind them.

"God's Word says that there is no greater love than for a man to lay down his life for his friend. Bruce did that for Sharee. It also says that we are to love our enemies; and in this case, Bruce went beyond our natural abilities to love to give someone else not just a chance to live, but a chance to live forever—a chance for salvation. We all talk about being like Jesus, but this…this was Jesus in action.

"'What things were gain to me,' Paul says in the scriptures, 'those I count lost for Christ.' Bruce has lost his worldly life to gain eternity. He has graduated from this earth. We don't think about the fact that God promises a place without sorrow, pain or death. That place is not here, but it is real. The place called heaven. That is where Bruce is now.

"Jesus bought us entry into heaven. He bought it with his death, burial, and resurrection. He paid the price. All we need to do is believe and accept what Jesus has done. Then we, too, can be in heaven when we die.

"And Bruce would want you to accept this gift. He wants every one of you in heaven with him." The Pastor paused. A breeze, soft and finger-trailing, slid over the crowd. "All you need to do is believe and accept Jesus' sacrifice for you. If you would like to do this now, bow your head with me. Let's pray."

෴

Sharee stepped out of the SUV, trying not to look at the field and the pond. The church office was straight ahead, the work buildings to its right. John's truck was parked a few spaces down from hers. She took a long breath. She hadn't seen him for four weeks. She didn't want to see him now.

The leave of absence Downtown Ministries gave her had ended Friday. She'd gone home to her parents for those four weeks, but even there the wounds bled. John had called every day, but talking to him proved hard. His phone calls were full of encouragement, full of references to God. She just wasn't there yet. Maybe her faith would never be the same. She just didn't want to hurt his. They both sensed her drawing away, yet all their conversations were similar to the one they'd had yesterday.

"Sharee, it's okay to be angry, to hurt, but you can't run from God. He won't let you." John's words came with a gentle entreaty and with a soft laugh. "I know, darling, believe me. I was there. You know. When can I see you?"

"I told you, I just need to…to work through this on my own."

"You are tearing me apart, girl." Then the quiet settled between them. "You are tearing us apart. Don't do this."

But she couldn't get a grip on the emotions, and she dare not let her thoughts or feelings surface. They would overwhelm her.

When he called this morning, he told her he was taking her to dinner. No arguing. He'd drive to Ocala. He thought she was still there, still at her parents, and she didn't correct that thought. But she couldn't do dinner. No tête-à-tête. No being alone someplace where her emotions might prove uncontrollable. She wasn't ready. Why couldn't he understand that?

She put her shoulders back and walked toward the work buildings. Better here. Better to meet him here and let him know she didn't want to see him again…for a while. At least, no dates, no…whatever. Seeing him here, on her terms, this once. Then not again. Unexpected pain tore with sharp fingers through her. A second later, she blinked hard and forced herself not to cry.

The door stood open. She took a step inside. Quiet and shadowed and cool. Something touched her. Peace?

A loud ringing caused her to jump. She twisted her head back and forth. John's neat workbench sat on her left, Pastor Alan's jumbled bench to her right. The ringing continued, and then she saw the phone on John's bench. She walked forward and picked it up just as it stopped ringing. The caller ID showed China Summers. The phone's face went blank, and Sharee put the phone down. A moment later, she heard a beep, and she picked it up again.

A picture showed on the phone's face. Sharee stared. China sat on a stone wall wearing a peasant dress, its hem hiked halfway up her thighs. The bodice of the dress had slipped down on one side to expose her bare shoulder. Sharee bit her lip, swallowed again, and fought the emotions rising in her. She started to sling the phone as far away as possible then stopped. The rising emotions, the frustration, threatened to bring the tears she'd tried so hard to keep under control these past weeks.

In slow motion, she put the phone down, turned, and walked out the door. Just leave, Sharee. Just leave. Her legs felt heavy. The car appeared farther away than when she came. As she reached it, she heard her name.

No. She couldn't face him now. She fumbled with the car door then yanked it open. A hand slammed it shut.

"Where are you going?" John's anger hit her, but as she looked up into his eyes, so did the pain. He caught her arm. "It's been almost a month. Were you just going to leave?"

She tried to pull free, but he held on. She fought against his hand, against his eyes, against his concern.

"Sharee." A guttural sound, almost broken.

"China left you a message." Tears started with the words. She tried to tug free again.

"What?" Complete bafflement.

"Yes. She sent you a picture." She wanted to lash out at him, to ask how many other pictures the girl had sent; but she couldn't. Maybe it was better this way. "John, I...this won't work."

"What won't work? What are you talking about?"

"Us. I...it's just...it's not going to work."

His fingers tightened on her arm. "Has something else happened?"

"No, I ...it's..."

"Do you think I'll let you walk away without a better explanation than that?" When she said nothing, he brushed his hands up and down her arms. "Let me help. Please."

"What can you do? I don't feel anything. I'm too dead." The tears mushroomed, spilling forth as her words broke. She dropped her head.

He tugged her to him, wrapped his arms around her. "It's all right. It's all right to cry. To hurt. It will get better." After a few minutes, she gained some control and pulled back. She had to leave. He was weakening her resolve.

"I can't do this yet. I need to be alone."

"You've been alone. You need to talk to someone."

"No. I haven't. I've been with Mom and Dad until last week. I need some time."

"Until last week? You've been back a week?" And when she said nothing, "You've been home, and you didn't tell me."

"John, please…"

"Please what?"

"We can talk later. Just give me time."

The dark eyes searched hers. His mouth twisted. "How long?"

"A couple of weeks. Give me a couple of weeks."

"A couple more, you mean. If I had my way, I'd take you to the mountains or some place. Just the two of us." He tilted his head to catch her gaze. "We could get married like we were going to and just leave for awhile."

"No, I…I have to get back to work. I can't."

"Can't? Or won't?"

"John." She prayed for the first time in four weeks. *Please, Lord, let him let me go.*

"All right. Two weeks, that's all. I will camp on your doorstep if you even try to stretch this longer."

She breathed a sigh of relief and stepped free of his arms.

Pastor Alan watched through the window as Sharee walked across the parking lot and headed for his office. John had said he'd given her two weeks, and those two weeks were up.

When he'd stepped into Alan's office a few days ago, he'd paced back and forth before stopping and meeting Alan's look.

"I'm concerned about Sharee. I can't seem to get past her reserve right now. The wall she's put up. We haven't talked much these last few weeks, and I've seen her only once since the funeral. She's making excuses not to see me. Of course, we agreed to put off the wedding. We couldn't go through with that so soon after Bruce's death." He began to pace again. "We've talked on the phone, but she's resistant to any help I want to give."

"Is she feeling guilty about Bruce's death?"

"I'm sure she is, but she won't discuss it. She's angry, too." John stared out the window. "I know the signs."

"Do you suppose that's why she won't talk to you? She's feeling guilty about Bruce's death—and doubly where you're concerned? How are you doing, by the way?"

John ran a hand through his hair. "It's hard. Hard to think about Bruce. He'd become a real friend. But it's different this time. Different from when Janice died. I've made peace with God's sovereignty. I can't say I wasn't angry for a while."

Alan nodded. He'd noticed that. Noticed, also, when it left.

"I guess, at first, I wasn't what Sharee needed. So, when she kept putting off seeing me that first week or two, I wasn't upset. I tried to help, but I was dealing with my own stuff. I should have been there for her. Earlier. I was almost glad when she went home with her parents. But within a week, I knew. She was having a harder time than I was, and that turned me around."

"But she still won't see you?"

His hand pushed the hair back again. "I wondered, you know, if she blamed me. Why didn't I see that Janice's mom was so…unbalanced after Janice died? Sharee went through a lot. If I'd suspected…"

"The blame game never ends. And never accomplishes anything. Don't take that up."

"Sharee needs help, Alan, but I can't reach her. I know the barrenness that anger and unforgiveness can bring into your life. I've come to a point where I trust in God's goodness, his righteousness. I don't always like what God…allows…but I trust. That's something Sharee taught me." The dark brows drew together. "And now she's struggling. Maybe she'll talk to you. In fact, I'll insist. I gave her two weeks to be alone, and they're almost up. If she doesn't want me parked on her doorstep, then she'll need to talk to you."

So, she'd come today. Coerced. Not a good way to start a counseling session.

As she crossed the parking lot, she glanced toward the sanctuary and stopped. China stood close to John, talking. The girl had shown up a short time ago and planted herself at John's side. John brushed paint on the large wooden doors that fronted the church, and China leaned toward him, laughing. Alan wondered how it made Sharee feel— seeing John and China together. Would it spark something to make her reach out to John?

A moment later, she turned away and headed to the office. She didn't see John's glance in her direction or the way his eyes followed her. Alan opened the door for her before she reached it.

"John said you'd like to talk to me." Her voice sounded stiff, wary.

He nodded. He indicated his back office and moved around to sit at his desk. Her reserve and the awkwardness she exhibited were alien to their relationship.

"Yes, I did. How are you doing?"

She took a seat across from him. "Okay. I'm getting there, I guess."

The listless, monotone of her voice bothered him. He waited a minute, studying her. "You've been through a lot. No one expects you to get through something like this in a hurry."

"Yeah."

"And how's John doing?" He knew, but he wanted to hear it from her.

"Right now? I think he's doing okay. But he and Bruce had developed a close friendship. I don't know how he feels about me being responsible for Bruce's death. He mentioned once that he feels responsible himself." She shook her head. "You know how he is. He said he blames himself for putting me in danger, for Bruce dying, because it was his mother-in-law. His *former* mother-in-law. He says he should have known. Of course, that's crazy. *She's* to blame."

Pastor Alan leaned toward her and sent a silent prayer to God. He'd heard the bitterness. "Sharee." He kept his voice low, soft. "At some point, you will have to find it within yourself to forgive her."

Sharee's face flushed. "She tried to kill me, to kill John. She killed Bruce."

"Did she? We're all blaming ourselves. I got to the church about the same time as Bruce did that day, but I stopped to call 911. I should have been with Bruce when he went barreling down the path to save you. He's the one who figured out what was going on."

"You said that before, but it didn't make sense."

"Daneen and I received a call from a woman saying her son had threatened to commit suicide. She wanted us to come talk to him. Bruce was in the office, and since he had dealt with thoughts of suicide himself, he offered to go with us. We pulled up at the house and knocked on the door, but no one answered. Then John pulled up. He'd gotten a call for him to meet us there. Well, a light went off in Bruce's head. Sure, someone would call for me and Daneen to come talk to them if they were feeling suicidal, but no one would call John. I mean, most people outside the church think of him as the maintenance man. They don't know the call God has put on his life. So, it didn't make sense to Bruce. He wanted to know why anyone would want us all away from the church."

"And he thought of me. Why?"

"Because you were the one targeted most times. Because someone had gone to the trouble of making sure John was out of the way. Bruce said instantly that you must be in trouble—and that you were probably at the church."

"Why did he think that?"

"Because Daneen and I were called away. No one would be there. I'd never seen him move so fast. He was back in his van before John and I figured out all that he was saying. We'd come in different cars. Bruce preferred to drive his, you know. It was equipped for him. We raced back to the church. Bruce got here first. He was out of the van, in his wheelchair, when I drove up. He yelled for me to call 911, and like an idiot, I took the time to call. I should have gone with him."

"The police said he flew right off the path and into the water to knock her off me."

"Yes."

"That was amazing."

"You were both close to the edge or it wouldn't have made any difference. As it was, it was a miracle."

She put her head down. "A miracle? For me, but not for Bruce. I...it hurts to think about it."

"If John hadn't insisted we build that path around the field for him to practice racing that wheelchair. If it hadn't climbed the hill to the edge of the pond, he'd never have made it to save you. He flew up that path and launched himself and that wheelchair right into the water. It was a miracle."

Tears flooded her eyes. He reached across and patted her hand.

"Sharee, it's all right to cry. It's all right to be sad and mad and wretched, but it's not all right to stay there."

Sharee covered her face with her hands. Her voice broke as she said, "I left him. I let go. To get her."

He rose, came from behind the desk and touched her shoulder. "You did what you had to do. You had to make a choice. Two people needed you. Bruce was right. You needed to save her—in more ways than one. It's why you need to forgive her. She needs to know God."

"I can't stand to think of it." She cried into her palms. "I can't."

Alan bent down and took her hands from her face and looked at her. "Sharee, you can. God will do that for you. You need to remember what you told us that day. You did what Bruce told you to do. Ultimately, it was what God wanted you to do."

She shook her hands free. "How can you say that?"

"You know how I can say it. It's true."

Daneen had slipped into the room. She touched Sharee's shoulder.

Sharee began to shake. She covered her face once more. Sobs racked her. Daneen bent close and held her. Alan sat back and waited. In a few moments, the sobs ceased. He handed her a bunch of tissue from the box on his desk.

"You can say you're angry with Lorraine, but, actually, you're angry at God. Aren't you?"

She blew her nose and looked at him.

"Face it, Sharee. God didn't do what you wanted. He could have saved them both. And neither you nor I know why he didn't."

Sharee put her hands over her ears. "It hurts. It hurts too much."

"Let me tell you this. Bruce prayed every day for you and John. For your safety, for the ministry that God has set before you, that Satan's schemes would be foiled. And physically, he exercised every day. He raced that crazy wheelchair around here all the time. We all thought he was going to race in some Paralympic games, but the race was different from that. He raced to save your life. The real exercise, though, was spiritual. He sought his Creator like he never had before." He let the words hang and squatted down in front of her. "I have to ask you a question, Sharee. What kind of Christian are you?"

He felt the movement from his wife and turned his head. "Careful," she mouthed.

"Pray," he mouthed back. She nodded. He lifted his own silent prayer.

"Sharee, are you going to let Bruce's sacrifice be for nothing? Do you remember telling me what you said to John a few months ago? You told John that if anything happened to you, like what happened to Janice that he was not to get mad at God again, not to leave the ministry, but to go on serving God? You said that the God we serve is worthy of that kind of love and devotion. Do you remember that?"

"Y...yes."

"Well, how easy was that to say? Without thinking that you might be the one to face such a situation?"

Sharee's eyes closed.

"If you don't forgive Lorraine, if you don't forgive yourself, and don't forgive God because He didn't do what you wanted, then you will destroy your ministry. Oh, you and John might still get married, still go to Indonesia, but the joy and the love of the ministry will be gone. John might not even realize for a while that you've changed, but you will know...inside."

"Alan," his wife warned.

He didn't look up. "She's not a child, Daneen. She knows her God—and the Word. Don't you, Sharee?"

Sharee dropped her head.

"But you've never had to face this type of reality before. You have a choice to make. We'll still love you, you know that. John will still love you. God will still love you, but if you make the wrong choice, your soul will be torn."

Her head rose.

"You have a choice," he repeated. "Don't worry about the feelings. I didn't say you had to feel like it. I said you had to make a choice. The feelings will follow. Some day when you least expect it, God will open your heart and pour in the feelings."

"I know." Her voice was low. "I know that."

"Sharee, forgive yourself. It was Bruce's choice, after all. His sacrifice. Think about that."

Daneen took her husband's hand and indicated the door to the outer office. "Give her time," she mouthed to him.

He rose. His hand brushed Sharee's shoulder. They moved through to the outer office.

❧

"God, where were you?" The cry escaped her mouth almost before the other two left.

I was with you. Not words aloud, but a still, small voice—somewhere inside.

"But I left Bruce, and he died."

I was with him.

Tears spilled down her cheeks. Was this bitterness and anger she felt so dangerous? "How can I forgive her? How can I forgive myself?"

No answer, but she knew. Alan was right. She knew she had to take the first step but didn't want to do it. She remembered John saying how he had not wanted to forgive Dean.

How arrogant was I that day, Lord, because I was able to forgive Dean, and he wasn't? And now? How am I going to forgive her? Why should I forgive her? She tried to kill me, to kill John. Her heart felt like a hard ball within her chest.

When you stand praying, forgive...

I don't want to. She sighed. How many times had John teased her about being stubborn? She'd never thought she was until now.

"She doesn't deserve forgiveness." Her heart heaved, moved inside her chest. Neither do I. Her mind went back to Pastor Alan's sermon. Bruce died for her.

I died for her.

Shocked, she sat upright. Jesus died for Lorraine Wicker—just as he'd died for her or Bruce or John.

She took a trembling breath. *I don't feel it, but okay, Lord. Okay. I'm willing.* Something hard and ugly gave way inside her. She put a hand to her chest and sat in silence for a while.

Looking up to the ceiling, she took another long breath. "Forgive me for being angry, bitter, and unforgiving. Help me come back to you."

The air softened around her, like butterfly wings. Tears pooled again. She sat still, feeling Him speak to her without words. *Love,* she thought with recognition. *Love... mercy... grace.* She lowered her head and cried.

The pain still simmered inside, but with a difference. She knew she'd have to this again. Each time she thought about it, she'd have to forgive again. Fear flew through her. What if I can't? What if I don't want to—tomorrow or the next day? The depth of her powerlessness startled her.

"Lord, I'm willing, but I need help."

She felt the butterfly wings again, and she caught her hands to her chest as if holding onto the Spirit inside. Another sound came—from the doorway. She turned.

John stood there. His gaze met hers, and in one step, he crossed the distance between them and pulled her into his arms.

Chapter 16

The wedding was, after all, not as rushed as Marilyn Jones had feared, or as hasty as Lynn's nightmares. Sharee stared at her reflection in the mirror. She and John and the congregation had needed time to process Bruce's death, to allow for healing, and to laugh again.

She had circled the date on the calendar—Saturday, September 15.

Now, she stood perspiring and nervous in front of this full-length mirror at the church. Ryann and Abbey brought the wedding dress over. It slid over her head and down past her shoulders.

"Wait, wait!" Abbey said. "Be careful, Ryann."

They settled the strapless gown around her, and Ryann held the back closed. Abbey pulled up the long zipper.

Marci and John's sister, Alexis, had left earlier to finish their own dressing. Sharee glanced at her mom who stood by the mirror, tears welling in her eyes.

Sharee touched her arm. "Are you all right, Mom?"

Her mother swiped at the tears and smiled. "You're so beautiful. I can't believe this day is here. You're getting married."

"I know." She swirled around, the gown's A-line skirt billowing around her. "But could you find out where the thermostat is for this room and turn it cooler?"

Her mom wiped her eyes. "Yes. Okay. But you look so beautiful. John won't be able to take his eyes off you."

"They say all brides look beautiful, just like all babies do."

"Tell her she looks beautiful, girls." Her mom headed toward the door, and Ryann and Abbey murmured their agreement.

"You do, and the dress is gorgeous, too," Ryann eyed the yards of white material highlighted with lace and beads and sequins.

Lynn rushed in with her flowers, followed quickly by Alexis. They both stopped and stared at Sharee.

"You look amazing!" Lynn said.

John's sister gave her a big hug. "You really do. Wait until John sees you."

"And look at your flowers. I thought they'd never get here. I had to

send Ryann's father over with the men's boutonnieres, and Daneen took
the bridesmaids' flowers to them. Just look how beautiful yours turned
out." She held up the bouquet of white roses. Accents of silver and plum
ribbon twisted here and there among them.

Sharee held her hand out, taking them and lifting them to her nose.
"Oh, they are beautiful and smell so good. You've done a wonderful job,
Lynn. Everything is perfect." She held the flowers aside and hugged her.

"Careful with the dress!" Abbey said, and she took the flowers from
Sharee's hand. "You still have about fifteen or twenty minutes to go."

"Yes," Lynn said, "and I have a lot to do." Suddenly she stopped.
"You did do the something borrowed, something blue thing, right? For
good luck? Well, if not, too late now. Oh, and here's a box that someone
dropped off yesterday. I forgot to give it to you. Another wedding present.
You can open it later. Gotta run!" She slipped back through the door,
pulling John's sister after her.

"Oh!" Sharee's hand flew to her mouth. "I've...I've forgotten...one
thing. Ryann, bring my purse, please." As Ryann went to get her purse,
Sharee glanced at the tag on the box. From the Intercoastal Hospital Staff
on 2-West. Sharee's eyes widened.

She remembered the note that had come from Cindy after Bruce's
death. The staff at the hospital had seen the whole thing on the news,
Cindy had written, including pictures of Sharee and John and the church.
She and the rest of the staff on 2-West had felt certain that during Sharee's
stay at the hospital that John was, in fact, on guard and protecting her from
something. They were glad she was safe but deeply sorry about her friend's
death. Their thoughts and prayers were with them. It was one of many
things at the time that had reduced her to tears.

"Abbey, would you open this for me?" She gave the box to her.

Ryann handed her purse to her.

Sharee took a blue sheet of paper from her purse and unfolded it. "Do
you remember this?"

Ryann put her hand to her mouth and giggled. "Yes. You've still got
it?"

"Still got it and him." Sharee grinned, showing it to Abbey. The
words "HE'S A KEEPER" were written in plain letters. "Now hurry before
Mother gets back. I need help. Lift up my gown, Abbey. Left side. Now,
Ryann, fold that up again. Smaller. Okay. Put it under the garter."

"What?" Ryann looked at her then started giggling. "You're gonna let
Mr. Jergenson find it, right? Oh, my goodness, when the others hear this!"

Heat rose in Sharee's face. "Don't tell anyone."

"Yea," Abbey chimed in. "Don't tell anyone." She winked at Ryann.

"Okay, girls, enough. Abbey, how are you coming with that box?"

Abbey tore the rest of the paper off and pulled the box open, lifting out a white foam protector. "Here, Ms. J, it's yours. You open it now."

Sharee pulled the foam pieces apart to reveal the fragile sculpture within. There were three figures on the stand. One was a knight with his sword drawn. He had his left arm held out to the side, shielding a young woman in a long white dress. A small gold crown sat on her head. In front of him was a fire-breathing dragon. She turned it over and read the inscription. *Sir Galahad and the dragon.*

Sharee laughed.

Ryann's nose wrinkled. "What's funny?"

"Nurse Cindy used to call John by that name—Sir Galahad."

"And he's protecting you?"

"Yeah, except..."

"Except?"

"It says Sir Galahad, but it could also represent Christ protecting his bride, the church. And the dragon is the devil."

"Like in Revelations?" Abbey asked. "Where Jesus comes riding out of heaven on a white horse?"

"Yes, something like that." She stared at the sculpture. "We have an enemy that seeks to kill, steal, and destroy, but we have a Savior that's greater."

She closed her eyes for a minute, thinking of Bruce. *Do I believe all that I say I do? Do I believe in heaven and eternity? If so, then Bruce is alive, in heaven.* She let the thought fill her.

She swallowed and handed the sculpture to Abbey. "Will you take this to Lynn and tell her I want it on the cake table? Don't let John see it. I want him to be surprised."

Abbey grinned at her. "Sure, Ms. J, I'll be back in a minute."

"Good." Sharee smiled at Ryann. "I'll go put on my necklace in the bathroom here. I need some quiet for a couple of minutes, but I'll be back so we can finish up with the veil and get my flowers." She gave the girl a hug and went down the hall.

Lynn had cordoned off the large lavatory near the dressing area, making it off-limits for all but the bride until the ceremony was over. Sharee hadn't thought much about it at the time, but now she hugged the privacy to her.

She stared at her reflection in the mirror on the wall. The dazed look engendered by Bruce's death had disappeared. God had worked in her heart. Not that there weren't times of sadness, but God had restored.

She slipped on the delicate diamond necklace John had given her. His strength and support, even as he went through his own process of grief, had buoyed her. She had almost shut him out after Bruce's death.

Thank you, Lord, for not letting that happen. Thank you for all you've done for us, and thank you for today.

She picked up the matching diamond earrings and leaned toward the mirror. Light hit one and sent a flash of color her way.

Behind her, the door to the bathroom swung open. China entered, closed the door, and then stood with her back to it. Surprise jolted through Sharee.

A soft smile curled China's lips. "Well, you won. The game is officially over."

Sharee turned. She hadn't thought of China in a long time. She hadn't seen her for months. "Game?"

"You'd really won before, you know."

"What are you talking about?"

"That night at the church when John spoke to the youth group. He told me that night, after the service, that he wanted me to stay away from him—and you."

Sharee noticed the sarcasm but said nothing.

"He thanked me for helping with Cooper while you were in the hospital but asked me not to come by again." Her smile lost its sweetness. "I'd made a copy of his key and stopped by to 'find my bracelet' after you went home from the hospital." The sarcasm was laced with hardness now. "You'll be glad to know he was the perfect gentleman. Well, not quite a gentleman. He threw me out."

Sharee lifted an eyebrow but kept herself from smiling. He'd told her more than once not to worry about China.

"Then after the funeral, you were so…well, not there, were you? I thought I might have another chance."

"And you sent him a picture on his phone, didn't you?"

"He told you? He blocked my access after that. He's really such a prude. So loyal to you." She made it sound as if it was something bad.

"China." Sharee held up her hand to stop her. "Why are you telling me this?"

"Because I thought you should know." She smiled sweetly and turned to go.

"Wait."

The girl held the door open but looked back at her.

"I've wondered about something. Did you talk to Dean at any time?

"The guy you were first engaged to?"

"Yes."

China looked as if she might not answer but then shrugged. "I heard Bruce on the phone with John one time. Bruce was picking up a ring for John—for you. The more I thought about it, the more I realized it had to be an engagement ring."

"And you told Dean?"

"Yeah. I thought it might create some problems. I didn't know if he still cared, but I remembered him being so possessive. So, I called at his work and left him a message."

"Interfering in people's lives is not a game, China."

The girl shrugged and turned to go again.

"Are you…do you…consider yourself a Christian?" Sharee asked.

China looked back at her. "I've been in church all my life."

"That's not what I asked."

Again, she shrugged. "I don't know. I don't know if it's that important."

Sharee stared. *Dear God, help her.* "If you had been in a garage all your life that would not make you a car. You are not a Christian because you go to church, you…"

"I know, I know. I need to accept Jesus as my savior. I know."

"I'll pray for you," Sharee said.

China laughed and let the door close after her.

Standing in the foyer of the church, her dad looked at her in a way that made her want to cry.

"Daddy…" Sharee started.

He put a finger to her lips. "It's okay, sweetheart. It's okay. It hurts. I can't say it doesn't, but it's right. He's a good man. He loves God. He loves you. What more could I ask? Your mother and I are very proud of you. You know that, don't you?"

She nodded. *If something doesn't change soon, though, I'll have tears down the front of this gown.* She clutched her flowers in tight hands.

Her father smiled, eyes alight. "Your mother cried most of last night, and then I had to throw water on her to get her up this morning."

"You what? You threw water on *mother*?"

Brian Jones grinned, looking, Sharee noticed, like John for a minute. "Yes."

"Oh, I bet you're in trouble."

"I am. Like the time we went horseback riding in Colorado, and your mother's horse took off up the mountain—in the wrong direction? When the crew finally caught up with her and got back to the ranch, it was almost dark. Remember how upset she was because we couldn't stop laughing?"

Sharee's heart lifted. "I do. Remember the time she thought she saw a bear when we camped at Juniper Springs in Ocala? We were telling everyone to watch out, when she realized it was only a sheepdog—that belonged to another camper."

"We've had fun."

"We have. Dad, I love you. I love Mom, too."

"And John?"

She smiled. "And John."

"I guess I finally have a son."

Sharee hugged him. "You do."

The music began. Lynn stepped from the corner where she'd been standing. "There's your cue, bride girl. Time to go."

Sharee and her father turned as Lynn pushed open the double doors of the sanctuary. They stepped forward. All the people in the church stood to their feet. The carpet had a white runner running the length of the aisle. Wine-colored rose petals were scattered along it. At the end, John and the groomsmen stood waiting.

Sharee's breath caught in her throat. Her legs began to shake. Her dad's hand tightened on her arm. She looked down the aisle, and everything blurred except John's face.

She saw his smile, but she couldn't move. Every muscle froze. She looked down. *Get your head up,* she seemed to hear Bruce say; and as she looked back down the aisle, she saw the warmth of John's eyes.

"I love you," he mouthed and put out his hand.

All her nervousness dropped away, and she walked down the aisle toward the man and the union for which she had waited thirty years.

♥

...To have and to hold...in sickness and in health...for richer, for poorer...forsaking all others... as long as you both shall live...

I hope you enjoyed reading *As Long as You Both Shall Live*.
Authors need and appreciate book reviews.
Could you please take a few minutes
to put a review on Amazon?

As Long As You Both Shall Live is Book 2 of the Dangerous Series.
You can find Book 1, *Amber Alert*, on Amazon in both print and E-book.
The last book in the series, *Looking for Justice*,
is also available on Amazon.
An excerpt from *Looking for Justice* follows.

Looking for Justice
Christian Contemporary Romance with Suspense

Chapter 1

Alexis Jergenson shoved open the door to the administration building of Appalachian Christian College and sprinted toward the stairwell. She'd left behind five years as a prosecuting attorney, and now faced her first day of class as *Professor* Jergenson.

Setting a precedent for tardiness had not entered her morning plans. The drive from her condominium to the college usually took twenty minutes, except for this morning's traffic gridlock caused by a four-car accident.

Gripping her purse in one hand and the handle of her briefcase in the other, Alexis took the short flight of stairs two at a time. As she rounded the corner to the second-floor landing, she crashed into a man coming from the other direction. Her purse and case flew from her hands.

He rocked backward and seized the handrail.

Alexis grabbed at his jacket to steady herself, but only managed to yank free his perilous one-handed grip. They stumbled backward and fell. His elbow gouged her side, a hand smashed her cheek, and the hard steps slammed against her shoulder and hip.

They hit bottom, and he rolled past her. Alexis groaned and didn't move.

Feet pounded in their direction, and high, excited voices filled the air. Alexis straightened her legs, rolled to her side, and sat up. She did a quick inventory. *Nothing broken*. She tugged at her skirt. Heat rose in her face.

Beside her, the man groaned, and with an awkward movement, pushed himself into a sitting position.

"Professor Stephens!" A female student stopped beside him. "Are you okay?"

Another student leaned over Alexis, but the babble of questions and comments from the growing crowd drowned his words.

"Luke!" A man's voice broke through the chatter. "What happened?"

Glancing up, Alexis recognized Don Jacobs, an English professor. He bent over Luke Stephens and offered a hand.

The other man shook his head, his hands slipped to his knee and did a quick examination. "Give me a minute."

"Professor Jergenson?" The academic dean, Cliff Smithfield, stepped into her line of vision. "Don't move. My wife is the campus nurse. She'll be here any minute."

Gingerly, Alexis stretched one leg then the other. She rolled her head. No sharp pains. "I think I'm okay."

"You took quite a tumble. Wait until Linda gets here."

"Really, I'm okay. Just bruised."

She started to stand, and he reached to help her. Her legs wavered. The staff member next to her put a hand out, also. Alexis managed a smile, straightened and settled her feet under her.

"Thank you. I'm okay now." She tugged at her skirt again, ran shaky hands over her upswept hair, and glanced at the man on the floor. She'd recognized him, of course, right before slamming into him.

"Professor Stephens, are you okay? Is your knee hurt?"

Green eyes shifted her way, but he didn't answer, just climbed stiffly to his feet. The female student beside him put a hand forward but drew it back.

"Luke?" Don Jacob's inquiry held insistence.

"I'm fine." Luke Stephens transferred his gaze to Alexis. "And you?"

The roughness of his voice surprised her. Had the fall caused an injury? She waved a hand. "No, I'm good. Bruised is all. But are you—" A hand settled on her arm, and she glanced around to find a woman in a pair of blue scrubs standing next to her.

"Hi. I'm Linda. The nurse. Someone told me you had a fall." Her eyes focused on Luke. "You, too?"

"Both of us." Alexis touched a spot above her right ear and forced herself not to wince. "But I've been told I'm hard-headed. That's a plus today."

"Well, why don't you come to my office? Let's give this a few minutes and see how you feel. We need to do an incident report, anyway."

Alexis shifted her gaze to the floor. Her purse was here somewhere as well as the briefcase. "I'd like to make my class first. I'll come by later."

"You're sure?" When Alexis nodded, the woman's glance went to Luke.

He dipped his head. "I'll do that, too, Linda."

Alexis straightened her jacket. The heat from her face hadn't dissipated. So much for starting her class with dignity.

"All right. I'll expect to see you both later. If you have any dizziness or any other problems, come immediately or send a student to fetch me."

The academic dean cleared his throat. "Okay, everyone. Give Professor Jergenson and Professor Stephens some room. Everything's okay. Classes have started. Don't be late."

With a rumble of conversation, the students dispersed.

"I don't think we'll have to hurry to either of those classes," a student said. Another person laughed and agreed.

"Hush!" A female voice rose above the laughter. "Professor Stephens could have been hurt."

Alexis gave a quick smile and glanced at the man. He had an admirer. Not surprising. Solid build, those startling green eyes, and young—at least, in this circle of academia.

The Dean nodded. "Well, come see Linda later. In the meantime, if either of you needs to leave class, don't hesitate to call me. I'll substitute if I have to."

"Me, too." Don ricocheted a look between Alexis and Luke.

Luke met it with a wry smile. "And my students would love that. You could bring another python to class like you did last semester."

Alexis arched a brow. "A python?"

Don chuckled. "You have to get their attention somehow. Okay. I'm off to class, but keep my offer in mind." He hustled down the hall. The Dean and his wife headed back in the opposite direction.

Alexis shifted to face Luke. "I am sorry. I was running. I was late. I shouldn't…" She stopped.

Those intense eyes, their color set off by the navy blue suit he wore, had lost their amusement and narrowed as he looked at her. With her heels, she was close to his height, but five foot eight was tall for a woman. That same height gave her an edge in the courtroom, and from the vibes coming from Luke Stephens, she might need help here, too.

Her guilt turned defensive as they stared at each other. She dropped her gaze from his and looked again for her bags. Well, she had tried to apologize.

"We usually tell the *students* not to run up the stairs."

The man's words caused her hands to tighten as she grabbed her purse and case. She straightened. "Oh?"

A student raced past them and disappeared up the stairs. His pounding feet echoed back down the hall. Alexis gritted her teeth. Wonderful. As if the man needed an exclamation point to his sentence.

He cleared his throat. "For their safety, of course."

"Of course."

He was just as irritating as she remembered. For some reason, the man had taken an instant dislike to her at the faculty and staff meeting three weeks ago. Later, she'd told herself she'd imagined it. As two of the youngest members on staff, she and Luke Stephens should be allies. Not that she didn't realize and admire the scope of intelligence around her, but the age of her colleagues here compared to those in Atlanta had disconcerted her.

She tilted her head. "I'll remember that."

"Good."

She narrowed her eyes at the word, and the twitch of his mouth sent a ripple of heat through her. If he thought this was amusing… But he just gave a nod and followed Don down the hall.

Alexis stared after him. Ignore the man. You've faced worse. She settled her purse under her arm. Her students couldn't be as unfriendly as Luke Stephens and not nearly as intimidating as a hostile judge.

She mounted the stairs again. At a walk.

Chapter 2

"Come on." Alexis made a kissing sound with her mouth, but he didn't move. Instead, he watched her with distrust, muscles tightened across his chest, stance rigid. She took a deep breath. He was gorgeous. Ah, yes, gorgeous.

She put out her hand.

He shook his head, the chestnut mane flying from the thick neck, nostrils flaring.

"Oh, you…beauty."

She flattened her palm and watched the horse's eyes shift. Neither moved for a moment, but just as she was about to drop her hand, the powerful neck stretched, inching forward. Soft lips brushed her palm but found nothing. He stamped and flipped his head.

Alexis gave a quiet laugh. The ride out into the country after classes today had paid off. Her first week finished, she had craved the distraction of something beautiful, totally unrelated to teaching. Approaching Don with camera held high, she asked where to go to get pictures of the fall foliage. She envisioned the pictures blown up and mounted on the walls of her condo. He'd grinned and directed her out this long, winding road that dipped and climbed at regular intervals.

Her gaze slid to her red Jaguar parked on the other side of the fence. When she spied the stallion galloping along its perimeter, she wrenched the wheel, zipped the car to a stop on the tiny shoulder and climbed through barbed wire. Of course, she'd seen the No Trespassing sign, but beauty like this couldn't be ignored; the sign could.

"Come on, boy." She clicked her tongue. "I have carrots in the car. Really." And not because she'd expected to find a horse, but because since moving from Atlanta to Tennessee, she'd fought off loneliness by eating her way through an abundant supply of Theo Classic Chocolate bars. Even organic, Fair Trade chocolate had calories.

She bent, shoved a strand of wire up and eased a leg between it and the second strand, holding her camera close to her chest. Her jeans caught on one of the barbs, and she unhooked it before sliding her whole body through. She cast a backward glance at the horse. Her tongue made more clicking noises as she eased open the car door.

"Stay here, big boy."

Alexis grabbed a couple of baby carrots from the bag on the front seat and turned back. The wind lifted the stallion's mane, and the late afternoon sun shot waves of light through it.

Like tongues of fire. Magnificent. She lifted the small Canon camera that she'd slung around her neck. Now here was a picture...

A whistle came from somewhere over the hill, and the horse shifted.

"Wait, darling, wait." Letting the camera drop back into place around her neck, she stuck out her hand, palm flat, balancing the carrots. The animal eyed it. Alexis made kissing sounds again. "Come on. It's good. I'm not teasing now."

The soft lips crossed her palm, and the carrots disappeared. A quick crunch followed, then another. A stray piece dropped from his mouth. She reached up and rubbed his nose.

Years had passed since she'd ridden. Her parents had thought it would help...

The wind whipped her hair, and she lifted her head, studying the skies. Dark clouds bunched and grew above them. She looked back to see the horse's head inching over the wire.

Grinning, she flat-handed another carrot his way. "Here you go, boy."

Leaves spun past them, and she scrutinized a stand of nearby trees. Sassafras, sweet gum, and hickory sent swirls of yellows, golds, and reds their way. She brushed her hand down the side of her jeans, pulled her phone out and began videotaping–the horse, the trees, leaves falling like rain.

To the right, the ground dropped away, and past the trees, the farmland descended to a small road. On this side, a fence hemmed in the land; beyond it, flat pasture stretched.

The wind whipped her hair across the phone. She grabbed the long strands with one hand, holding it back, and peered through the lens again. Leaves tumbled and spun past her vision. *Okay.* This was what she drove out here to see–autumn and all its glory.

A whistle brought her head around and the horse's head up.

She'd heard it before, but it hadn't registered. A rough voice called a name she couldn't understand.

"Here, boy, take it." She offered the last carrot.

The call came a second time – impatient, rough. *Uh oh.*

The third whistle was closer, louder.

"Shoo." Alexis waved him away, but he didn't move. "Go. Take off." She put a hand on his neck and shoved. "Don't get me in trouble. Some people are protective of their property."

She glanced at the No Trespassing sign. At least, she stood on the correct side of the fence now.

To her left, at the top of the rise, a silhouette appeared. The person stopped and looked down at them. The stance, the hat, and thick jacket marked him as male. Alexis pulled her shoulders back and stared, narrowing her eyes to see him better.

Dark clouds had scurried from the west and banked above him, forcing the sun to shoot rays of light through their darkness. A flicker of caution leaped through her–a familiar feeling, never far away. She started to edge back to the car but stopped.

Don't be paranoid.

A bridle or halter hung from the man's shoulder, and when he started forward, she noticed the limp. Her watchfulness dropped ten degrees. Coming downhill would be hard. She eyed the sign again and stifled the desire to grab the horse's mane and lead him uphill. That move might not be appreciated.

The stallion stood still a moment longer before whinnying and trotting uphill. When the horse approached, the man reached out and rubbed a hand down his nose. He pulled a large carrot from the coat's pocket. The horse chomped and slobbered, and a minute later, the man slipped the bit between the horse's teeth and another part of the bridle over his head. His hand ran along the neck, patting again. Words spoken in an affectionate undertone reached her ears before he lifted his head to look her way.

Recognition sent a sharp jolt through her nervous system.

He came the rest of the way down the short hill, leading the horse, and stopped in front of her. Stormy green eyes met hers. Neither spoke. Jacket, jeans, and boots transformed him from the college professor she'd knocked down on Monday into a cowboy.

He hadn't been happy then; he wasn't now. She vacillated between walking to her car and holding her ground.

Luke tipped the Stetson back on his head and broke the silence. "Anyone ever tell you that feeding someone else's livestock is off-limits?"

Alexis cast a look at the stallion whose lips still evidenced slivers of orange veggies. From her carrots or his? Either way, she was busted. He must have noticed hers before feeding the horse himself. But whatever compassion she'd had while watching him walk downhill vanished.

"That's the first thing you've got to say to me? Not hello or how are you, fellow professor?"

"My first thought was, have you knocked anyone else down lately?" A half-smile appeared for an instant, but it disappeared, and he warded off her response with a lifted hand. "And my second was did you track me down to apologize?"

"Apologize?" Her voice rose. "I apologized already or tried to. Why would I—" She remembered his sharp, indrawn breath from that morning. That combined with his limp today meant something serious. Five days had passed.

A gust of wind sent leaves swirling between them. She hadn't seen him again this week. He taught Bible and business classes. Business classes were held in the Quad building, but students packed his Bible classes down from her office on the administration building's second floor. She'd recognized his voice as it drifted into her office that first afternoon and every afternoon since. Her free time coincided with his class, but he never came past her office. She assumed he disappeared down the back stairwell afterward.

She crossed her arms and lifted her chin. "I had no idea you lived here. Don sent me this way when I asked where to get pictures of the trees, the leaves. When I saw the horse, I had to stop. I... He's beautiful. But I'm sorry if the fall on Monday hurt your leg."

"The leg is fine." The words contained an edge that let her know the discussion had ended.

Okay. Wonderful. So, he didn't want to talk about it.

A car zipped past, and she realized she hadn't seen or heard another car since she'd stopped. She stepped back from the fence and away from him. The man was disagreeable, and being alone with most men made her uncomfortable. So many had that predatory look, letting their eyes slide over her like she was livestock on display. It didn't matter what she wore – business suits for the courtroom, modest dresses for evening, a pair of jeans and a loose shirt to run to the store – men were predators.

Yet, Luke's deep-set eyes had never left hers. His clenched jaw reflected some strong emotion, though. As a lawyer, she'd learned to read faces. So, what was she seeing now? Before she could decide, he grabbed a handful of the stallion's mane and threw himself forward onto its back. The horse circled and stamped.

Luke straightened, pulled on the reins and looked down at her. A stab of lightning lit the sky behind him. "You'd better head into town. We're going to have a gully-washer, and the roads flood around here."

She looked past him. Heavy clouds packed the sky, and the wind bent the trees to his right.

He nodded toward her car then turned the horse. "That Jag won't make it far on flooded roads. Good evening, Miss Jergenson."

Alexis watched until they disappeared over the rise. *Into the sunset.*
Yeah, so apropos.

She climbed into the Jag and turned it back toward town. The man's
scowl from the moment of introduction at the staff and faculty retreat until
now made her wonder if he didn't like the idea of pre-law classes being
offered at a Bible college.

During the job interview, Cliff, as academic dean, mentioned the
opposition that rose when he first advanced the idea. With all the
challenges directed at Christian beliefs these days, he told her, a number of
students had applied to law school. Offering preparatory classes would be a
win-win situation – good for the college, good for the students. But not
everyone agreed.

She pressed her lips together. Well, whatever the reason, she was
persona non grata in Luke Stephens' life.

Rain splattered her windshield. She flipped on the wipers and glanced
at her GPS. A white Honda Accord flew past going in the other direction.
Glancing in the rearview mirror, she saw the car's red brake lights flash,
and it swerved on the wet cement. She wrenched her attention back to the
road. The drops grew in size and intensity. She flipped the wipers to high
speed.

On the other hand, maybe he had discovered her secret – that she
wasn't a Christian. Yet, the Dean said the President agreed on her hire. She
understood their desperation. They'd spent money advertising pre-law
classes. Then, four weeks before the semester started, the professor they
hired backed out. Alexis had received a call from half-way around the
world informing her of the opening. Her sister-in-law had patched a call
through from some tiny village in Indonesia to tell Alexis she needed to
apply. She'd never learned how her sister-in-law knew of the opening, but
the timing was right. Her desire to leave Bradley & Associates, to leave the
past and the memories behind, had balanced with the need for another,
different career.

Still, all the other professors were Christians. The Dean had asked her
simply not to say anything; they'd assume she was, too. In a year,
however, they would look to hire someone whose beliefs coincided with
theirs. Fair enough.

Although her conscience tweaked her, their desperation mimicked
hers. Her client's death had come as a shock and added an exclamation
point to her own problems. She'd needed a new place and a new career.
Perhaps then the haunting memories would ease.

Alexis squinted through the downpour and slowed. Shoulders along
this part of the road didn't exist, just ditches. A line of rain pelted the
windshield, dropping a gray curtain around her, obscuring her vision. She

jerked and hit the brakes, sending the car into a slide. Heart pounding, she gripped the steering wheel and held tight. The car slowed and stopped. The front wheel on the passenger side hung over the ditch.

She sat a moment, insides jumping. Heat radiated throughout her. Her back wheels were on the asphalt. That was good, wasn't it? In her mind's eye, she could see the Jag flipped on its back in the ditch. She swallowed and straightened. Could she back out? She'd need to do that. Slowly. She didn't want to spin out going backward. Her dad's instructions from years ago crossed her mind. *Don't overcompensate.* The rain drummed against the roof, and her stomach quivered. Stop it. You're all right. Just get moving.

She put the car in reverse, eased on the gas. Nothing. She pushed harder on the pedal. The tires spun. Come on. Come on. A sudden bounce and the car shot backward.

She yanked her foot from the gas and let the car slide. It whirled in a circle, slowed and stopped. Her heart reacted like a light with a short in it. She took two deep breaths and lowered her head against the wheel. Where's a paper bag when you need it?

After a minute, her heart leveled; and she raised her head. The rain had eased, and she could see that the road before her dipped into a gully. The downpour had erased the asphalt and filled the ditches on either side. Luke's words came back to her, and she understood what he meant. The Jag's body hugged the ground, great when taking curves at high speeds, not good at getting through flooded roads.

The trouble with being new in town is that she didn't know alternate routes, and neither she nor her GPS had any idea what roads would be passable now. Her eyes focused on the rearview mirror again. No other cars had come this way since the white Honda, but the danger grew the longer she sat there.

Okay. She made a slow Y turn and headed back the way she came. Even Luke Stephens would shelter her until the rain stopped. Wouldn't he?

∿

Groaning, Luke backed up from the fireplace and dropped into the lounge chair. He'd been desperate enough to jump on the horse and ride back without a saddle in spite of his leg. Feeding and stalling the stallion and the two mares had eaten away more time, and the pain mounted with each passing minute.

When he got inside, he tore the bathroom cabinet apart looking for the pain meds even though he'd quit taking them some time ago. His head dropped back against the headrest.

Twice now, the woman had caused him more pain than he'd dealt with in the last year, and pain did things to him he didn't like. He'd wanted to take her head off, only God wouldn't let him. The strong rein on his spirit had choked back his words.

He took a deep breath, glad of the hand that had kept him from saying things he would regret. The woman had not meant to cause him pain. Something stirred in his soul. He opened his eyes and stared at the ceiling.

What is she doing here, Lord? Someone special to You?

Leaning down, he pulled off the boot and rolled up the left leg of his jeans. He'd overdone it. Walking as far as he did, and downhill at that, had pushed things too far. Not to mention the fall on Monday. Amazing that neither of them had suffered a broken bone or worse. God, again. He remembered her apology, the flush staining her cheeks and her indignation. His mouth curved into a smile.

Luke stretched his neck and rolled his shoulders. The room darkened around him. The rain started, a few scattered drops that grew into a thunderous cascade. Moments later, a torrent hit the roof. Luke turned his head and stared through the large window facing the front of the house. The downpour grayed and blurred the image of the huge tree outside.

Good thing he'd fed up. The stallion, the two mares, and Farley would ride this out in the barn. Maximus never liked the rain nor the thunder and lightning accompanying it, but he'd be fine in the closed stall. The dog would keep him company. The mares at the other end of the barn would be fine, too.

He opened his eyes and watched the tree outside bend and shift in the wind. The line of rain increased only to drop to nothing a moment later. Then it returned with mounting intensity. The meteorologists had predicted a series of squalls. That's why he'd gone to find Maximus.

And found her.

The lash of the wind and pounding rain filled his ears. He rolled his shoulders again. With the number of low places on the road between here and town, she'd never make it in that car. His truck sat higher, which was one of the reasons he'd bought it.

Not the main reason, of course; that had to do with starting over – after the divorce. He'd bought the truck and this house with twenty-five acres. Four years later, it felt like home. And the pain of someone who couldn't live with the "new" him had dimmed.

Or so he'd thought…until he saw Alexis Jergenson.

Lightning stabbed across the sky and jerked him back to the present. Rain pummeled the ground. How far had she made it before the storm broke? Numerous gullies and valleys made the road between here and the main highway treacherous during storms. Someone would need to rescue her.

Meeting her at the faculty retreat along with the other new faculty members had shaken him. She had reached forward to shake his hand, and the dark depths of her eyes and the way her long straight hair swung as she nodded at his introduction brought back memories he didn't want. Too much like Teresa. Too pretty. The sight of her had sent pain and anger ricocheting through him, surprising him.

Thunder rumbled. He sat forward. If the woman needed rescuing, he'd have to do it. Who else knew she was out there? He groaned and sat forward. Pain or not, he needed to find her. She'd be somewhere between his place and the bridge.

He headed to the front door, threw it open and almost collided with her.

Again.

She'd raised her hand to knock, and her hair and jacket dripped water. She looked like foliage curling beside a waterfall, droplets clinging to her eyebrows, her eyelashes, and mouth.

Rain and wind blew into the house as they stared at each other. Lightning tore across the sky. Luke grabbed her arm and dragged her into the foyer, slamming the door behind her. She jumped and slid further into the hall.

Even dripping wet, she was still one attractive woman. And, like Teresa, she probably needed the proverbial bullwhip to beat the men off.

His jaw tightened. Pretty women were Trouble. Capital T. "You're drenching the floor."

She jerked her head around, and scooted back to the rug against the door, clutching her purse under one arm.

"Better?" she asked. Cynicism filled the word. "You were right about the rain. I've never seen it come down like that. The road flooded right in front of me. And you're right about the car, too. It won't make it through puddles the size this storm is dumping. I didn't know where to go, so I—" She stopped, eyeing him with a look he could read easily enough.

She wasn't any happier being here than he was having her. When he said nothing, her gaze shifted past him to the living area. The crackle of the flames in the fireplace reached him.

"Do...do you mind?" she asked, trying to hide the shakes starting in her shoulders, "if I stay until it stops?"

He kicked himself inside. Quit being a jerk. She's wet and cold. Not every pretty woman is selfish and unfaithful.

Pushing past his reluctance, he indicated the room behind him. "Sure. The fire will warm you in no time."

Author Biography

Linda was born and raised in Florida. She is married with two grown sons, a daughter-in-law, and three grandchildren. At twenty-six, she discovered the miraculous love of Jesus. God blessed her with a passion for the written word—especially mysteries and romantic suspense novels, from Nancy Drew to Agatha Christie, from Dee Henderson to Kristen Heitzman.

She speaks about and works against human trafficking. Linda also blogs on this subject as well as commitment to Christ on her Website: www.lindarodante.wordpress.com (Writing for God, Fighting Human Trafficking).

To learn more about her books, this series, and the author, please visit www.lindarodante.com.

Made in the USA
Middletown, DE
21 March 2016